Raisins
and Almonds

Books by Kerry Greenwood

Raisins
and Almonds

A Phryne Fisher Mystery

Kerry Greenwood

Poisoned Pen Press

Copyright © 2002 by Kerry Greenwood

First U.S. Edition 2007

10 9 8 7 6 5 4 3 2 1

Library of Congress Catalog Card Number: 2007924779

ISBN: 978-1-59058-168-1 Hardcover

Poisoned Pen Press
6962 E. First Ave., Ste. 103
Scottsdale, AZ 85251
www.poisonedpenpress.com
info@poisonedpenpress.com

Printed in the United States of America

Dedicated to Jean Greenwood
incomparable
with thanks to Dennis, Mark and Benjamin Pryor,
Arnold Zable, Ashley Halpern, Lily Grossman aleha ha-shalom,
David Greagg, Jenny Pausacker, Richard Revill,
J. Cosmo Newberry III, Lee Kennedy and Susan Tonkin.

Beneath my little one's cradle
Stands a clear white goat
The goat set off to trade
In almonds and raisins.
There will come a time, my child
When you will journey far and wide
Remember this song I sing today
As you travel on your way.
Raisins and Almonds are laden with spice
You will trade in merchandise.
This is what my child will do.
Sleep, my child, lue-lue-lue.
   —from *Rozhenkes mit Mandlen*
    (*Raisins and Almonds*), Yiddish lullaby,
    translated by Arnold Zable.

Chapter One

trans 1.4. polyisoprene

The ranked books exhaled leather and dust, a comforting scent. The noise of the Eastern Market—the roar of traffic and voices and feet—was almost inaudible inside *Lee's Books New and Secondhand,* prop. Miss Sylvia Lee, a haven of peace and scholarship at the top of the city. Miss Lee's shop was always ordered, always quiet, and always scented with the gum leaves she bought from Miss Ireland on the upper floor: an arrangement of gum leaves and poppies was her favourite decoration, and when there were no poppies she made do with gum leaves alone. She specialized in abstruse works in Latin and Greek, though her concession to popular taste was the brightest point in the shop: a table of yellow-jacketed novels for railway reading. The space was small and closely packed with volumes in leather bindings. The shelves extended to the ceiling, which was white. The room was lit by a large electric light in the middle, and a working lamp over Miss Lee's desk. Miss Lee herself wore sub fusc garments, a skirt of a dark colour and a beige or white blouse and a cardigan under her neat working smock. Her mousebrown hair was cropped short. She lived across Exhibition Street in an apartment, a perfectly self-contained young woman, who required no masculine attentions, merely wishing to get on with her own neat life in peace.

Miss Lee was adding up a column of figures. Her pencil moved smoothly up the pence, then the shillings; and she was about to write down the total when it happened, and she was never afterwards able to forget the sum of eleven pounds, twelve shillings and eight-pence halfpenny.

The tall man in the long black coat, who had been examining Volume 9 of Hansard for 1911—for which Miss Lee had long abandoned hope that someone would acquire for their library—exclaimed in a foreign tongue and dropped the book.

She dashed from behind her counter quickly enough to support him as he sank to the floor. He held out one hand, palm upwards, as though inviting her to notice its emptiness—or was it the small wound on the forefinger?

His eyes opened wide for a moment, and he spoke again. Then he convulsed, limbs flung out like a starfish, so abrupt and horribly strong that Miss Lee was forced to release him. His head hit the floor and she heard his teeth gnash, a dreadful grating noise echoed by a rattling in his throat. As she grabbed her ruler to lay between his teeth, he convulsed again and lay still.

She stood with the ruler in her hand, gripped so tightly that the edge cut into her flesh. The young man was dead, that was plain. What to do next?

She walked steadily to the door of her bookshop in the Eastern Market and said to her neighbour the teashop lady, 'Mrs. Johnson, can you call a doctor? One of my customers....'

She was proud of herself. Not a quaver in the voice. And as Mrs. Johnson's scatty assistant was chivvied out of the shop to call for Dr. Stein, who had consulting rooms in the next building, she walked back into her shop and sat down rather abruptly behind the counter to wait for some help. She clasped her hands together on her shabby calf-bound ledger, to stop them from shaking.

For there was nothing she could do for her customer now, and one must not give way.

◇◇◇

Phryne Fisher was dancing the foxtrot with a sleek and beautiful young man. She was happy. She was agreeably conscious that she was gorgeous, from the turn of her brocaded shoe with the Louis heel, through the smoky-grey stockings of the sheerest silk to the Poitou gown, tunic and skirt of heavy, draped, amethyst brocade threaded with a paisley pattern in silver. A silver fillet crowned her black hair, cut in a cap like a Dutch doll's. She had a huge amethyst in silver on her right hand, a wide band of engraved silver around one upper arm, and the same stones in her ears. She smelt bewitchingly of Floris honeysuckle and knew, without doubt, that her partner appreciated her. He would not, otherwise, have spent a small fortune on the purple orchid which decorated her shoulder. Another young man might have spent the money, but only a devoted and intelligent young man would have ascertained the colour of the dress on which it was to be worn.

His name was Simon Abrahams. Phryne's Chinese lover, Lin Chung, had been forced to go to Shanghai on a silk-buying trip, and Phryne found that she had rather lost her taste for plain ordinary young men. Searching for a diversion, she had collected Simon from a public dance hall. He was not conventionally good looking. His nose was high bridged, his eyes dark and set deeply into their sockets, and there were shadows under them which spoke of childhood illness. He was not tall, being a few inches above Phryne's five feet two, but he was beautifully made and stunningly dressed, and there was a flavour about him—his diamond tie pin a little too large, perhaps, his gestures emphatic beyond the usual Public School rule, his voice quick and emotional—which made him as exotic as a tiger lily in a bed of white daisies.

His skin was olive, his hands graceful, and he danced like an angel, which was how Phryne found herself competing in the Foxtrot Competition run by the Jewish Young People's Society at the Braille Hall, which was hung with a truly remarkable number of balloons and streamers.

Here, thought Phryne, relaxing into her partner's embrace, I am the exotic. I am the—what was the word? I am the *shiksa*, the foreigner, the non-Jew, and how nice they are being to me. I wonder how much trouble the poor boy is going to get into for taking me as a partner, and not one of the nice girls his mother wants him to marry? He really does dance like a dream.

They slid to a halt and the judges conferred. A stout lady in satin nodded vigorously, and the bald gentleman next to her waved a hand wearily, as though abandoning the dispute. '*Nu?*' she heard him say. The dancers all stared at the judges. Balloons wavered in the hot air.

'It's decided,' said the bald gentleman. 'The best dancers are Simon Abrahams and his partner Miss Fisher, but the heat goes to Rose Weinberg and Chaim Wasserman, because they are both members of the Jewish Young People's Society.'

'Shame!' yelled Chaim Wasserman. 'If they're the best dancers, then you can't give the heat to us.'

'He's right,' said the young man to Phryne's left. The room then broke into at least three arguments, all of which had ferocious supporters. Phryne was fascinated. In an instant, everyone had an opinion and someone's ear into which to yell it. One faction was for awarding the prize to Simon and Phryne; after all, they were the best dancers and who were we to start discriminating against non-Jews, for goodness' sake? Another was to award it to Chaim and Rose, who danced well and were both members and good persons besides if you overlooked their uncle Marek, and anyway Marek was not anyone's fault except maybe God's and He presumably had a purpose in creating even such persons as Marek. A third was denouncing the chairman, not for making such a decision, but for having the bad manners to say that that was how he made it, the chairman having been a *schlemiel* since early childhood, it was well known. She was about to suggest to Simon that they find a chair, as she didn't want to miss any of the debate and it seemed likely to go on all night, when an old man in evening dress pulled at Simon's arm and led him out of the hall into the kitchen. Phryne followed.

'Simon, your father wants to talk....'

'Later, uncle,' said Simon, dragging against the urgent fingers, 'I will talk to my father later. In any case I told him, I dance with whoever I like and I like Miss Fisher.'

'No, no, he wants to meet the lady, he sent me to fetch him this Miss Fisher. If you would do us the honour, gracious lady,' said the old man, bowing from the waist. Phryne gave him her hand, and he kissed her fingers punctiliously. He had a heavy accent which turned all his w's into v's and vice versa, but it was not precisely a German accent. Phryne appreciated his politeness in continuing to speak English rather than his own language.

'My *father* wants to *talk* to Miss Fisher?' asked Simon, suddenly sounding like the crowd in the hall. '*My* father wants to speak to *Miss Fisher?*'

'I told you, suddenly you haven't got ears? This way, if you please, lady.'

He led Phryne on his arm out into the night and opened the door of a very big car. Simon got in beside her, evidently puzzled and apprehensive.

Seated in the back seat was a stout elderly gentleman in the most beautiful cashmere coat Phryne had ever seen.

'So, Miss Fisher, I am Benjamin Abrahams and I am honoured,' he said, taking her hand and looking into her eyes. He had the same intense, brightly dark gaze as his son, and Phryne could not look away. 'You are the private detective, are you not, Madame?'

'I am,' she agreed.

'Then I have to ask you a favour. My son has spoken much of you. He says you are an honourable woman, a woman of courage. In many matters his head may be turned, but for such a young one his judgment is beyond his years.'

'Thank you,' said Phryne, 'but...'

'Wait,' said Mr. Abrahams. 'Don't say anything yet. I don't offer you money, Miss Fisher, though I will pay you. But this is the situation, an awful thing. There is a bookshop in the Eastern

Market. I am the landlord. My tenant is a lady called Miss Lee, a single lady. Today a man died in her shop.'

'Terrible,' murmured Phryne, conventionally.

'Death is not so terrible, always it is there. But this was particularly bad. It was a Jew. His name was Simon, a student from Salonika. He was poisoned. The police say that they do not know how the poison was delivered, and by the time they found out—the body was taken to the hospital, you see—the clues had all gone. Miss Lee you understand is a neat person, she had swept the floor, cleaned the shop—after such a happening it is a human thing to do, is it not? The man was certified dead by the good Doctor Stein, who is also a Jew, and the police....'

'Who have they arrested?' asked Phryne. 'The doctor?'

'No,' said Mr. Abrahams. 'They have arrested Miss Lee. The victim was often in her shop, and owed her money. Therefore they suggest that she gave him tea, as it might be, with strychnine in it. There is strychnine in the rat poison she used.'

'Miss Lee?' objected Simon. 'It is absurd.'

'So, it's absurd,' agreed his father. 'So we ask Miss Fisher to fix it.'

'But, wait, if it's that absurd, they'll release her,' said Phryne, vaguely uncomfortable under the dark eyes of both father and son.

'Such a high opinion of the justice system you have, hmm?' asked Mr. Abrahams.

Phryne did not reply. Such a high opinion of the justice system she didn't have.

'Indeed. But there is this, a more serious matter. The victim is a Jew. The doctor is a Jew. I am a Jew. Australia is not very anti-Semitic—the argument is rather between the two Christian sects, between Catholic and Protestant. But the possibility is always there. I do not think that we will have pogroms here—I hope it is foreign to the national character. But no one likes strangers and we are strangers, and in Europe the *shtetls* are burning again, the little towns inhabited by Jews. We are exiles, wanderers; we have no home. There is nowhere where we are safe, really safe.

This murder, it is likely to raise all sorts of bad feeling between Christians and Jews.'

'I think you're exaggerating,' said Phryne.

'My grandmother was murdered by a Cossack,' said Mr. Abrahams. 'My father and my aunt also. My mother and I fled here because our only remaining relative lived in Gatehouse Street, and when we landed we had one suitcase and forty pounds Australian or they would not have let us land. We came from a village which had lived and traded with the Russians and Poles for generations, and then they turned on us and slaughtered us in one night. There is a saying, Miss Fisher: "Do not love anything, or a Cossack will take it away." Anything can turn the opinion of the people, and then what would become of us?'

'I still think that you are exaggerating,' said Phryne. Mr. Abrahams took her hand and sighed.

'Beautiful lady, you can say whatever you like to me, if you will solve this murder.'

'If I take the case,' temporized Phryne, 'I can only tell you the truth. I mean, I can't fix the result. If it's a Jew murdering another Jew, then I can't cover it up.'

'I accept that,' said Mr. Abrahams.

'And I cost ten quid a day,' said Phryne.

'*Oy*,' said Mr. Abrahams, and grinned.

Chapter Two

cis 1.4. polyisoprene

Detective Inspector John 'Call me Jack, everyone does' Robinson sighted the neat figure in a town suit and the two café curtains of black hair and sighed. The Hon. Miss Phryne Fisher, as ever was, he thought, large as life and twice as natural, and about, by her stride, smile and general demeanour, to make his day uncomfortable. It looked like a nice clear case. Frustrated spinster falls in love with attractive tall dark stranger. Tall dark stranger does not return the favour, or perhaps seduces and betrays her, and she gives him a friendly cup of strychnine tea. Easy, clear cut and simple, and here came Miss Fisher to complicate things.

Wishing he was at home in the undemanding company of his cattleya orchids, Jack Robinson intercepted the visitor at the door.

'Well, well, Miss Fisher,' he began, 'nothing to tax your well-known skills in this case.'

'Oh, no?' Phryne smiled guilelessly into the policeman's face. He winced. Miss Fisher was at her most dangerous when she was smiling guilelessly. It was a sign that someone, somewhere, was about to be shaken down until their teeth rattled and the

Detective Inspector was uneasily aware that he was the closest available target.

'Yes. Open and shut,' he continued. 'Frustrated unmarried woman falls in love with a customer, he doesn't notice or perhaps he takes advantage of the situation, and Bob's your uncle, she up and poisons him. Picture the scene. He comes into her shop, she never expected to see him again after the way he treated her. But there he is. She puts the rat killer into a cup of tea. He drinks it, drops the cup—splash!—and falls dead. Curtain.'

'Oh, very good,' purred Phryne, peering around the bulk of the Detective Inspector to look into the shop. 'Keep on in that vein and you'll have a script for Metro Goldwyn Mayer. Call it "Starved of Passion"—starring, oh, I don't know, Theda Bara?—and you'll be able to retire on the proceeds.'

'Miss Fisher, have you any evidence to the contrary?' said the policeman, a little stiffly. Phryne fixed him with a green gaze.

'I won't know, will I, unless you let me have a look at the scene of the crime.'

'That's quite against the rules,' he began, and Phryne waved a dismissive hand.

'Absolutely, can we take that as read? Come on, Jack dear, you're a just man. What can you lose, except an official reprimand for leaping to the wrong conclusions?'

'Come in,' said Jack Robinson, as he had known he would from the first sight of that extravagant purple feather in the small black hat, and Miss Fisher ducked under his arm and stood still at the door, surveying the small shop.

'It's in apple pie order for a scene of the crime,' she commented, looking at the ordered shelves and sniffing the smell of lysol, gum leaves and leather.

'The prisoner cleaned it carefully. Not a fingermark, and of course she washed the cup.'

'The cup?'

'The tea or whatever the poison was in.'

'Oh, that cup. The one which was dropped so dramatically in your script. You know—Dot will advise us on this—but I'd swear that this floor has been swept and polished recently, but not washed. Eh, Dorothy?'

'Yes, Miss.' Miss Fisher's personal maid and companion sniffed, then crouched and ran a finger along the American cloth. 'This floor was waxed with Shi-noleum, recently, and since then it has been swept and then buffed with a soft cloth around a broom. Waxed floors spot if you spill anything wet on them, and they pit if you spill hot water on them—melts the surface, you see. Then you have to put on more wax. When I was a maid, I remember, the missus once went crook because of a dropped cup of tea. I had to re-do the whole floor.' Dot folded her arms in her dark brown cardigan and sniffed again. 'And I can't smell wax, Sir. Disinfectant and gum leaves, but no wax. Shi-noleum's got carbolic in it, and that's a real noticeable smell. Miss Fisher's right. Nothing wet's been spilled on this floor, not for weeks.'

'Hmm.' Phryne made a slow circuit of the little shop, touching nothing. The books were ranked by subject and were largely in unknown languages, although one shelf appeared to be devoted to Hansard, Collected Sermons and novels by Walter Scott—all, Phryne imagined, unsaleable except to the insomniac or those customers who possessed a piano with one leg half an inch short.

Miss Lee's desk contained ranked pens, a bottle of William's Superfine Ink As Used By Royalty, a pen knife marking the place in an invoice book, an eraser and a perpetual calender, a sheaf of business cards and a list of telephone numbers. The only signs that a woman worked in the bookshop were a packet of Ladies Travelling Necessities and a small box of Bex powders.

Open on the desk was a ledger with a half-completed sum and a pencil which had rolled into the centre of the book. Behind Miss Lee's high stool was a little curtained alcove which contained a gas ring with kettle, a tap with sink, one cup, one saucer, one teaspoon, a strainer, and one small brown teapot. Phryne opened a tin and found it half-full of hard ginger biscuits. The other tins contained sugar and tea. A small amount of milk was curdling quietly in a small jug.

'Miss Lee did not entertain, it appears,' she said to Jack Robinson. 'Only one cup. Did you find another one?'

'No,' he admitted, 'but she had plenty of time to get rid of it.'

'All right, Jack dear, you must have more on her than this romantic tarradiddle about unmarried women. What happened according to Miss Lee?'

'She says—and she's sticking to it like a good 'un—that the deceased came into the shop just after Miss Lee opened in the morning—about ten past nine. She's seen him before, he often came in and bought rare Hebrew and Greek books. She had him on her order book as Mr. Simon Michaels, a scholar, but he has been identified as Shimeon Ben Mikhael, a native of Salonika. In Australia on an entry visa due to expire next week.'

'Who identified him?' asked Phryne, listening to the carters screaming insults at each other out in the Eastern Market.

'No one, we can't find anyone who knew him. He lived in a lodging house in Carlton, in Drummond Street. He was carrying his passport. Salonikan, but he's a Jew all right.'

'And?' asked Phryne, wondering if her good opinion of Detective Inspector Robinson was about to be shattered.

'So we have to be real careful. You know what's happening in Russia. I'm not going to have no pogroms in my patch, not never,' said Jack Robinson stoutly. 'I started my career in Carlton, and they're nice people, not mean whatever slang says. They look after their own in a way which ought to make us ashamed. And they're funny. Many's the laugh I've had with old Missus Goldstein, and a bit of a warm by her stove in the shop. She used to make me eat chicken soup and tell me I was too thin for a growing boy. So I'm not having even the suspicion of a shadow of a doubt about this case. It's personal, not political. And there ain't no Jews in it but the coincidence of the victim's being from Salonika.'

Phryne put down Miss Lee's tea cup onto its matching saucer. It was a sturdy piece of white china, with a blue ring. Coles, she guessed. It was spotless, as was all of the area behind the plain brown curtain.

'I take your point, Jack, and it does you credit. Oddly enough, it is precisely that matter which has brought me into this case. My employer feels exactly as you do about the Jewish angle. But I don't think that you have a very good case against Miss Lee, and you'll feel really silly if you bring the wrong woman to trial. Now, tell me about the death—Miss Lee's version.'

'He was standing here,' said Robinson, placing himself next to the bookcase full of unreadables at the far end of the shop. 'He was holding a book in his hands. Then he collapsed, Miss Lee ran to catch him, he jerked out of her grasp and flopped like a landed fish—strychnine does that to you—and then he died. Death was certified by Doctor Stein at ten o'clock. Miss Lee wasn't affected at all. Walked into the market and called for help as cool as a cucumber. Sat behind the desk and waited for them to take the body to hospital, then cleaned her shop as though it had been an ordinary day. That's what put the duty officer on to her. She was too calm.'

'What was the book?' asked Phryne. Robinson stared at her. 'What was the book?'

'Yes, it's a reasonable question, isn't it?'

'I don't know,' admitted the Detective Inspector.

'And where did he fall?'

'Just where you're standing, Miss. Leastways, that's where Dr. Stein found him, and he was as dead as a peck of doornails by then. Why do you want to know about the book?' asked Robinson, obscurely worried that he might have missed something.

'Just being careful, Jack dear. Have a look, Dot, can you pick out the book that's out of place?'

Dorothy examined the shelves with a housekeeper's eye. 'They're not in any order, Miss, but they're a little dusty—it's a very clean shop but no one can have wanted these books. See, there's a little line of dust at the edge of the shelf. It's either this blue one, Miss, or this dark one.'

Dot pointed out a volume of Hansard for 1911 and a volume of sermons for those of riper years.

'They both look entirely deadly, Dot—sorry, Jack, I didn't precisely mean that. Hmm. Have you examined the books?'

'No.' Robinson was biting his bottom lip.

'Well, do you want to, or shall I?'

'I'd better take charge of them, I suppose. Look here, Phryne, do you really think Miss Lee's innocent?'

'Yes. Her story is coherent. Your story about the dropped cup isn't fact, Jack dear—unless she caught it in mid-air. And how else could she have got a relative stranger to eat a strychnine powder? I suppose you've noticed that there are Bex in the drawer.'

'Yes, Miss, all the powders will be removed for testing, and the milk and the water and the leftover tea. She had rat poison in her possession, Miss Fisher. She bought a small packet of Henderson's Rat Killer. And we can't find it.'

'What does Miss Lee say?'

'Nothing, Miss. She won't say anything at all. We took her in and she told us her story, and since then she won't say a word more. She says she never left the shop and she was seen in the market, walking fast. She's hiding something and I reckon I know what. Homicide.'

'And equally it could be a hundred other things. Can I talk to her?'

'Why not?' asked the policeman rhetorically, and led the way out of the shop.

Miss Lee was ushered into the visiting room of the Women's Prison to meet her unexpected visitor. Female homicides were rare, and the prison population of drunks, whores, thieves and child-abandoning good girls, after a certain amount of bridling, had decided that she was one of the quiet ones and should not be tormented or affronted, in case she ran amok in some spectacular way. They attributed the fact that she was taken to see her visitor in the Governor's sitting room as evidence that she was a real dangerous criminal as well as—self-evidently—a lady.

The escorting wardress pushed Miss Lee not ungently through the door and shut it behind her.

'Miss Lee? I'm Phryne Fisher.' A spectacularly fashionable vision rose and gripped her hand. The woman was small, dark, and fizzing with energy, and she made Miss Lee fatigued. She was drawn to sit down beside Miss Fisher on a couch, and real tea was pressed upon her. She held the cup and saucer dazedly. She had adapted to being held captive by dropping into a light trance, obeying every order instantly, and trying not to think about her situation. Having retreated into this state, it was proving difficult to withdraw herself from it, and the world seemed to contain too many blurry Phrynes in far too many distracting black hats with purple panaches.

However, this appeared to be tea, and she might as well drink it. Miss Lee's sense of self, which had been absent, winged back and lodged in its accustomed place as she sipped very good Ceylon tea with just the right amount of milk and sugar. Nightmares might happen, she might be dragged from her shop into the street, exposed to shame and locked up with a lot of dissolute noisy women, but tea remained comfortingly real. Her visitor waited until she had finished the cup, gave it to a young woman in a brown cardigan to refill, and returned it to her before she spoke.

'Miss Lee, I am tolerably certain that whatever happened in your shop the other day, it was not the film scenario which our excited Detective Inspector Robinson has told me. Have you heard it?'

Miss Lee did not smile, but her tense mouth relaxed a little. 'Yes. I thought it was most imaginative.'

'Oh, I agree, and you wouldn't have thought that a man of his staid appearance had been reading Marie Corelli, would you?'

'Elinor Glyn,' demurred Miss Lee.

Phryne looked at her. She was a strong-featured young woman, with washing-blue eyes, a firm mouth and chin, and a carefully controlled mouth. She had been allowed to keep her own clothes, and was dressed in a sensible skirt, a warm jumper and thick stockings. Her taste in colours resembled Dot's: brown and beige and umber. Her hands were hard with work, the writer's callus on her forefinger still stained with ink. They were folded in her lap, trembling a little under geological tension.

'It's because you behaved like a lady, you know,' said Phryne. Miss Lee looked at her visitor. 'Because you didn't shriek and tear your hair and rush out into the road screaming. That's why Jack Robinson thinks you're a murderer. Did you ever hear anything so silly?'

'No,' murmured Miss Lee.

'Exactly, and we can't allow this to continue. Miss Lee, I am actually being retained to investigate this matter by Mr. Abrahams. Do you know him well?'

'Yes, he's my landlord.' Phryne detected no blush, no lowering of the eyes, which should have been present in such a proper young businesswoman if her relationship with her landlord was closer than a commercial one. 'He's a very generous man, whatever they say about Jews. He let me the shop at below market rent for my first year—I tried to pay him back, but he told me I had to build up substantial capital first, and I do find rare books for him sometimes. I believe his wife is a pleasant woman.'

'Why do you think that?'

'Because of the books she reads.' Miss Lee studied Miss Fisher for a long moment, visibly made up her mind, and went on in her brisk, no-nonsense voice. 'It's a little game I play, Miss Fisher, guessing what people are really like by their choice of books. Mrs. Abrahams isn't sentimental—no Marie Corelli or Florence Barclay for her—she likes biographies. Always of people like Elizabeth Fry, you know—Florence Nightingale—strong women who made a difference in the world. I just found her a copy of *Travels In West Africa* by Mary Kingsley. She likes stories with a happy ending if possible and she tries to like modern novels, but she usually sends them back for me to re-sell as second hand. Therefore I think she is a nice woman with a social conscience, who perhaps wishes that she had been given the chance to do something brave or dangerous. Mr. Abrahams is a romantic. He doesn't read novels but he likes poetry, and he's self-educated, I believe. I'm chattering, Miss Fisher, because I am nervous.'

'Miss Lee, if you were not nervous, you would be certifiable. I had my doubts about Jack's story, and now, having met you, I am certain that you are innocent.'

'How are you certain?' asked Miss Lee.

'Because I cannot believe that you would make so many mistakes, if you wanted to kill someone,' said Phryne.

Dot said, 'Miss,' warningly—she was worried by Miss Lee's pallor—but Miss Lee herself nodded and said, 'Thank you. That's the argument I would use myself, Miss Fisher. I am capable of murder, I suppose—we all are, are we not? And assuming I had a reason to kill poor Mr. Michaels—which I did not, I liked him—then I would not have done it in such a way that I can't imagine how he was poisoned.'

'You didn't offer him a cup of tea, or water? To take a pill, perhaps, or a powder that he had in his pocket?'

'No, why should I? I would not like someone else to use my cup and there's a teashop practically next door. I only make my own because I can't leave the shop without someone to mind it. And anyway you know how it is, Miss Fisher, the moment I pour my own tea someone comes in with an enquiry about the next Agatha Christie and the tea gets cold anyway.' Dot nodded. 'I can't abide cold tea. So I usually take just a little milk from home and have mine when I can borrow Gladys from the printer's to mind the shop for quarter of an hour. If someone was taken ill in my shop I would escort them into the teashop to sit down. Mrs. Johnson would look after them. No, he must have taken whatever it was somewhere else, and it began to work in my shop.'

'Possibly, but we need to consider every angle. I know you've done this before and I know you're probably bored out of your mind repeating it, but could we go through it once more in excruciating detail? Dot will take notes and I'll ask questions at the end.'

'You believe that I didn't do this?' asked Miss Lee, with her first sign of emotion.

'I am proceeding in a certain knowledge of your complete innocence of the charge,' said Phryne quietly.

Miss lee sighed and leaned back in her chair. She rubbed both hands over her face and through her short, mousy hair.

'I live across the road in an apartment at number 56 Exhibition Street. It is an old house and I live on the second floor—I was pleased to get my flat, because it has windows onto the lanes: they're more interesting than the main street, and it's quieter. My landlady lets rooms on the ground floor, and she provides meals for her lodgers, but I prefer to take care of myself—I never really relish someone else's tea, and I've got a gas ring to boil myself an egg in the morning, and a toaster, a rather superior electric one. Mr. Schwartz from the hardware in the market gave me a discount because I found a copy of *Riders of the Purple Sage* for him—he's a Western fan. I buy my supplies for the morning when I leave the shop in the evening, and I usually have a sandwich for lunch and a little dinner in one of the food shops along Exhibition Street or the cafés in Chinatown—I haven't been to half of them yet and they spring up every day like mushrooms. Or I might have a proper lunch one day, and a sandwich for supper on the way to the theatre or the movies. And there's the stock if I lack something to read. It's a life I always wanted, Miss Fisher. No house to keep, no potatoes to peel, no floors to scrub. When my mother—and she was a tyrant, mother was, God help her—finally died three years ago and left me a little money I swore I'd never scrub a floor again, never cook a meal. Of course, I had to do a certain amount of cleaning in the shop to begin with, but now it's paying its way I can afford a charwoman, and the luxury is positively sinful. It's Mrs. Price, and her son dotes on mysteries…I'm running on, aren't I?'

'Keep talking, Miss Lee, this is just what I want,' said Phryne, and Dot's pencil flew across the stenographer's notebook. Dot had laboured long at Pitman's, and was pleased that her skill was so far equal to the clear, low-pitched voice.

'That morning, I rose as I usually do at seven-thirty, collared the bathroom ahead of the opposition, washed and dressed, made myself an egg and some toast, poured the rest of the milk into my little jug and went down the stairs.'

'Were you carrying anything else?'

'My smock. I had brought one home to launder—one gets filthy handling old books, they are surprisingly dirty. I remember Miss Ireland saying that flowers are the messiest trade, but books are close. I had Miss Veering in the market make up three smocks for me, after I got vilely dirty unpacking an auction delivery. I don't like aprons, they look matronly and they don't cover the arms and shoulders. My smocks are made of mid-brown cotton with an inwoven paisley pattern, long sleeves with an elasticated cuff and a round neck. I can just fling them on if a dusty delivery comes in and not worry about ruining my own clothes and yet not look like a housewife. It was cold so I wore my brown coat with the fox-fur collar and my brown felt hat. I was carrying the smock over my arm. I had the jug in one hand and my key in the other. I don't usually carry a handbag, they're cumbersome. I put my key in my pocket and left the building and shut the front door behind me. Then what happened? My shop is almost opposite the apartment house. There were a lot of carts and drays, and I was careful crossing the road. I bought a newspaper from the boy on the corner of the lane as I came into the market, and a muffin from the muffin man. It was a cold morning and that little hot paper package warmed my hands.'

Phryne was getting used to the crisp voice and could see Miss Lee, confident and neat in her coat and hat, the smock over her arm, the jug in one hand and the muffin warming her other palm. Phryne remembered the taste of cinnamon muffins and resolved to reacquaint herself with their hot soggy sweetness.

'Then I said hello to my neighbour Mrs. Johnson, unlocked my door, picked up the letters from the first post, and hung up my coat and hat on my peg, put on the smock and rolled up my sleeves. There was a big box of books due—I wonder what has happened to it?—from a Ballarat deceased estate. Then I opened the letters.'

'What were they?'

'I cannot exactly remember—they should still be there. An order, I think; yes, one was an order because I entered it in my order book. You can consult the order book, Miss Fisher, I can't remember the customer's name. A few people came into the shop, but it was early, the market doesn't really clear of the grocers and fruiterers until about ten, but some of them buy books and I like some time to myself. I ate my muffin before it got cold. I sold some novels—they will be in my day book—and I talked to one woman about an atlas; I didn't have one to suit her.'

'What was she like?'

'A stoutish woman, not very young, wearing her best go-to-town clothes, a dark blue suit a bit too small for her and a lumpy black hat with a bird on it. You know, one of those with a wide brim. I did think it was odd that she should want an atlas—she didn't seem to really know what an atlas was, could not believe me when I said that the reason the map looked oddly shaped was because Mercator's projection mapped a sphere onto a flat page, not because there were bits snipped out. But there's no accounting for people, Miss Fisher. And she was probably buying it for someone else, anyway. What next? Two young men looking for a book about the odds and horse-racing—I sent them away with a nice solid tome on statistics, which ought to keep them gainfully occupied for a few months. Then Mr. Michaels, who came to ask if I had the book he ordered—a rare one in Latin which I had actually found in a French auction. He was so anxious about it that he came in almost every day to ask if it had arrived. I carry books in most languages, of course, if the customers require them, and I supply the University with all the classics and textbooks in Latin, Hebrew, Aramaic and Greek. Professor Gregg was good enough to say that the University is very pleased with my services.'

For the first time Miss Lee's voice faltered.

'Oh, dear,' she said sorrowfully. 'I was really beginning to do quite well. Now what will become of my shop?' she wailed, and put her hands to her eyes.

Phryne moved to allow Dot to supply a handkerchief and a hug, and presently Miss Lee recovered herself. That had been a cry straight from the heart, Phryne thought, and yet some scant five minutes later Miss Lee was back in firm control of her face and voice, though her hands gave her away, clenched together.

'I'm so sorry,' Miss Lee apologized. 'Well, Mr. Michaels. He came in, asked about the *Theatrum Chemicum Brittanicum*, which is still on its way from France, then wandered over to the Great Unsaleables.'

Phryne laughed and Miss Lee smiled. 'You know how it is at auctions, one has to buy a lot of rubbish to gain the thing one requires? Well, I have my share of volumes which no one will ever want, but one never knows in the book trade, so I keep them on display in a case. Then—well, then it happened. I was doing some accounts, and I heard him make a strange little sound, then I caught him, he had some sort of fit, and then he died. The rest you know. I went next door, the ambulance was called. They took the body away. I knew he was dead. There's an absence in death, the person isn't there any more. I was shaken, so I cleaned the shop, reverting to type, perhaps. I swept the floor and re-shelved the books and then the police came and here I am.'

'Did you have a cup of tea that day, Miss Lee?'

'No, I didn't have time.'

'And you didn't leave the shop that morning?'

'No,' said Miss Lee. Phryne looked at her. She was trying to conquer something—distaste? Finally she managed it.

'Of course, I had to go to the lavatory, and I asked Gladys to mind the shop for the time I was away—five minutes, perhaps.'

'Because of your condition,' hinted Phryne. Miss Lee blushed as red as a poppy.

'Yes. Of course, I had a packet of necessities in my desk. Oh, Lord, and that policeman must have found them.' Miss Lee tried to cool her cheeks with her hands.

'And that's why you didn't tell him you had left the shop and why he thinks you're lying,' said Phryne, triumphantly. 'Miss Lee, I must go, thank you for your time. I will have you out of here as soon as may be. Meanwhile, if Jack Robinson comes back and asks you if you left the shop, tell him. He won't be shocked, he's a married man. By the way—what happened to that packet of rat poison that you bought?'

'The policeman asked me that. I don't know. I left it under the sink. The corn chandler's shop attracts rats, and I came in one morning to find a huge great brute scurrying behind the shelves. So I bought some poison, but I hadn't even opened the packet.'

Dot made a note of this reply. Miss Lee asked gravely, 'Miss Fisher, don't give me any false comfort. Do you really think that you can prove me innocent?'

Phryne took the offered hand. 'There are more gaps in Jack's theory than in Mercator's projection,' she said. 'I will prove you innocent, Miss Lee, even if it means finding out how poor Mr. Michaels died. You can trust me. I'll be back,' she said.

'I shall always be in when you call,' said Miss Lee.

Phryne gave a slightly startled laugh and Miss Lee was escorted out. The office door opened and Phryne and Dot walked in and stood before an acre of desk.

'Look after Miss Lee. My advice is that you supply her with remand comforts, visits, clean linen and put her to work in the library, strictly no floor scrubbing,' Phryne told the governor of the prison, a bleak woman in grey. 'She didn't do it.'

Chapter Three

Nigredo is called the Raven.

—Elias Ashmole,
Theatrum Chemicum Brittanicum 1689

Phryne swept past Mr. Butler and paused in the doorway of her own sea-green, sea-blue parlour in her bijou Esplanade house. She needed a bath to rinse the prison smell off her person, and she wanted to sit down and take off her rather tight shoes, but it was a very pretty picture.

Dot's policeman, Hugh Collins, who had been a faithful kitchen visitor, had been let into the parlour, probably on the urgent petition of the girls, to tend to something which whimpered. Phryne could not see into the grocer's box, but both her adopted daughters were deeply concerned. The fairer Jane's countenance was creased; the darker Ruth was biting the end of her plait, which she always did when she was worried. September holidays had brought the girls home from school, and they were dressed in the warm colours they affected when at home rather than the severe school uniform, designed to iron out from any female body the slightest shred of sexual attraction. Jane was in green and Ruth in red, and the fire lit their faces: Hugh's sharpened with concentration, the girl's with concern. They looked like Rembrandt figures, strange in the modern parlour like the inside of a shell and surrealistic. Phryne stood still until there was a sharp yap. Hugh said, 'There, that's done it, poor little bitch,' and the creature in the box stopped whimpering.

'Miss Phryne,' exclaimed Ruth, leaping up and dragging Jane with her. 'Look what we found. Mr. Collins fixed her leg. He reckons someone kicked her! How could anyone kick a poor little thing like that?'

'There is always someone willing to kick puppies,' said Phryne, kneeling down next to the carton. A wretched scrap of damaged black and white fur shivered on an old jumper.

'Girls, I don't...' she began, to be met by two shocked faces.

'Oh, Miss Phryne, please,' said Jane, catching at Phryne's hand. 'She's only a little dog.'

'Little dogs grow up,' said Phryne reluctantly. 'I really don't want a dog, girls.'

Jane recovered first. She gave the puppy a final caress and stood up. 'Come on, Ruthie,' she said to her adoptive sister, clearly resigned to the loss of the animal as she had been resigned to other losses.

'She's only a puppy, and if we put her out she'll die,' protested Ruth. Phryne was entirely unprepared for this assault on her emotions. Reflecting that the object of the argument was not only an infant but injured, could conveniently decease any moment and might as well do it in comfort; she patted the girl's shoulder.

'All right, Ruth dear, as long as you and Jane look after it you can keep it. Now tuck the box in the chimney alcove, injured creatures need heat. Have you got a name for her? Hello Hugh, how nice to see you again. Perhaps we should have some tea, it's a vile day outside, an early north wind, and...' she continued, and was embraced by both girls, their faces against her own. She caught sight of the group in the mirror: the laughing Ruth and the exultant Jane, embracing Phryne, Jane's unplaited hair flowing like silk across her broad-cloth shoulder and breast, supporters to her Dutch-doll face. She turned and quickly kissed each glowing cheek, coloured as gracefully as geranium petals.

She hadn't actually wanted a dog, but then she hadn't wanted daughters either and they had turned out to be very interesting and hardly any trouble at all, considering.

'Thank you, Miss Phryne,' said Jane. 'She won't be any trouble. We'll walk her and wash her; and Mr. Collins thinks she's a sheepdog so she won't grow too big.'

Despite a private feeling that she had heard that tune before, Phryne allowed them to help her into her chair and remove her shoes and Mr. Butler handed her one of his special cocktails, which she savoured quietly. A hint of almond, perhaps? Was that noyau, certainly cherry brandy, and…as always, she gave up. Mr. Butler's cocktails were his own sacred mystery. The girls sat down on the floor with the box, and Hugh Collins resumed his place at Phryne's wave. Dot sat on the arm of his chair, an impropriety which she would never have allowed herself if the friendship had not progressed to consideration of marriage.

'How did you get involved in this, Hugh?' asked Phryne, sipping her cocktail. Constable Collins and Dot had tea.

'I was coming to deliver a parcel for Dorothy, Miss Fisher, and the girls said they'd found a puppy. Poor little thing had a dislocated hip, but I've put it back. Some mongrel kicked her, I expect.'

'Oh, well, poor little creature,' said Phryne. 'Make sure that she's fed, won't you, Ruth?' Ruth was the sensible one, who had engineered her own escape from bondage and serfdom. Jane, more intellectual and destined perhaps for the medical career she craved, would be thinking about something else. Jane always was. It was part of her slightly distracted charm.

They did her credit, Phryne thought, looking at Dot refilling Constable Collins' tea cup. Dot was well dressed and solidly respectable, though at her first encounter with Phryne she had been desperate, dishevelled and heavily armed. Ruth, rescued from slavery in a boarding house, was clean and combed and becoming delightfully plump, her devotion to food destining her for a domestic career. Mrs. Butler said that she showed promise as a cook, but was 'too bold' with spices and heavy handed with pastry, though she made excellent soup and was an angel with anything involving yeast. Jane, rescued from far darker bondage, was thinner and paler, and clever in an offhand vague way which alternately exasperated her adoptive parent and astonished her. As long as someone was around to make sure that Jane got on the right tram with the right change and then got off at the right stop for her examinations, Phryne was convinced that all available academic honours would be hers. The boarding school, which also housed princesses and diplomat's children, had accepted the orphans without surprise; after all, their background might be dubious, but they were the adoptive children of the Hon. Miss Phryne Fisher, well known to be extremely rich and exception- ally well-connected, being the daughter of a Duke. She was also socially adept to the level of *Ipsissimus* and not to be crossed by any organization that wished to remain in the mode.

Therefore Ruth the slavey and Jane the whore's daughter mingled with the daughters of the upper classes, and quite liked each other, each side considering the other unbearably exotic.

And although the north wind scoured the unreliable spring outside, inside Miss Fisher's parlour everyone was getting on splendidly.

The girls had settled down on the hearth rug. Ember the black cat had walked in, sniffed the canine scent, hissed briefly, then analysed it as a small dog with no immediate desire to chase cats. Ember had ascended to Phryne's knee with a precise leap and was now sitting in sphinx pose, nose to the fire, blinking occasionally and looking, as Jane said dotingly, perfectly Egyptian.

'Nice to see you, Hugh dear, are you off duty or have you left the force?' asked Phryne. The large man grinned. He owed Phryne a lot. Because of her he had entered for his detective's exams with his Sergeant's recommendations and was on the way to becoming Detective Constable Collins.

'No fear, Miss Fisher, I'm on nights. Just dropped in for a word with Dot and one of Mrs. B's ginger biscuits when the girls came in with that poor little mutt. I'm glad you're going to let them keep her, Miss Fisher. Nice little stocky body, I reckon she's a crossbreed, not too big and going to make a good guard dog. Need a guard dog in St. Kilda, with all them alleyways behind the houses.' Constable Collins basked under the affectionate regard of everyone in the room except Mr. Butler, who instinctively knew who would walk, brush and care for the new acquisition, and Phryne, who was conscious of being manipulated. Then she remembered Hugh's mention of a parcel.

'Oh, of course, it's your birthday next week, Dot dear, isn't it? We've an appointment with Madame tomorrow, don't forget, for your suit. If you really insist on a suit?'

Dot nodded. When offered a handmade garment of her choice as Phryne's birthday gift, she admired all the beautiful evening dresses that Madame Fleuri constructed for the fattest purses, if not the best figures, in Melbourne. But what she wanted was a dark brown wool suit made with Madame's exquisite tailoring, finish and style. Dot wanted a garment that she could wear for the rest of her life. Oddly enough Madame, who was really French, understood this desire. 'If you still 'ave this garment, Mademoiselle,' she told Dot at her first fitting, 'you can be married in it, and even buried in it in the fullness of time; and while you 'ave my suit, you will never be without something respectable to wear.' Phryne was delighted to see the Parisian couturière and the lady's maid smile at one another with perfect understanding.

However, puppies and constables and handmade suits aside, there was the case, and Phryne wanted the opinion of her family. She told the story of the young man dead in the bookshop, Miss Lee and the prison interview, and the Jewish connection as seen by everyone involved in the matter, Jack Robinson and Mr. Abrahams alike. The girls thought about it. Dot leaned against Hugh Collins, who shyly embraced her. The fire crackled. The puppy snored faintly in her exhausted sleep. No one spoke. Then Ruth commented, 'There are Jewish girls at school. One of them's terribly clever—Jane talks to her. Mostly they're standoffish, stick together and don't talk to the gentiles—they're all very rich, of course. One of them's Mr. Abrahams' niece, I think, if he's the man who owns half the Eastern Market; she was talking about it, eh, Jane?'

'Mmm?' Jane had been staring into the fire.

'Pay attention, can't you? Rebecca Levin, isn't she Mr. Abrahams' niece?'

'Yes, I believe so. I like Rebecca. We were talking about Euler's Grand Equation, you know, which links the five fundamental numbers. It's such a pretty thing,' said Jane, who had never been induced to regard clothes with anything but passing interest. Ruth sighed affectionately. 'Becky wants to do science at University, she's fascinated with numbers. She told her father that it's well known that there's a whole system of prediction based on Kabala, which is a Hebrew invention, so there's no reason why she should be doing something anti-religious by going to University to study pure mathematics. She says that her uncle will pay her fees if her father won't. They're all expected to learn, you know, even the girls. We met Mrs. Levin, remember, Miss Phryne, at the school concert? With Becky's sister, Anne.'

'Oh, yes, voluble lady in puce, as I recall, very chatty about how pretty her girls were. I'm glad they're clever,' replied Phryne, whose memories of the school concert were not compelling enough to feature in her autobiography when she got around to writing it.

'Yes, really clever,' agreed Ruth. 'But nice with it. Anne has to make sure Becky has breakfast and walks the right way home, just like I do with Jane. Mrs. Levin invited us to tea last week, but we were going to the dentist so we had to refuse.'

'Accept for this week, or would you rather invite them here?' asked Phryne.

'We've never seen their house, so we'd rather like to go there, Miss Phryne, but it depends on which would help your investigation,' said Jane, still staring into the fire and appearing to think about something else—perhaps Euler.

'Go to their house, and tell me all about it,' said Phryne. 'What did you make of Miss Lee, Dot?'

Dot, suddenly conscious of being embraced by Hugh Collins, sat up abruptly and blushed. 'I don't think she did it, Miss. I'd be lonely living like she does, but I reckon it's what she's always wanted. She wouldn't be likely to fall for any man, tall, dark or handsome, but if she did I reckon she'd pick well. Even if it all went wrong, she'd retreat back into her room and shut the door, not go looking for revenge like someone on the movies. The story's silly, Miss, like you said, a movie script. And there hadn't nothing been spilled on that floor, I'd swear my life on it. But there's something missing—how did he get the poison? And who killed him and why? I reckon that Miss Lee's the easiest target, Miss, and it's real hard to prove a negative, like Jane was explaining to me the other day. We have to find out who that man was and why someone killed him—and how they did it—before the law's going to let Miss Lee go.'

'Aren't you being a bit hard on Detective Inspector Robinson, Dorothy?' asked Hugh uneasily. Dot removed herself from the arm of the chair and sat down on the couch with Phryne.

'No,' said Phryne quickly, before Dot could reprove her friend. 'We understand his position entirely: he needs a murderer and Miss Lee looks good on a superficial inspection. But we don't think she did it and we need to look at Mr. Michaels very hard. Now what other information can we get, hmm? I've seen the scene of the crime but it had been extensively tidied. Nothing out of place—Miss Lee is a neat woman. Nothing unusual in the shop that I can think of offhand.'

'You need the autopsy report,' said Hugh.

'Can I get it?'

'I don't see why not,' said Hugh Collins, redeeming himself instantly and causing Dot to return to her perch. 'I'll just borrow a copy from the file.'

'Not yet,' said Phryne. 'I'll ask Jack for it. Then if he refuses you can borrow it for me, and I shall get it back to you as soon as I can get it photographed. Also I need to know what was in his pockets, where he lived, and everything known about him—but I'll ask Jack, Hugh dear. Let me keep you in reserve in case official channels fail me.'

Phryne smiled at the young Detective Constable to be. She did not want to blight his career unless it could not be helped. But she was determined to remove Miss Lee from the custody of the law.

The telephone message which was delivered just before lunch confirmed her resolution. Miss Lee, allowed comforts, had a request for some books to while away the hours in her cell. She had never had time before, but she was being lodged and fed without any effort of her own, so she was intending to learn Latin.

Phryne resolved that the books would be collected that afternoon and went back to the fire.

After a good lunch—the weather might be unreliable but the new asparagus was bang on time, and Phryne adored asparagus, lightly steamed and dipped in melted butter—she called Jack Robinson and asked him to adorn her dinner table. He declined, pleading pressure of business.

'Where are you going this afternoon, Jack dear?' asked Phryne.

'Back to the Eastern Market. Tell you what, Miss Fisher, why don't you sort of accidentally meet me there by Miss Lee's shop at about three? I've got all the neighbours to speak to and it's an interesting place; you'll like it and you might see something that I miss.'

'What a nice proposition,' said Phryne. 'See you there.' She rang off, called for her coat and hat, and walked through to the kitchen. The girls were occupied with a cooking lesson, and Phryne went out on Jane's learned discourse on the chemical interaction of water and bicarbonate of soda in scone dough.

'Very interesting,' said Mrs. Butler, 'but if you don't mix them fast and get them into the oven quickly, they won't do you credit.'

'Quite,' agreed Jane, wiping flour onto her face.

Phryne parked the Hispano Suiza in the Spencer Street Oil Shop where the car had been rebuilt. John Lawless was always pleased to see both Phryne and the machine again. She left the car in the care of that greasy young man, who was already sliding a polishing cloth over the gleaming red coachwork, and hopped on the Bourke Street tram.

She paid her penny and slid her punched paper ticket into her left-hand glove. It was a sunny day with a cold wind—typical of Melbourne in spring, which showed the city at her most capricious and uncomfortable. Bitter dust made Phryne sneeze. She lit a gasper and blew smoke pleasurably out the door as the tram clanked down the Bourke Street hill past William Street and the courts, Queen Street and the lawyers, Elizabeth Street and the GPO and passed all of the great emporia—Buckley and Nunn's, Myers, Coles, and Foy and Gibsons. Surprising numbers of women, hats askew, breathing heavily, crowded past the stylish figure of Miss Fisher, carrying paper dressmaker's bags and squashy parcels. Phryne noticed that Myers was having a sale and stopped wondering about them.

Ting ting went the conductor's bell, the tram laboured up the hill, and Phryne stood up, balancing carefully on the crosshatched wooden floor. More than one delicate example of the cobbler's art had gone the way of all footwear when the heel had caught in that flooring. This happened so commonly that the cobbler at the corner of the Eastern Market had a small sign outside, advertising 'Get You Home: Heels Mended, Sixpence'. He had been known to ritually bless the name of the Tramways.

She alighted at the corner of Bourke and Exhibition and stood outside the dress shop, admiring the market.

It was a three-storey building made like a rather restrained Palladian cake, with once-white frosting and pillars and a dark stone facade. Phryne knew that it was three storeys on one side and one on the other, occupying as it did a sloping site. It had none of the baroque tiled additions and riotous ironmongery of the main provisions market at the top of Victoria Street. The Eastern Market, she thought as she crossed Bourke Street and walked towards the main entrance, was the place to buy anything small or strange. Because rents of the stalls were so low, odd crafts could afford an outlet. She walked out of the cold wind under the verandah and heard the market noise and smelt the market smell. She stood still to appreciate it, her back to the tiny leaded window of Miss Jane Trent, Umbrella Repairer. Phryne loved markets.

Although most of the wholesale fruiterers were based at the Victoria Market, a few supplied the barrows which went out every day into the street. The tubercular soldiers from the Great War who had been told to get an outdoor occupation sold choice fruit, vegetables and flowers from them, and they were stored overnight in the basement of the Eastern Market. Phryne could smell the new spring blooms which she most enjoyed, which came before the roses—hyacinths, crocuses, freesias—and also a wave of mandarins and lemons from a barrow trundling past. She heard the rumble of carts, the whistle of caged birds from Lane Bros., who had one live finch in a cage above a whole flock of speckled chickens, and Wm. Gunn, who had a huge cage full of finches above a pen in which one very red-combed rooster glared aggressively with mad bird eyes through the mesh. As Phryne walked, she heard the language of the carters, one of whom was begging his fellow in extremely emphatic terms to move the flamin' euphemism of a cart so that decent working men could get past and earn a crust, or he would knock his sanguinary block off. The cart was one of the few horse-drawn drays left, and clearly belonged to someone who was not taking the spirit of the go-ahead get-ahead twenties seriously. When Phryne came around to the head of the wagon, which had wedged itself at an angle in one of the entranceways so that nothing could get past it either way, the driver had worked himself into such a temper that he had torn off his coat, leapt down, and was offering to fight anyone and everyone.

For a moment, Phryne enjoyed the spectacle. The tunnel to the undercroft was lit with electric bulbs, which lent such a strange and glaring light to the faces that they looked like a Dante illustration of demons and sinners, though sorting them out into sinner and demon was beyond Miss Fisher—they all looked equally villainous. She surveyed the cart and its relation to the trucks, blinked, and realized that it was fixable, though the solution was not evident to anyone in the middle. Picking her way between fuming hoods and yelling drivers, she went to the head of the horse, which was standing patiently enough, took it by the headstall and began to turn it. The dray body perforce came too, and as it was higher off the ground than most of the trucks, it passed over the bonnet of a Dodge without scratching the paint. The horse came placidly with Phryne, the owner gradually becoming aware that the dray was moving away. 'What're you doing?' he yelled.

'I'm shifting your cart,' said Phryne coldly. 'Don't speak to me in that tone of voice, and you as much use as a steampowered grapefruit. Come along, Dobbin.'

'You let go o' my nag!' the drayman screamed, bringing a promising riot to a halt as the rest of the drivers stared.

'Certainly,' said Phryne promptly, releasing the headstall. 'If you continue down that way I see no reason why this should not work. In fact, I'll come with you,' she added, hopping up onto the dray seat and gathering the reins. The horse, who had been very bored with standing still until his hoofs ached with all that human noise assaulting his fringed ears, was not going to stop, so the driver had to run after the dray and fling himself aboard. The trucks fell in behind and the flow of traffic into the undercroft of the Eastern Market resumed.

Phryne had never been under the market before. She relinquished the reins to the driver as he flung himself into his seat, and remarked affably, 'This is like the crypt of a church. I had no idea it was here. Where does it come out?'

'Little Collins Street,' replied the driver, utterly unable to decide on a proper reaction. This sheila had taken control of his horse when the stubborn brute had walked the wagon into a corner, and was now coolly chatting in a society voice as though nothing particular had happened. She was obviously a lady and he did not really feel like chancing his arm by crossing her.

Generations of men who had refused to pull forelocks kept his gnarled hand away from his cap, but he replied civilly.

'See, Miss, this is where the wine cellar is for the whole of Melbourne, it's nice and cool but it ain't damp, they say that's good for plonk. My boss keeps his drays down here, though the nags are stabled up above. The stallholders store things here too. Trouble is that they banned us from bringing the big trucks into the market, so now all the produce mostly goes to the Vic market—pity really, I always liked coming into the city. This is where I leave me dray, Miss. Let me just help you down.'

Phryne accepted a hand and jumped lightly down onto cold clean cobbles.

'There's a staircase over there, Miss,' said the drayman from the horse's head. 'Take you up into the middle of the market.'

Phryne nodded and smiled and walked in the opposite direction. The drayman was about to call after her, but thought again. That, he realized as he uncoupled the tug girth and allowed his horse to walk out between the shafts, was a determined woman, and his mum had always told him not to get in the way of a determined woman.

Phryne followed her nose to a side of the market which was clearly a cellar. Wooden walls had been built and from behind them came a strange rumbling noise and a strong medicinal smell. A slightly glazed watchman was sitting in front of the gate, which was fixed with a strong iron chain and padlock. The rich smell came mostly from him. Phryne judged it to be rather good port and hoped that it belonged to someone who could afford to lose a few bottles. This cellar occupied a fair chunk of the undercroft, which now smelt less of wine and more of horses and almost overwhelmingly of oranges. The barrows were being loaded with new fruit, and the scent was strong enough to sting Phryne's eyes. Trucks chuntered past, their drivers alert in the half-light, half-dark.

The rest of the cellar appeared to be occupied by piles of boxes, sacks, mountains of chaff-bags and half a real haystack. The roof was supported by heavy beams, soot blackened, and the stone ceiling between was of vaulted brick which might once have been red. She found the staircase and climbed up, emerging onto the central floor of the market, which was buzzing with people.

The Eastern Market was Phryne's sort of market. She sauntered past little shops selling all manner of fascinating things, like sequins and beads and feathers for hats, eye veils and galoshes and singing birds, bunches of snowdrops or hyacinths and a pound of galvanized nails wrapped in a paper poke, toffee apples as bright as red glass and red glass Venetian apples as shiny as toffee.

She watched a huge carter swing the hammer down onto a 'Gauge Your Strength' machine and heard the bell ring as she walked down the iron-lace staircase to the lower quadrant, which sold guitar strings and framed art moderne prints of ladies in Russian dress and sad clowns, sheet music and baskets, and packets of cooling feverfew and chamomile tea from Broadbent and Sons, Herbalists.

By the time she had found her way back to the main entrance to Miss Lee's shop, Phryne was carrying a new shopping basket which contained her own purse, a posy of blue hyacinths, a copy of 'The Basin Street Jazz', a packet of autumn-coloured sequins for Dot, a packet of flea powder for her new arrival and a blue leather collar and lead into which, she feared, the puppy would certainly grow. Phryne also had a one-ounce paper of strychnine—price two shillings—bought from a nearby chemist, who had asked her to sign the poisons book, which she had obligingly done, and no one had questioned whether Miss Jane Smith was actually her name, or asked her why she wanted such a deadly poison. This was instructive, she felt. For herself she had purchased a slightly off-centre silver ring with a big flawed sapphire in it, wrapped around with beautifully made silver snakes, and for the girls two small silver rings made of daisies.

She was sitting down in Mrs. Johnson's teashop and examining her purchases when an official voice said, 'Well, Miss Fisher? Visiting the scene of the crime?'

'Jack dear, do sit down, have some tea?'

'Thanks, don't mind if I do.' He sat down heavily in the red-painted chair and rummaged for his pipe. Phryne opened her gold cigarette case and offered him a gasper, but he shook his head.

'Cut your wind, those things will, Miss Fisher. Two teas, Mrs. Johnson,' he said to the hovering attendant. Phryne did not speak until he was sipping his strong liquorish black tea, loaded with sugar. She showed him the chemist's packet, done up with sealing wax.

'What's that?'

'Strychnine. I just bought two shillings' worth, enough to kill several horses, and no one asked me why I wanted it.'

'Hmm. Well, I can't find Miss Lee's rat poison. The autopsy'll be this afternoon, do you want to come?'

'Not particularly, Jack dear, if you tell me about the report.'

'I'll do that. I don't like this any more than you do, you know.'

Phryne sipped her tea, which was very good, hot and strong. Her feet hurt and she was suddenly very sorry for Miss Lee, cut off from this bustling and fascinating place, which changed all the time. Detective Inspector Robinson evidently caught her thought.

'Miss Lee's asked for some Latin grammar books—you know that? I never met a murderer who wanted to further their education on remand. I'm going into her shop to get her a grammar and some writing paper. Oh, and I've something to show you, too. Come on,' said Robinson, laying four pennies on the table to pay for the tea.

He unlocked the shop and looked around helplessly at the books all marked in foreign languages. The shop smelt dusty and unloved.

'I'll find her a grammar or two,' said Phryne. 'What have you got to show me?'

'What was in the dead man's pockets,' said Jack Robinson, opening a paper bag with 'Evidence, not to be removed' on it. He laid out the contents on Miss Lee's desk.

'Hmm. Two passports, I see. One British, one Greek. Looks like the same photograph.' Phryne looked at the dead man's face: serious and very young, dark and Middle Eastern. 'His visa, about to run out, as you said. A pen knife, a wallet, a purse which closes with rings—I've never seen a man with a purse like that—a packet of Woodbines and a box of wax matches. Purse contains five pence ha'penny. Wallet contains several letters in a language which I don't know, a script I don't know, either. It must be Hebrew—it's not Greek, anyway, Jack dear.'

'And these scraps, which is more of it, whatever it is. Plus these drawings. They look old,' said Jack gloomily.

Phryne unfolded a piece of parchment, and stared at the drawing. It was inked in black and coloured in red and gold. It seemed to show a red lion being burned on a golden fire. Underneath were letters. *Aur*, she read. 'Hmm. That's Latin for gold. There's a lot more but it makes no sense, at least not to me. I need a classicist. What did your experts say, Jack?'

'We asked one of our own members, he can read Hebrew, and he says it don't make sense, it's just a jumble of letters, like a code.'

'And the Latin?'

'Haven't seen about that yet. Do you want to do me a favour, Miss Fisher? I don't want to put all this through the evidence book in case it proves to be something which might cause a breach of the peace. So I'll lend it to you, if you guarantee to let me know what it's about if it's germane to the case. Is it a deal?'

'You're trusting me very far, Jack dear,' said Phryne gently.

He took her hand and clasped it. His forgettable face was blank with worry.

'I do trust you,' he said. 'Is it a deal?'

'Deal,' said Phryne. 'And I know just the man to ask.'

Chapter Four

Albedo is the flight of the white dove.
—Elias Ashmole,
Theatrum Chemicum Brittanicum 1689

Phryne left telephone messages for the beautiful Simon Abrahams and his elusive father, who were both out according to their maid. Phryne dined early because of the girls, and retired to her leaf-green bedroom with a couple of books on Judaism, a glass or two of champagne, and a headache.

This became rapidly worse as she read her way through Mr. Louis Goldman's *The Gentile Problem.* The Jews, he proved, had always been people apart and distinct by custom and appearance, devoted to their own laws, which enjoined education, careful diet and cleanliness on their followers. This meant that, preserved from plague in filthy medieval cities, they had been accused of witchcraft and burned. They had been forbidden any business except that of lending money at interest, and they had been tried and condemned for usury. The Jew of Venice with his 'my daughter! my ducats!' did not seem comic to Phryne any more as she stared at the illustrations: Jews burned in fires, drowned in rivers, hanged higher than Haman. Instead she heard Shakespeare's Shylock saying, 'Hath not a Jew eyes? Hath not a

Jew hands, organs, dimensions, senses, affections, passions? Fed with the same food, hurt with the same weapons, subject to the same diseases, healed by the same means, warmed and cooled by the same winter and summer as a Christian is? If you prick us, do we not bleed? If you tickle us, do we not laugh? If you poison us, do we not die? And if you wrong us, do we not revenge?'

Except they had not revenged. Nowhere had the Jews, driven like cattle and slaughtered like them, fought back against their oppressors; and Phryne caught her lip, wondering what commandment she was outraging by wishing for just a little rebellion, just one uprising, since the brave Queen Esther had told the Persian King that she was a Jewess, and the Jews had hanged Haman and his sons on the gallows they had thoughtfully built for the Semites—which was the feast ever after of Purim.

Of course, that did explain why neither Abrahams was available. It was Saturday, which was *Shabbes*, the Sabbath, and they could not talk on the telephone during *Shabbes*—that would be work. Presumably.

Phryne finished her glass of rather good French champagne and slid down into her dark green sheets. The wind was tormenting the tree outside her window, lashing the branches against the house. It was a restless, uncomfortable sound, and she could not concentrate. She laid the book aside, put out her lamp and closed her eyes, but the constant scratching at the glass irritated her so that she sat up, meaning to find another book or perhaps dress and go out to a certain nightclub which might yield her some interesting company. Her own house seemed silent as Phryne swung her feet to the floor, her silky nightdress sliding off one pale shoulder.

Something attracted her gaze to the window, and she saw two bright points, like eyes. She was so surprised that she sat quite still for perhaps ten seconds. Then she rose and moved towards the window and the little lights. She had almost reached the casement when a shrill howling broke out downstairs. Phryne was distracted, and when she looked again whatever it was had gone, if it had ever been there.

'Well, what did you make of that?' she asked the black Tom Ember, who had been reposing as usual at the foot of her bed. Ember really appreciated silk sheets. He had looked up when Phryne had moved, but appeared uninterested in whatever had been at the window. The wailing noise, however, galvanized the cat. He ran to Phryne's door and demanded to be let out immediately and not a second later, and when she opened the door he leapt down the stairs and vanished out of sight.

Phryne followed more slowly. She knew what the howling was. A small puppy had woken up and missed its mother, its siblings and its nice warm nest, and was telling the entire house that it was really unhappy. She hoped to get to the as-yet-unnamed beast before Ember, who appeared to be seriously displeased.

Phryne paced down the staircase into the parlour and turned on the light. The grocer's box padded with an old jumper was still in the chimney corner, but there was no warmth left in the ashes. She knelt down and looked in, and a small desperate creature tried to fit itself into her hand, stopping in mid-howl and whimpering.

'Poor little pest,' said Phryne, lifting the puppy and cradling it to her silky breast. 'I'll bet you're hungry and you are certainly cold. Let's go and warm you some milk, shall we, and we'll put your box next to the stove.'

It was one thirty by the kitchen clock. Phryne stoked the slow-combustion stove with chunks of red gum, lowered the lids and waited for a while until the firebox began to roar. Then she found a saucepan and heated some milk and water, half and half for a dog. She poured it into a saucer and watched the little dog wriggle and lap, reflecting how strange it was to be sitting in her own house at such an hour on such an errand. The rest of the house was asleep. Dot was asleep in her tower, and the girls in their bedroom under the jazz-coloured comforters. Phryne could hear Mr. Butler snoring in the Butler's suite, beyond the pantry. It was strange to be awake, Phryne thought, when everyone else was so firmly in the land of nod.

Ember walked into the kitchen and sat down at Phryne's feet, tail curled around black paws, looking inscrutable as was his wont. The clock ticked. The electric light banished the darkness but made the garden outside Phryne's house as black as a pit, and she felt suddenly uncomfortable, as though someone was watching her. She pulled the creamy silk close at the front, swore and stood up, taking the poker. Action, she reflected, was always better than unease.

She unlocked the back door with its huge key and stood in the doorway, scanning her own domain. One tree, tall. One shed, whitewashed. Three garden beds, grey in the darkness. One small patch of lawn. Nothing else, no sound but the wind and no movement but the trees bowing under the wind. She stared out into the night, poker raised, for some time before she closed and locked the door again and returned to the puppy.

It had clambered back into the grocer's box, and was washing itself inefficiently with a small pink tongue like a scrap of ham. Ember, watching it with close attention, cleared the box lid with one complicated leap which took him into a reclining position with the puppy snuggled up to his side. He dipped his gaze and licked the top of its ragged black and white head, then began to wash its milky face.

'Ember, it's a dog, *canis*, you know, not *felis*,' Phryne informed him. Ember appeared unenlightened by this news. The kitchen began to warm. Phryne, fascinated, made herself some Dutch cocoa from the tin with the lady in a white cap on the front and sat sipping it, her bare feet on the hearth stone, the uncurtained windows as black as black glass, and listened to Ember's rising purr.

She put herself back to bed half an hour later, and the night seemed to have quieted so that she fell easily asleep.

All of which went close to explaining why, when Phryne woke suddenly to voices at her own front door, she was annoyed.

'Eight of the clock on a Sunday morning, what an hour!' she exclaimed, as Dot tentatively enquired if Miss Fisher wanted to see the apologetic young man now downstairs with a bunch of hyacinths (white) in his hand?

'Oh, all right, Dot dear, but I'm not getting up yet. Tell Mr. Abrahams that if he cares to breakfast with me I will be delighted to see him in a quarter of an hour's time. Open the window, Dot dear, and bring me coffee, I want to see the spoon standing up in it.'

Phryne extracted herself from a tangle of green sheets and quilt, went into her own bathroom, made certain contraceptive preparations and washed her face. That was as far as she was intending to go in the way of hygiene, and her cream negligée which supplemented the remarkable appeal of her cream night-dress should be decent enough for a chat with a nice young man before Phryne went back to sleep. The insertion of her diaphragm was almost second nature now, with a young man in the offing. She stood at the window, looking out, until the rising wind chilled her and she wrestled the casement shut.

There were green leaves on the sill, recently broken, but whether they had been snapped off the parent stem by a climber or a possum or the weather, who could tell?

Simon Abrahams, who was escorted up the stairs to Miss Fisher's boudoir by a very respectable maid carrying a covered tray, stopped at the door and stared in a way which would have caused his mother to clip his ears. The room was lush, and the bed in which Miss Fisher reposed was hung about with cobweb-fine black gauze embroidered with ivy leaves and grapes. He looked aside and saw his own faun's face in a mirror wreathed with garlands. The bedchamber was opulent, unrestrained and entirely shameless he was glad to say, and he walked forward, his feet sinking into a velvety carpet like moss.

'Simon dear, do come in,' said the vision in the big bed. She was draped in milky Chinese silk and looked both sleepy and cross. He thought her very beautiful and dangerous, and sat down carefully on the edge of her bed and took her hand reverently between both of his own, raising it to his lips to kiss.

'Green leaves, lady?' he said in his lightly accented voice, noticing them on her pillow.

'For spring,' she replied, and he presented his hyacinths. Phryne leaned forward and drank in the scent, and he had a dizzying feeling that he was actually going to fall down her cleavage.

The maid uncovered the tray, taking the flowers and placing them in a vase of exactly the right dimensions. She poured Phryne a cup of coffee from the copper pot, opened the napkin to reveal freshly made bread rolls, and left. Miss Fisher buttered a roll lavishly and poured coffee for her fellow breakfaster. Then she seemed to be struck by a thought.

'Simon, I'm sorry—can you eat with me?'

'Yes, of course,' he said, 'unless you were responsible for dosing my co-religionist with rat poison,' he added, taking a roll and breaking it. 'In fact, even if you were I would presume that you haven't a reason for killing me, eh?'

'Aren't you supposed to only eat kosher food?'

'You've been researching us,' he said slowly. 'Yes, my mother keeps a kosher house. No, I see no reason why your coffee, your cherry jam and your bread should not be perfectly all right. I can't eat dairy food at the same time as meat, that's all, and I'm destined never to taste *moules marinière* or bacon, but that's no great loss. And we keep the Sabbath, so we don't do anything but rest on Saturday, which is something of an impediment in a world which doesn't do anything on Sunday...including get up early, I had forgotten. But my father taught me never to be negligent to beautiful ladies, so I came as soon as I decently could to apologize for not returning your call yesterday.'

He gave her a lopsided smile which was very hard to resist, and Phryne's mood was already improving under the onslaught of real coffee, hyacinths and charm.

'I had a disturbed night, with all that wind; and the puppy which the girls have wished on me started howling. I shall go back to sleep presently, but for the moment I am pleased to see you,' said Phryne, sipping the black caffeine-rich brew and surveying the young man.

He was very decorative. His hair was curly, and she wondered idly what it might feel like under her hand. His bright brown eyes were as alert as a fox's; indeed there was something foxy about him, except that he had the unshakeable confidence of being his mother's favourite or only child. His close-shaven jaw was slightly shadowed, his tie pin was a little too emphatic, his suit a little too formal for so early in the morning, and his buttonhole of a pink rose quite outrageous according to the canons of public-school taste. Phryne was very pleased with her acquisition.

'Delighted,' he murmured, looking into her eyes. She bit into a crust and the young man dragged his gaze away and caught sight of her bedtime reading. He shuffled quickly through the books.

'Ah, yes. Mr. Goldman.'

'Have you read it?' asked Phryne, spreading cherry jam on her roll.

'Yes, certainly. "The Jewish problem is not a Jewish problem, but a gentile problem, and only the gentiles can solve it." The trouble with being a Jew—apart from being Chosen and presumably God knew what he was doing when he Chose us—is that we have no home. There really is no place where the Jews have not lived for years and felt safe which has not turned against them. We exist everywhere on sufferance—here, for example.'

'Here?' Phryne sat up a little. 'There have been no pogroms here.'

'No, but immigration is restricted. If there was an emergency somewhere—Russia, for example—and the Jews had to flee, as they fled in 1492 from Ferdinand and Isabella in Spain, where would they go? Our own assimilationists would keep the Russians out, saying that there was no room in this country for the sweepings of the Soviet ghettos as they said about the immigrants fleeing the Czarist May laws in 1881. The Jews who have been here for a couple of generations—and Australia has only been settled for a few generations, you know—would keep the others away because they are afraid of turning even this laconic place against us. They are afraid of there being too many Jews attracting too much attention and envy. We have not forgotten Ikey Mo in the *Bulletin* in the nineties, you know.'

'The *Bulletin* in the nineties hated everyone,' objected Phryne. 'Along with Ikey Mo there was Johnnie Chinaman and Jacky-Jacky the aborigine and Paddy the drunken Irishman; and they weren't keen on women, either, looking on my own sex, as I understand, as the root of all evil. But what's the solution? If your own people want to restrict immigration, what is to be done?'

'A homeland,' said Simon, and his face shone with a pure light of dedication.

'Where?' asked Phryne, putting the tray on her bedside table.

'Palestine…'

He looked so beautiful, his long lashes lowered over the bright eyes, that Phryne reached out and caressed the curly hair and the smooth cheek. Simon Abrahams nestled into the touch and kissed her palm, and Phryne gasped. Her hand dropped to the broadcloth lap, and Simon made the same noise. She undid his tie, shucked his coat, took the studs from his sleeves. 'Come and lie down with me,' she whispered.

He took the rose from his coat and shed the petals over Phryne. They slid down her shiny black hair and were scattered over her pillow and her breast.

From then on, it was simple. She lay and watched him undress, shedding broadcloth and linen, young enough to pull impatiently at the shirt where the buttons would not release their grip. The slim body emerged like a flower from a calyx: long legs, slim hands and feet, a wiry body used to some hard labour. He was entirely naked when he slid down alongside Phryne in her silken bed, and the cream nightdress was already cast aside.

Cool morning light made an icon, strangely religious, of the young man with the Middle Eastern face. Phryne felt him shiver as their bodies touched at a thousand points, and she ran both hands down his smooth back, her fingers curling over the muscular buttocks and sliding inward to cup the denuded genitalia in a gratifying state of excitement.

Jews, Phryne had been told, did not enjoy sex as much as gentiles because of circumcision. As she sank into a bath of sensuality, she was pleased to have this statement proved as idiotic as she had first thought it.

His fingers trapped her nipples and she gasped aloud, closing her eyes as the clever hands moved down her body and caressed in a circular, fiery motion, so delicate and so skilled that she did not immediately feel the change as the fingers were withdrawn and both bodies closed, joined, with a snap like a tensile steel spring.

Simon Abrahams' knowledge of women had been almost entirely theoretical. He had been sorely tempted by the light ladies who walked St. Kilda Road and by the flaunting damsels of the Eastern Market, who haunted the street-level shops when all the rest of the city was respectably dark, looking for a friend to take home with them before the market shut at nine o'clock. He was conscious of his duty to marry a suitable young woman and have children in due course, and meant to do so. But he had never expected to be seduced by a woman so beautiful, so strong, so sure of her own desires. She was as pale as bone china and as strong as he was; he felt lithe muscle under the smooth skin as she slid from under him and they rolled, so that he was lying flat on his back and the woman was riding him, her breasts in his hands, her mouth on his. She moved like a dancer, like a mating animal, like something out of a hermit's fever-dream. She lay under him with her legs wrapped round his waist. Surprise had delayed his climax; now it overwhelmed him. Her red mouth smothered his cry and matched it. He embraced Phryne as she collapsed onto his chest and panted for breath.

He felt tears trickle down his cheeks and tasted salt on his mouth. He was crying.

Phryne untangled their limbs and lay down beside him, and he put his head on her breast. She felt him sob and said gently, 'Simon?'

'Oh, Phryne, oh, beautiful lady,' he whispered. 'I never...I never thought that the love of woman would be so...so...'

'Overwhelming?' She was still breathless, and her body burned under his hands. Her voice, however, was light and almost careless.

'Well, gentle lady, you wanted me,' he said, hurt. 'Was that all you desired, Phryne?'

'No, I desire a great deal more than that,' she returned. 'I am not intending to cast you from my door now that you have given me your all, Simon dear—don't be melodramatic. You're very beautiful,' she kissed him once. 'And you're very skilled,' she kissed him twice. 'And as you see,' she kissed him a third time, 'you have more to offer me.'

Simon Abrahams found that, as usual, Miss Fisher was correct.

Phryne woke at noon and surveyed the room lazily. Dot had been in and removed the tray, contriving as she always did to ignore any extra tenants in Phryne's bed. The sun was shining in that half-hearted watery unreliable way which marked the season as spring and the city as Melbourne. The wind appeared to have died down. The noises of the house came to her as she turned her head and picked rose petals from her surroundings. Something with a very high-pitched howl was making its wants felt: the telephone bell announcing that the outside world was still there and desirous of establishing contact with Miss Phryne Fisher. She heard Mr. Butler's even tread as he went to answer it and Dot yelling something to the girls, who appeared to be in the kitchen. All normal, even comfortable sounds, after the strange night and the delightful, if fraught, morning.

Sprawled asleep across half the bed was a long-limbed young man of surpassing beauty. His eyes were closed, his expression beatific, his arms outspread, his hands out and half-open, half-curled. He could have been a renaissance painting, except for the love bites which marked his olive throat with round red patches, darkening into black. Phryne wondered what had prompted her to bite him so hard, and shivered at the remembrance. If she had been his first lover—and she suspected so—then this was a youth of truly remarkable amatory skill, who needed only a little cultivation to be superb.

She knew that she could not keep him. He had to go back to his father and his family duty. But while she had him, Phryne meant to enjoy him.

But she was hungry, and it was lunch time. Also, whatever message he had come to deliver had been lost in the translation, so to speak, and it might have been important. She slipped a considering hand down his face, from brow to nose to lip, and he woke enough to kiss her palm.

'That's how this all started,' she observed. 'Wake up, my dear Simon, it's lunch time and I'm starving.'

His bright eyes snapped open and he sat up, startled.

'Oh, Phryne,' he said. 'Oh, Phryne,' he began again. 'I never asked, you know, I never asked all those things one is supposed to ask. You just ravished me out of all my senses,' he said complacently.

'And very nice too,' said Phryne, throwing back the sheets and rising. 'Come and have a bath. You didn't need to ask me,' she added, taking his hand and leading him to her bathroom where the tub was quite big enough for two. Over the roar of the taps, she commented, 'You would have touched my diaphragm, that meant I would not conceive. And anything else can be settled now.' She put both hands on his shoulders and looked into his eyes. 'Thank you for your love and your body,' she said very deliberately. 'But I can't keep you, you belong to your family; and you can't have me, I belong to myself. Is that clear?'

'Yes,' stammered Simon. 'But…does this mean that you have had your will of me, that you….'

'Curb this tendency to melodrama. I do not intend to cast you aside like a soiled glove, either. Dear Simon,' she said, kissing him and helping him into the bath, scattering orchid bath salts with a liberal hand, 'you shall come and lie with me again, if you please, and we shall have a love affair of which your mother will never approve. Now, what did you come here to tell me?'

Simon Abrahams sat in warm water and sponged Phryne's white back while he racked his brains to recall what had brought him to her house so early on a Sunday morning.

For the life of him, he could not remember.

Chapter Five

Rubedo is the ascension of the red queen.
—Elias Ashmole,
Theatrum Chemicum Brittanicum 1689

Phryne pushed back her chair. She had lunched well and her young lover appeared to be coming to terms with his new status. Simon had refused cream soup but accepted lamb chops and pureed vegetables, and was now eating new strawberries with enthusiasm.

'What do you make of these, Simon?' she asked, laying the dead man's notebook and the strange engravings on the table. He puzzled over the black letters.

'No, I can't read them. It's Hebrew, but it's some sort of code, or maybe just a jumble of letters. No, that doesn't seem likely, does it? But the parchments—I've seen something like them before.' He turned the picture of the red lion around, mouthing the Latin. 'It's doggy enough, medieval, probably. I have it, Phryne—alchemy.'

'Alchemy?' asked Phryne, sprinkling castor sugar over her strawberries and applying cream liberally.

'Yes. I don't actually know anything more about it, but those drawings apparently depicted chemical operations. Mercury entered into it. And salt. I've got a friend who's a real expert on alchemy. His name is Yossi Liebermann. They call him Joe.

Been studying it for years—the study of a lifetime, thus Yossi. He says it is connected with Kabala.'

'Kabala?'

'Far too complicated for me to explain,' said Simon. 'We can go and talk to him, if you like. He should be home. Oh, and I've remembered what I came to tell you. My father has talked to his people in the Carlton factory, and they knew this dead man, Shimeon Mikhael. He was a mystic, they said. People were a bit afraid of him. He was a Torah student, a good one, they said. He knew a lot. But he was waiting for the Messiah to come, and that's always been a dangerous thing, my father says. He's invited you to dinner tonight, can you come?'

'Certainly,' said Phryne. 'I am very anxious to get Miss Lee out of quod, though I have no doubt that she is furthering her studies while there. Good. Well, if you would like to use my telephone, you can reassure your father that I have not eaten you alive, and call your friend.'

'Oh, he's not on the telephone, Miss Fisher. He's a bootmaker, and he lives in Carlton. But I'll telephone my father. Mother worries,' he explained.

Phryne ate strawberries and cream and smiled.

Carlton was unimpressive under a harsh light and the wind-blown dust of an unseasonable north wind. Phryne, who disliked dust as much as the cat Ember—neither appreciated having their sleek black fur ruffled—pulled her cloche firmly down and wished she had not chosen to wear a looseish, buttonless crepe de Chine coat and carry a pouchy handbag, as it was difficult to keep her ensemble together in a manner which was both decent and fashionable.

After five minutes of walking, she would have settled for just decent, or even partially effective.

Lygon Street, however, was always fascinating, even on a Sunday when all the shops were shut. Phryne noticed the Kosher Butcher's sign, and the strange angular black writing on the window. She turned the corner past the hardware shop into a street of little houses, dominated by the huge red brick wall of the Nurses' Home. Yossi Liebermann, it seemed, lived in Faraday Street in a boarding house, and Faraday Street was entirely lined with resting vans and horseless drays. This had meant that Phryne had to park her own car in Lygon Street and walk directly into the gale. She wished for a huge safety pin to secure her coat. She was confident of her ability to make this fashionable, if necessary.

The hot wind grabbed at her hair and pulled at her garments. She lost her grip on the edge of the coat and it bellied and flapped like a sail. Phryne Fisher was about to lose her temper with her garments, and her young man watched with some interest as she dragged the coat off and rolled it into a loose, crease-forming bundle.

'There are times when I swear I consider that all fashion designers hate women,' she snarled. 'Give me a man who designs clothes that can be worn in weather! What's the number of the house, Simon?'

'Here, I believe.' Simon opened the front door of a small single-fronted house. Simultaneously he put his fingers to his lips, reaching up and touching a little tube, like a metal casemoth, nailed aslant inside the doorway.

'What's that?' she asked, coming in gladly out of the dust into a dim hallway and a very strong smell of soup. Someone was making stock. Phryne smelt an odd addition to this domestic scent: something like glue?

'It's a *mezuzah*. It's a bit of the Torah, the Book of Laws, the part of the bible which tells us to love God,' he said. '*Shalom, Yossi*! How are you, old fellow? This is my friend, Miss Fisher.'

A thin young man, already balding, stooped down and took Phryne's hand very gingerly, as though she might bite. 'Delighted,' he said in a thick accent which was not quite German or Russian but had elements of both. 'Simon, I have no fitting place to entertain a lady, you know that, and it's Sunday, only Kadimah will be open…'

'Never mind, Yossi, Miss Fisher is investigating a mystery, the death of Michaels in the bookshop in the Eastern Market. My father has retained her.'

Yossi's dark doe-like eyes had been examining Phryne closely, though without offence; a strangely dispassionate gaze which took account of her youth and undoubted sexual allure without being personally affected in the least. Now he exclaimed, 'Well, then, if your father knows about this, Simon, it is all right. Of course, please, lady, come in. There is only the kitchen to sit in, or perhaps the yard, would you care for some tea? It is a hot day,' he continued, leading the way down the hall, which was long enough to play cricket, and down an unexpected step into a large kitchen which was full of light, people and the mixed scents.

A plump woman in an apron turned from the stove, where she was adding an onion to her stock. Two young women looked up from the big table, where they were assembling sequin-covered buttons next to a boy who sat in the corner, draped in a prayer shawl, reading a thick book. A young man in his shirtsleeves stopped in mid-pour of a glass of tea from a silver samovar and stared. Three young men stood up in the yard outside, dropping newspapers and hats at the sight of Phryne, bare-armed and dusty.

'Yossi, Yossi, you *schlemiel*, how could you bring me Mr. Abrahams without any warning?' exclaimed the woman furiously, bustling forward to take Simon's hands. 'Come in, come in, sit down—girls, put away the sequins and help me, find the good tablecloth, the good glasses, quickly, quickly!'

'Don't trouble yourself, Mrs. Grossman, we just came by on the off chance that Yossi was at home. This is Miss Fisher, she's working for my father, trying to find out who killed Michaels in the Eastern Market.'

'Miss Fisher,' said Mrs. Grossman, raking Phryne with a hard glare, then relaxing. Phryne wondered what Mrs. Grossman had found in her face which reassured her. 'Sit down, sit down, please. This is an honour. Don't trouble yourself, he says,' she grumbled, flinging a snowy tablecloth over the wooden table,

freshly wiped by one of the silent girls. 'Here is Mr. Abrahams'
son and a distinguished lady visitor and my house looks like a
cattle market, and he tells me not to trouble myself! *Oy, vey*, men!'
She dusted the crockery as her daughter put down the tray.

'Let's all say hello, shall we?' asked Simon a little uneasily.
'Phryne, this is Fanny and this is Helen.' The two girls shook
hands. They were dark, with curly hair tied up with red ribbons.
Helen, the younger, gave Phryne a mischievous smile which flashed
across her face for a second and lit it like a shooting star. 'This is
David Kaplan, his brother Abe, and their cousin Solly, they are all
newly arrived here from Poland.' The three young men, who had
squeezed into the kitchen, all bowed and squeezed out again as Mrs.
Grossman flapped her apron at them as though she was chasing
chickens. 'Out, out, you've been introduced—what's the matter,
never seen a beautiful lady before, eh?' They returned reluctantly
to their newspapers, but Phryne could feel their attention.

'This is Phillip Grossman,' said Simon, and the young man
in shirtsleeves, who had looked round frantically for his coat and
not found it, offered Phryne the hand with the glass of tea in it,
blushed, and was only saved from destruction at the hands of
his mother—who would not have been happy if he had spilled
it on her hand-embroidered tea-cloth—by Helen, who took the
glass, patted his shoulder and abjured him in a whisper not to
be a *schlimazl*.

'What's the difference between a *schlemiel* and a *schlimazl*?'
asked Phryne, sitting down on a hard wooden kitchen chair and
noticing that of all the clean kitchens she had been in this was
undoubtedly the cleanest, and probably the poorest.

'Ah, well, a *schlemiel* means well but he is clumsy and fool-
ish and things don't work out the way he expects. A *schlimazl* is
just unlucky. If he made umbrellas it would stop raining. If he
winds a clock, it stops. If he inherited a coffin business people
would stop dying. To him it all happens badly,' said Simon. 'Eh,
Mrs. Grossman?'

'Easier if you give the lady an example. Picture the scene,'
said Mrs. Grossman, spreading her arms. 'A café. A customer. A

waiter. The customer is wearing his best suit, hoping to impress maybe a young lady, eh? The one who spills the soup into his lap, that is a *schlemiel*. The one on whom the soup is spilled—a *schlimazl*.'

'Abraham ibn Ezra,' announced the boy in the prayer shawl and yarmulke unexpectedly. His siblings looked at him with slightly exasperated affection and his mother with whole-hearted adoration. There was no doubt who was Mrs. Grossman's favourite son.

'My son, Saul.' Mrs. Grossman was bursting with pride. 'He is studying Torah, all the time Torah and Talmud, we are all so proud of him! What do you want to say to us, *bubelah*?'

'Rabbi Ezra,' said the boy, lowering thick lashes over bright eyes modestly. 'He said about the *schlimazl*, "If I sold lamps/the sun/in spite/Would shine at night." He was a poet in the twelfth century.' With this bit of information, Saul dried up and went back to his text. Phryne was impressed.

'He is preparing for his bar mitzvah. Mr. Abrahams is his friend, his father not being here to see him—Yossel, God rest his soul in peace, *alav ha-sholom*, he would have been so proud! Rabbi Cohen says Saul has a real gift.' Mrs. Grossman wiped her eyes and poured out tea from the samovar—thin, straw-coloured and flavoured with lemon—into thick glasses in silver holders wrought in Europe with delicate artistry. Like the tea-cloth, these were clearly treasured possessions and perhaps all that Mrs. Grossman had been able to bring from her old life in a city or a village or a *shtetl*; and perhaps she had left her own house in flames as she fled with one suitcase and several children from city to port until she finally fetched up, so improbably, in Australia, which was after all the end of the world. Phryne asked.

'We called it the *Goldene Medina*,' said Mrs. Grossman, arranging little almond biscuits on a silver plate. 'Have a biscuit, please, Mr. Abrahams, Miss Fisher. The golden land, Australia, where you could pick up nuggets in the streets. We saved for years, Yossel and me, working, working, always picking up anything we could do—my Yossel was a carpenter. I could embroider, but also paint and gild and carve; he taught me, what my father would have said I didn't like to think, but he said, Yossel said, we must leave Russia, the new laws are killing us, and when the war comes the revolution will follow and maybe then they will be glad to see the back of us, they hate Jews, but they hate Christians too, and unless you want to see our Philo a soldier and our little Helen a whore, we must leave...*ai, ai*, what a time, we worked all the hours God gave, but he was right, my Yossel *alav ha-sholom*, the revolution did come and they did let us leave, and they let us take some goods, too, only the one big box, and the children's clothes, but we made the frame of the trunk out of gold, and stitched heavy cowhide over it, and then we sat with our hearts in our mouths, *oy*! in case the customs men dropped it and it split and showed the gold....' She rocked herself as she spoke, and her son Phillip took her hand. 'We came down into Germany where they did not want us either but let us pass, and they stole my mother's silver spoons as we passed the border and took a ship for Australia. It was so funny, we had only what we stood up in and our papers and the children, and I was pregnant with Fanny, and in the hold we had a treasure which we couldn't get at.'

'I remember the ship,' said Phillip quietly. 'I was seasick for days and we met bad weather and Papa prayed. I remember his voice and thought that as long as he kept praying we wouldn't sink.' He gave a half-apologetic smile and his mother cried, 'Well, *did* the ship sink? So, we heard at some places that they were killing the Jews in Russia, that we had escaped in time because they had closed the borders, that our old village was burned and gone. My dear Yossel *alav ha-sholom*, he told me that the revolution would treat us no better than the Czar had. Then we came here—I remember, we saw this Australia first from Fremantle, a terrible dry dead flat place, and my little Philo said, "*This* is the *Goldene Medina*, Mama?" and I was so disappointed I could have cried, but when we got to Melbourne there were people waiting—it was so strange, we were standing on the deck looking at the quay and I took Yossel's hand, I was suddenly so afraid, what had we done, leaving our own place and coming to this new country, and then someone yelled from the shore, "*Shalom aleichem!*" out loud, like that, so that anyone could hear and know it was a Jew speaking, and I was so relieved that I cried anyway, *nu*, where was I? Please, Mr. Abrahams and lady, have some more tea.'

'What happened then?' asked Phryne, sipping more hot, thin, refreshing tea.

'We were safe then. Yossel spoke to Mr. Abrahams, and he took charge of the trunk and paid us the full gold price for it, and we bought this house, and then just when we were settled and we all had jobs and we were happy, my Yossel he took tuberculosis and died, *ai, ai*, he lasted long enough to see his son, and then he was gone. My Yosselah, *alav ha-sholom*. God rest his soul, he was a good man.' Mrs. Grossman wiped her eyes with her apron. 'But we are doing well. I keep a boarding house and Mrs. Hallenstein sends me some of the new ones from the boats, so I have a household to feed and they have a good kosher home. My daughter Helen makes buttons and my daughter Fanny works in an office and my son Philo—who would have thought he would grow so tall?—he has his own shop in the Eastern Market, a picture frame maker. And my Saul is a son of the Book. And we are all happy except that Yossi brings me distinguished visitors without any warning.'

Phryne took Mrs. Grossman's hand and said, 'We are very glad to be here and your house could not be any tidier or cleaner if you had ten years' notice. I like this tea. Do you buy it locally?'

'King and Godfreys,' said Mrs. Grossman promptly. 'But maybe you can come again, and we will make you perhaps some French coffee, and my seed cake which I make better than any woman in Faraday Street, though I say it myself; it was my mother's recipe. Now I will not intrude any more on this business of the death, a terrible thing, such a young man.'

She collected her daughters and bustled away. Yossi Liebermann and Phillip sat down at the table, pushing aside the plate of biscuits, and Simon laid out the Hebrew notes and the strange pictures on vellum. They looked at them for some time in silence. Phryne saw a white bird rising out of a black cage, a red-robed woman crowning herself with gold, and a face perhaps of the moon with the subscription 'Luna'. In the middle of the flames, brilliantly red and gold, a small pale couple lay, crowned, limbs entwined, clearly making love. Phryne looked at the tiny female face blank with ecstasy and fought down a pang of lust.

'This is alchemy,' said Yossi. He touched the picture of the copulating couple with one hardened forefinger. 'This is the mating of the Golden King and the Silver Queen, which is sun and moon. You see, there are their names.' He pointed out 'Sol et Luna' in the margin of the brightly coloured painting. 'I don't know what this is about.' He laid aside a list, in Latin, and a block of dark Elizabethan printing. 'But this relates to the Kabala.'

'How do you know?' asked Phryne.

The stooped young man replied, 'These are verses which point to it. "*Immitens formas et influxus in Jacob sive subjectum Hominen*", which means "Letting forth shapes and influxes into Jacob or else the subjected man". Jacob means Israel, and there is the tree. But this is Christianized, not the original Hebrew Tree of Knowledge. That is fortunate, because I would not have been able to talk to you about our own sacred mystery, but this is possibly medieval, no later than renaissance, and I think it is part of the angel magic practised by such as John Dee.'

He smoothed the delicate painting with his work-ruined fingers. There was a supine naked man at the bottom of the page. From his genitals grew a tree, and each branch carried a globed fruit in which Hebrew letters and a Latin or Greek word or phrase was written. Perched on each branch was a creature: a dove or a raven or a snake. Crowning the whole was a king on a throne wearing the most magnificent purple robes.

'What does it mean?' Phryne asked.

Yossi sighed. 'Lady, that is the study of a lifetime, of many lifetimes, and I have only one and also a living to earn. But since I am begged by my friend Simon, I will tell you this much. The alchemists sought for the philosopher's stone, which would transmute base metal into gold. They used the holy Kabala in their study. Indeed, some of them were not even interested in the stone for its wealthy properties, or because it was to make them live forever. They wanted knowledge—to know everything. Myself, I am content to know a little. I do not think men were meant to know everything. I think such knowledge would burn us as Semele was burned by Zeus' fire. However, they said that they would reach perfection; the stone would make base metal into gold because gold is a perfect metal. The Kabala, it describes the works of Creation. There are ten paths, ten branches. It is a way of describing the world which can be used to call an angel or a familiar spirit, to make a golem.'

'What is a golem?' Phryne was fascinated.

'A servant made of clay or brass. Rabbi Elijah of Chelm made one, and it caused him a lot of trouble. He set it to sweep out his house, and it didn't stop until he had no house. He sent it to catch fish and it caught a whole lake's worth but didn't bring them back because he hadn't told it to—a golem has no mind. He animated it by writing the word of life on its brow, and killed it by rubbing out one letter, which means "death". This is called the use of the divine names, it is found in the *Sepher Yetzirah*, and that is all I can tell you about it, lady, I have taken vows.' Yossi was apologetic but firm.

'I have not, and I don't believe that this is mystical, it's all in the book, and it's philosophy, Yossi, not religion,' argued Simon.

'The rabbi says it's all romance,' offered Saul. Both young men looked at him. Phryne was expecting them to squash him, as one does with little brothers, but both of them, instead, listened.

'What else does the rabbi say?' asked Yossi.

Without closing the book, Saul blinked, took a gulp of Simon's tea, and recited: 'It is called Sephirot because it states that there are ten palaces—that is the Hebrew word for ten,' he added kindly, for Phryne's sake. 'But the top three cannot be contemplated by men. The lower seven are populated by angels praising God always, and through the palaces, from the lowest to the highest, the soul rises until it is at last one with En Soph the mystical and transcendent.' At the mention of this name, Yossi drew in a sharp breath. 'Rabbi Moses de Leon in Spain wrote a lot about it, but my rabbi says that a life of contemplation is better spent on the Torah.'

'There go your secrets, Yossi,' said Simon. 'Truly the little brother is a master of learning, *nu?*'

'But…please excuse me, Mr. Abrahams,' said Saul, 'I have seen a diagram like this before, and I don't think it was Christian. The name was the same as on that picture.'

'What name, Saul?'

'*Adam Kadmon,*' said Saul, and returned to his text.

'Primeval man,' said Simon. But the effect on Yossi of this statement was notable: he paled to the colour of junket and snatched his hands away from the parchment as though it had been especially prepared by the Borgias for one of their favourite enemies.

Without a word, he ran down the hall and into the street. Simon Abrahams and Phryne watched the door clap to behind him with astonishment. Even Saul looked up in mild surprise, all the emotion of which this scholarly child seemed capable.

Mrs. Grossman came back into the room, attended by her daughters, in time to hear the door slam. 'That Yossi,' said Mrs. Grossman. 'Poor boy, he works all day and then sits up talking all night at the Kadimah, enough to turn his brains. Excuse him, Mr. Abrahams. Have some more tea. Then Saul will read for us.'

'And you sing,' insisted Phillip.

'No, no, I only know old songs,' protested Mrs. Grossman, delighted but making a ritual objection.

'We insist,' said Simon, and Saul leaned forward to the book.

His voice was a boy's voice, cracking with manhood, and the tones and cadences of the language were utterly foreign to Phryne's ear. But the image of the boy, tucked in the corner of the workaday kitchen, his curly hair topped with a white and gold yarmulke, the striped tallis around his shoulders, his ink-stained boy's finger running the wrong way along the black letter text, stayed with Phryne as an epitome of the experience of all of

Australia's Jews: a people who treasured learning, and who never forgot their past or relinquished hold of their future.

Saul accepted the boiled lolly he was given with royal condescension. Learning, to him, was sweet. Mrs. Grossman sat down and without preamble began to sing, a quavering lullaby in a strange tongue, and Simon whispered the translation to Phryne as she listened.

> *'In dem bishe micdosh…*
> *Beneath my little one's cradle*
> *Stands a clear white goat…*
> *There will come a time, my child*
> *When you will wander far and wide.*
> *Remember the song I sing today…*

Schluf-sie, mein kind, schluf,' she concluded. Then she sighed, seized her son Phillip and hugged him hard, and summoned a smile.

'You will give my greetings to your father,' she said to Simon. Phryne shook hands all round, and Mrs. Grossman accompanied them to the door. As she was leaving, the older woman pressed a packet into her hand.

'Just a little tea,' she protested. 'A few biscuits. Nothing.'

Phryne was touched. 'Thank you,' she said, and went out into the dusty street feeling warmed and a little dislocated, as though she had been away in another country and had come back with unexpected swiftness to somewhere which ought to have been familiar but which looked odd and alien.

'That's a nice song,' she said, wrestling her coat over her shoulders. Simon caught the edges and bodily wrapped it around Phryne.

'It's the one lullaby which everyone knows,' he said. 'There isn't a Yiddish child in the world who wasn't sung to sleep with *Raisins and Almonds*. My own mother sang it to me. Now, Madame,' he bowed, 'are you coming to my father's house to dine?'

'Yes, I am.'

'Then perhaps you could drop me in the city, where I can get a taxi, so that I can prepare myself fittingly.'

'Certainly. Is this white tie—what should I wear?'

'Just ordinary evening clothes. Mother likes to dress. I don't think Father could care, but he's a merchant at heart, bless him.'

'Thank you, and what do you make of Yossi racing off like that?'

'I don't know what to think, Phryne.'

They had found the big car again, and Phryne tore off the offending coat and flung it into the back before she climbed into the driver's seat. It was such a hot day and the car had not been parked long so she tried the self-starter, and it worked. The engine turned over with a muted roar like an annoyed tiger. Simon, realizing that he was not going to be needed as a wielder of starting handles, climbed up into the seat next to Phryne.

'Is he usually that jumpy?'

'Well, no, I would have said that he was calm, like Saul. A lot of study does tend to disconnect one from the real world.'

'He must know something, Simon; you need to find him again and extract it. Was there anything odd about the words Saul used?'

'No, it's just the word for primeval, "of earth". *Kadmon*. Adam as the first man. I never studied the Kabala, so I really can't tell you any more. Are you going to collect that truck?'

'No,' said Phryne, giving the wheel a deft twiddle. The truck passed, the driver yelling opprobrious epithets. It would not have been fitting for a lady to reply, so she only raised a finger or two in the appropriate gesture.

'One thing I will say, Miss Fisher,' yelled Simon Abrahams, holding onto his hat as the Hispano-Suiza belted down Swanston Street past the brewery in a cloud of dust. 'Life with you is always very interesting!'

'Thank you,' said Miss Fisher. 'Here's the station. See you at eight.'

And because she was both hot and dirty, Phryne beguiled the rest of the afternoon by taking her maid, her adopted daughters and their pestilential new puppy to the beach, where she contemplated the difficulties of the Kabala from one of her favourite thinking positions, neck deep in sea water.

Chapter Six

The mating of sol and luna is conjunctio.
—Elias Ashmole,
Theatrum Chemicum Brittanicum 1689

Dinner, Phryne thought, might well be sticky in more than just temperature. As she allowed herself to be dressed in a Greek-inspired floor-length gown, she observed, 'Dot, I need you to make me a list.'

'A list, Miss?' Dot fastened the heavy gold necklace. It was made of old French coins, and it had matching long earrings.

'Yes. Miss Lee said that she sold "some novels" and then had a discussion with a woman about an atlas that morning—call it "the fateful morning"—and then there were a couple of young men buying a book about statistics. We need to find Miss Lee's customers. I want you to go through her order book—Jack left it on the downstairs table—and make a list of what she sold. How many people do we need to find, and how do we do that?'

'They should have come forward already, Miss,' observed Dot, flinging the filmy dress over Phryne's head so skilfully that not a hair was disturbed on the Dutch-doll head. 'There's been enough about the murder in the paper.'

'I know, but they haven't.' Phryne surveyed herself in the glass. The dress had an underslip of solid white silk, over which the delicate draperies of the overgown flowed. It was suggestive but not obscene.

'And how do we find someone who has just come into the Eastern Market on the off chance—they might be from anywhere,' continued Dot. 'They might have just come into the city for the day from—oh, I don't know, Bendigo—and might not read the papers.'

'Or they might have been run over by a tram just outside, or be deaf and dumb, or living in a cellar,' agreed Phryne. 'Yes, I know. It's going to be very difficult. But we need to find them. Also, can you call Bert and Cec for me? Ask them to lunch. The Eastern Market is full of carters and labourers. I need to know what happened to that rat poison, and I need someone on the inside. I have a feeling that this all centres on that market.'

'Why?' asked Dot.

'Just a feeling. Oh, and Dot dear, make sure that Mr. Butler locks all the doors and windows tonight, will you?'

'Miss…' said Dot, her brow creasing in a frown. 'Is this case dangerous?'

'No more than any of the others,' said Phryne airily. 'Now, how do I look?' She turned, watching the draped chiffon fall into place. 'Nice. Very nice. Tomorrow you can go and see Miss Lee again and extract from her memory every detail about her customers that morning, all right? And now I really must go,' she added, patting Dot on the cheek. 'Won't be late. This evening may be something of a trial, I fear. Mrs. Abrahams cannot possibly approve of me.'

Phryne arrived at the Abrahams' East Kew mansion in her big red car and drove it neatly up the driveway to park next to the big Rolls. A driver, collar unbuttoned, leapt to his feet and dropped his newspaper and his cigarette at the sight of one slender leg revealed up to the thigh as she alighted. Phryne grinned at him.

'Mind her for me, will you?' she asked.

'Strewth,' said the driver. 'She's a beaut, ain't she? Lagonda?'

'Hispano-Suiza. Observe the stork on the radiator cap. You're the Abrahams' chauffeur?'

'Yes, Miss,' he said, self-consciously adjusting his jacket. He was a young man with curly fair hair like fleece and a rural drawl.

'Been here long?'

'Three years.'

'Good place?'

'Yes, Miss, fair bloke, the Boss, always extra if he keeps me out late, lashings of tucker but foreign, but I like foreign. The Missus is hard to please, but she's a good sort. I'm saving up for a farm, so it suits me to live in. You come for dinner? I'll ring the bell for you, Miss,' he said, escorting Phryne along a garden path and up several steps to an imposing front door.

Whoever had built this house, thought Phryne, had a lot of money and a burning desire to enrich the working stonemason. It was made of solid dark stone, with bow windows and heavy window ledges under a red tiled roof. Phryne had observed the gargoyles as she came in. The architect had evidently been inspired by a visit to Notre Dame de Paris. The front door was set with gems of coloured glass, complex and beautiful, through which light glowed.

A butler opened the door, and Phryne farewelled her escort and stepped inside.

'Miss Fisher? This way, Madam,' murmured the functionary from his starched height. He was perfect right down to the gold studs in his shirt and the sable solemnity of his bow tie, of such a perfect butterfly shape that it must have been either (unthinkably) stitched into place or the product of a long and devout apprenticeship.

The hall was high and painted in a pale cream to show off a treasury of paintings. Phryne exclaimed in delight, and went over to examine what she was sure was a little Renoir of a child with a cat. The small face smiled out of the canvas, creamy skin against tortoise-shell fur. She was aware of air moving and turned to find herself being examined by a pair of dark unreadable eyes.

'It is beautiful, yes?' asked the woman.

'It is,' said Phryne honestly. 'Quite lovely. My name's Phryne Fisher,' she held out her hand. 'Thank you for inviting me to dinner.'

'My son's friends are our friends,' replied Mrs. Abrahams, barely touching Phryne's fingers. 'Do come in, Miss Fisher, we are having drinks in the library.'

She led the way. There was a faint trace of accent, Phryne thought, following her hostess' rigid back along the hall and through a solid oak door. But Mrs. Abrahams was not what she had expected. She was dressed in expensive tailored clothes, certainly—a rich plum silk dress which set off her golden complexion and her black hair. Her legs were clad in silk stockings as fine as Phryne's own. They probably shared the same shoemaker and certainly the same couturière. Mrs. Abrahams was impeccably turned out, and even with her black eyes and scraped-back shiny black hair had no flavour of the exotic at all. Mrs. Abrahams, in fact, did not look any different from any one of Phryne's acquaintances, and she was oddly disappointed. All the verve and enthusiasm which characterized Mrs. Grossman was flattened and quenched. In an attempt to fit in, Mrs. Abrahams had lost her flair. But she was very beautiful, and Phryne wondered where she had found the interesting panache of diamonds and feathers which decorated the left side of her sleek head.

The library was lined with books which looked as though they had been read and contained a gasogene on a tray, an array of interesting bottles, and three male Abrahams. They sprang to their feet when Phryne entered and Simon came forward to take her hand, kissing it with a certain fervour which indicated that he remembered their encounter with pleasure.

Whatever difficulty Phryne was having with the mother, the son, uncle and husband were instantly explicable. Simon was the picture of a successful, well-loved and confident young man, chafing a little at the restrictions of his father's house and alight with some idealistic purpose. Chaim Abrahams was self-effacing and stout but a little rubbed at the edges, as though time had not treated him well, though his suit was first class and his corporation extensive. Benjamin Abrahams was thick set, strong, middle aged, and prosperous. Phryne looked for the phantom cigar that always hovered in his mouth when convention would not allow him a real one. His handclasp was firm and warm and he beamed on Miss Fisher.

'The Hon. Detective Lady!' he exclaimed. 'What can we fetch for you? A little sherry, maybe, or would you like a cocktail?'

'Sherry, if you please,' murmured Phryne. She tasted it with pleasure. It was amontillado, to be sipped with reverence. The company sat down in comfortable chairs which could have been real Chippendale and surveyed Phryne, who surveyed them back with perfect poise.

'The pictures in the hall are absolutely beautiful.' Phryne opened with a conventional remark. 'Have you been collecting for a long time, Mr. Abrahams?'

'Since I arrived in Paris just after the war,' said Mr. Abrahams. 'They are a good investment, and besides they are beautiful, *nu*? I have a big canvas in the drawing room you will like, I think, if you care for the later Impressionists. Of the earlier I have alas only a few pieces—they were too expensive for me then; now, they are worth thousands, then only hundreds, but I did not have the hundreds, eh? But Toulouse-Lautrec I could afford, the Pissaro and some Sisley, also some rare books and drawings, manuscripts. I brought them with me when we left and came here; also my dear Julia has exquisite taste and she ordered the decoration of this house to set them off.'

Mrs. Abrahams waved off the compliment with a negligent hand. She was good, Phryne considered, a very finished product of some English finishing school, perhaps.

'Cream walls, yes,' agreed Phryne. 'With just touches of old gold and bronze. Very stylish. But what do you think of the art moderne, then?'

'Myself, I have no taste for it,' admitted Mr. Abrahams. 'But Simon likes it. See, there on the mantelpiece: the bronze girl. Simon dotes on her.' He grinned and Mrs. Abrahams stiffened, and Phryne reflected that it was going to be a very trying evening if this continued. She got up and examined the bronze.

It was very fine. The figure was of a young girl caught in a windstorm. Her finely detailed hands and face were made of ivory. She wore a decorated cloche hat and a raincoat which the wind was blowing so that the cloth flattened against her body and billowed behind her like a bell. Under the heavy cloth Phryne saw a froth of lacy bronze petticoat. One hand was holding her hat, and the other was grabbing her rebellious garment. It was innocent, charming and accomplished, and Phryne liked it very much.

'A lovely thing,' she said to Simon. He smiled and his mother made a harsh hissing noise. Mr. Abrahams patted her arm but he might as well have been patting the slender carved mahogany arm of his chair. Phryne knew the signs. This was a maternal lioness on guard against a predator who was stalking one of her cubs. This could be borne, as Phryne knew that her intentions were honourable. However, if this dinner was not going to be unbearably dull, she needed to get Mrs. Abrahams alone. An explanation would either clear the air or expel Miss Fisher from the house—and either would be preferable to this subdued hostility.

'Mrs. Abrahams, perhaps you could show me the paintings in the hall? I should like another look at that Renoir,' she asked, and the lady of the house accepted reluctantly.

When the door had safely closed on the slightly puzzled male faces, Phryne said, 'What have you got against me, Mrs. Abrahams?' and watched the closed face come alive in dazzling rage. Porcelain, she fancied, cracked as Julia Abrahams demanded, 'What do *you* want with my *son?*'

'I just want to borrow him,' said Phryne sweetly. 'I'll give him back when you want him. I know I can't keep him, and I won't hurt him.'

Mrs. Abrahams cocked her sleek black head and considered her visitor. When she spoke again, her voice had the same lilt as her husband's.

'You *don't* want to marry him?'

'No.'

There was a pause, then Simon's mother demanded, 'What's *wrong* with him?'

Phryne released the laugh she had been suppressing, and after a moment Mrs. Abrahams joined in. Her finishing school poise slid from her like a cloak from the shoulders, and she laughed so hard that she had to lean her immaculate back against the wall.

Phryne, who had been wondering what a sensual man like Benjamin Abrahams had seen in his stiff cold wife, was enlightened. Her whole attitude had changed; her immobile face was mobile, and she was hiccuping with mirth. Finally she groped for a handkerchief and wiped her eyes.

'*Ai*, what a pickle I've been in,' she confessed. 'Ever since Simon told us about you. Such a beautiful lady—he's been singing your praises for days, and then Bennie employed you to get the excellent Miss Lee out of jail, so you would be close to my son and you could not fail to notice his…his…'

'Infatuation,' Phryne completed the sentence. 'Don't worry. I can manage him. He is not,' she added, her hand on the door, 'the first young man in that condition that I have seen.'

'No, he wouldn't be,' agreed Mrs. Abrahams. 'You must call me Julia. Come and look at the Renoir, now, and let's not make liars of ourselves. It's a pretty thing, isn't it? I was so angry with Bennie when he bought it, it took all our savings. But he told me he'd buy me a fur coat when he sold it, and he made our fortune just after that with the Michelangelo red-chalk Madonna, so I got my fur coat and kept the girl and the cat as well.'

'The Michelangelo? Oh, please do call me Phryne, Julia. I have a feeling that I heard about it. I was in Paris, just after the war.'

'You were? It was the coup of my Bennie's career as a dealer. After that he packed up and moved here, because one cannot count on two miracles in a lifetime. There we were, Bennie and me—I had married against my father's wishes; he did not like Ben because he was so poor and he thought I was wasting my expensive education, but we were in love, and we sold pictures and objets d'art. Ben went to all the auctions of deceased estates, and in one Italian sale, an old man who died without heirs, he bought a big trunk of drawings and etchings for a few francs because he thought it might contain some of the Hokusai screen pictures popular in the nineties—that's what he could see at the top. They were an inspiration to the Impressionists, you know, and I used to remount them as pictures and we could always sell them. It was difficult, because they were printed on very cheap paper. We hauled the trunk home to our atelier, which was freezing, it was the middle of winter, so cold that ice was forming on the *inside* of our windows, and we upturned it so that all the prints and scrolls fell out onto the oilcloth. And Bennie was unrolling them and sorting them while I was making coffee, and I heard him say a very rude word.'

'And she turned and saw me unrolling a full length red chalk sketch of the Madonna, a study for a sculpture, perhaps. On vellum so old that it cracked,' said Mr. Abrahams' rich voice from the door. 'And I said "Look, Julia," and she looked, and there were the initials in the corner, clear as the day Michelangelo drew them, and she sat back on her heels and said, "First, some coffee, and then we rejoice that God has not forgotten us." But I was so nervous that when the coffee came I spilled it, though not on the Michelangelo drawing. Come, beautiful ladies, if you have finished with the Renoir we can sit down, hmm?' He led the way into the library and they sat down again. Julia sipped her sherry, smiling, and her male relatives exhaled a breath of not-very-well-concealed relief.

'Then what happened?' asked Phryne, agog.

'Oh, then we carried it together—*such* a journey, we were terrified that something would happen to tear the miracle from us—into the Ile de Cité to the Sotheby's man; and the relief when we laid it on his table and Bennie gave him the receipts for the provenance—they had to check of course that the dead count's family had such a thing in their possession, but it was clear title, inventory entries right back to the day they bought it from Michelangelo's estate. The dead man had no heirs, so we weren't taking anything away from anyone, such a great thing the Lord did for us. And we didn't have any money for a celebration so we had to walk back in the snow, you remember?' she asked fondly, and Benjamin Abrahams chuckled.

'I could smell trouble in France—there were synagogues desecrated and much anti-Semitic *dreck* in the newspapers. The Protocols of the Elders of Zion, *feh*! Even when everyone knows that it is a Russian forgery, they were reprinting it. So when the chalk drawing was sold, we came out here to join my brother Chaim—he was not doing well in business and wanted a position, and he's family, of course, and a great help Chaim is, my right-hand man, eh Chaim?'

'A *mitzvah*,' said Chaim. 'A blessing.'

'No, no, Chaim, don't say that. You're too modest. I couldn't have managed without you,' said his brother.

Chaim shook his head, smiled, and took some more sherry. It was evidently an old argument. Mr. Abrahams continued, 'So I came here and bought a house and a little property—we are very lucky. And you, Miss Fisher?'

'Phryne, please. I was born here and I was very poor until a lot of young men were killed in the Great War, and then I was suddenly rich and hauled off to England. After I left school there wasn't anything for me to do but Good Works or flower arranging, so I ran away to Paris; and then I came here because a man hired me to find out if his daughter was being poisoned by her husband. I like it here. I bought a house in St. Kilda. I have a maid and a staff and two adopted daughters, a cat called Ember, and just yesterday my household was increased by a new puppy. I've been very lucky, too,' said Phryne, who was always willing to count her blessings.

Mrs. Abrahams beamed upon Phryne. This wealthy young woman was content in her independence and would not give it up to snare a rich boy, even one so beautiful and attractive as her son Simon.

'Tell me, do all the Jews in Melbourne speak with one voice about policy?' asked Phryne. 'There seem to be a number of views on immigration. And Palestine.'

'No, no, *one* voice? Ten thousand voices. There is a divide in the Jewish community,' responded Mr. Abrahams. 'Those across the river, the "gentlemen of the Mosaic persuasion" as they call themselves—Carlton thinks that they are compromising their Jewishness away, so that they forget that they are Jews—marry Christians, and cease to have an identity. People who do well move from Carlton now to East Kew, staying on this side of the city. The Jews who have been here longest live in Caulfield and Camberwell. They think that Carlton is running the risk of pogroms because they are so different, speaking Yiddish in the street, even wearing sidelocks and gabardine like the Hasidim in St. Kilda. Carlton thinks that Caulfield has no guts and that they are all imitation Christians; Caulfield thinks that Carlton is obstinately different and foreign and, well, Jewish, and is going to get us all killed.'

'Who is right?' asked Phryne, allowing the butler to seat her at a snowily draped dinner table.

'Both, of course,' said Benjamin Abrahams. 'There is something to be said for keeping a low profile and possibly even for restricting immigration. It has worked in some places.'

'But not forever,' said Simon, alert, from next to Phryne.

'No, nothing works forever,' agreed Mr. Abrahams.

'The only solution is Palestine,' said Simon.

'No, no, no,' said his father. 'What is there of the Holy Land now but mud and swamps and deserts and Turks? And Arabs? It is not ours any more. We were dispersed. We are exiles.'

'Then it is time we went home,' said Simon. 'Two thousand years wandering, it is enough. Already we have bought land there. Now that Zionism is established and we have a clear goal, we must go forward, purchase the land from the Arabs, and build a Promised Land again.'

'Palestine does not flow with milk and honey any more,' argued his father. 'It flows with dirty water and diseases. It is a dead land, and dead land cannot be resurrected. Besides, are we farmers? Can I milk a cow, turn a harrow, reap corn?'

'When they let us be farmers, we were,' protested Simon. 'There is the fruit-growing colony at Shepparton. And the settlers at Berwick have even their own Torah.'

'Enough,' scolded Mrs. Abrahams. 'We invite an accomplished lady to dinner and what do we give her? Arguments about Zionism. She does not wish to hear them. Neither do I. We talk of other things,' she declared, and the conversation, dragged by the neck, was diverted into a discussion of art which lasted through three courses.

The food was delicious if, as the driver said, foreign. The entrée was extremely good chicken bouillon, clear and salty. The roast was a conventional baron of beef, surrounded with crisp vegetables including roasted pumpkin and rich, garlicky wine sauce. Dessert was a collation of sliced exotic fruit: pineapple, mango, banana, pawpaw. Phryne was looking about for cream when she remembered a laborious chapter in Mr. Goldman's book on the concept of kosher and the separation of milk dishes and flesh dishes, and accepted black coffee without a flicker.

The butler set an ashtray in front of Miss Fisher and she lit a gasper, complimenting her hostess on an excellent dinner. She drew in the smoke with pleasure. A really good dinner always made Phryne feel virtuous and benevolent, prone to love the whole human race.

The effect, regrettably, wore off fairly quickly.

Mr. Abrahams lit a cigar, leaned back, and asked, 'And what has happened with the unfortunate Miss Lee?'

'I've spoken to her, and I'm convinced she didn't do it. However, I don't know who did or why, and until I do Jack Robinson isn't going to let his prime suspect go free.' Phryne ran through her investigations so far, which had yielded remarkably little, and said, 'I need to know what is in those papers, and I need to know quickly. No one can read the Hebrew letters. Can you recommend a learned man for me?'

Husband and wife exchanged glances.

'Yes, well, yes, we know who might be able to read them, but…he's a difficult man,' said Mr. Abrahams carefully, consulting his wife with a waggle of one eyebrow.

She nodded and said slowly, 'Difficult, yes, but it is possible that Phryne could handle him. I don't think he's met anyone like her before, Bennie. Neither have I, hmm?'

'His name is Rabbi Elijah,' said Benjamin. 'He lives near you, in St. Kilda. He is a very holy man, very learned, but…'

'Difficult?' finished Phryne.

Mr. Abrahams nodded ponderously. 'Difficult.'

'I'll go and see him tomorrow. Can you give me a letter of introduction?'

'I don't think that would help. He is…'

'Difficult,' conceded Simon. 'I can take you to him, but the only one of us Godless almost-gentiles he would speak to is Yossi Liebermann, and you had such a startling effect on him, Phryne…'

'What happened to Yossi?' asked his father, and Simon described Yossi's abrupt exit from Mrs. Grossman's house.

'Too much study, it turns the brain in the end, especially studying the Kabala, that is not meant for humans to understand,' commented Benjamin. 'Also of course he would not be comfortable in the presence of so beautiful and stylish a gentile lady, lest his purity be smirched, I beg your pardon, Phryne.'

'Not at all—a compliment, to have such an effect.'

'Poor Yossi,' sighed Julia. 'His mother had such hopes for him. He's a good shoemaker, a craftsman. Then he started reading all the ancient writings, the old Rabbis and now—' She sighed again.

Mr. Abrahams objected mildly. 'He is still a good shoemaker and he is working well, even though he stays up all night, Lily Grossman says, making experiments and stenches and burning her table. Did I tell you that young Saul is almost bar mitzvah? We will need to arrange the reception.'

'He is a good boy, Saul,' said Julia, brightening. 'The reception will be in the house in Faraday Street?'

'Yes, if it can be managed,' said Mr. Abrahams, smiling at his wife.

'Of course it can be managed,' she said sharply. Phryne saw a ghost of the same expression of slightly irritated efficiency which she had seen on Mrs. Grossman's face as she chivvied her children to prepare for the visitors. 'I will talk to Lily about it, Ben. You want a good spread?'

'Yes. Everything as Yossel would have wanted. His father was a good friend, a real *mensch*,' he explained to Phryne. 'And the boy is a good boy.'

'Yossel would be proud,' agreed Julia. 'I will arrange it.'

'About Rabbi Elijah.' Phryne inserted a word into the conversation.

'Rabbi Elijah? Difficult,' said Julia, unconscious of the irony.

'How do I get to see him?'

'You go to his house—Simon will take you—but make sure that he doesn't see Simon. To him we are as bad as the unobservant, almost as bad as the *meshumad*.'

'*Meshumad?*'

'The Apostates. Those who embraced the Christian religion without threat of torture,' explained Simon. 'We are not Orthodox enough for the Hasidim, the Holy Ones. Perhaps he might prefer an honest *shiksa*.'

'Simon!' reproved his father, but Phryne smiled.

'Perhaps he might at that,' she agreed, patting Simon's hand. His mother smiled.

Chapter Seven

Without counsel purposes are disappointed:
but in the multitude of counsellors they are
established.

—The Holy Bible, Proverbs 15:22

'I really can't remember anything about it,' protested Miss Lee. 'I already got the novels wrong, that was Wednesday.'

'Yes you can, Miss, you just have to close your eyes and put yourself back there and it's all in your head, just like a moving picture, that's what Miss Phryne says,' Dot instructed. 'Now, you're opening the shop and hanging up your coat and putting on your smock. Go on from there.'

'I unlocked the cash tin and just as I was taking out my stock book a young man came in and asked if I carried newspapers, and I told him I didn't.'

'What did he look like?'

'An ordinary young man,' said Miss Lee. 'Oh, dear, I can't do this. He had a serge suit and an umbrella—I would have said that he was a clerk. In any case he was only in the shop for less than a minute. I broke my pencil, then, and I was sharpening it when the bell tinkled and…'

'Yes?' prompted Dot. Miss Lee's brow creased with effort. 'You're doing very well, you know.'

'The bell rang, I looked up from my pencil, and there was a delivery man with a big box. It was my auction books from Ballarat...yes. I asked him to put it in the corner and I checked the invoice—there was something wrong with the invoice—what was it? Ah, yes, it had a blot over the list of contents, I couldn't read it. You have to be careful with dispatch notes, they fudge the orders sometimes; and if I was to sign it without checking what was in the box I couldn't complain if the one valuable book was missing and all the dross was there. Dross always is, somehow. I've never lost a set of Victorian sermons in my life...I made the man wait until I checked the volumes, then I signed it and he went away. After that there was Mrs. Johnson looking in for her cookery book, which I sold her, then this absurd woman and her atlas. Then the two young men and then Mr. Michaels. Poor boy.'

'Tell me about the carter,' said Dot. Miss Lee ran her fingers through her short hair and groaned.

'He was just a carter, in gloves and boots and overalls and a greasy cloth cap—rather stout like they often are; dark, I thought, and gruff. But he did look at the books while I made him wait. I really didn't see his face, Miss Williams. Is it important?'

'Probably not,' conceded Dorothy. 'What about the woman with the atlas?'

'Oh, my dear, she was raddled and forty if she was a day, dressed in a rather tight dark blue suit and a perfectly absurd hat. It was a broad black straw with half a seagull on the side and shells all round the crown, I noticed it particularly because I really wanted to...visit the convenience, and she was holding me up. She was asking me such silly questions and all I could see of her was this awful hat. She was small. About five foot.'

'And common?' asked Dot, who had strong views on style.

'Oh, very. And foreign. Then two young men, friends; I gathered that they worked in the city. They had nice suits—a little loud perhaps. They were probably mechanics, or maybe something horsy.' Miss Lee's fine nose crinkled. 'They had a rather...gamy smell. Then after that it was quiet and I could go to the convenience, and when I got back there was poor Mr. Michaels and this all happened. Will this help?' she asked, and Dot patted her hand.

'Yes,' she said with perfect faith. 'Miss Phryne will find them.'

Phryne Fisher had dressed carefully for her encounter with Rabbi Elijah. She wore a black suit, the straight skirt reaching almost to her ankles, and a close-fitting black hat. Simon was impressed at how decorous she looked until she gave him a sensual smile which disturbed his equanimity.

'What do I call this rabbi?'

'He probably won't speak to you; don't be too offended, Phryne. He isn't supposed to talk to...er....'

'*Shiksas?*'

'Er...yes. Call him Rabbi, if he speaks to you. Also, you must not touch him, in case you might be ritually unclean. Menstruating, you know,' blushed Simon. 'But you might catch his interest if you can show him the papers.'

'I can but try,' Phryne shrugged and got out of the car.

'He lives over there—and—what luck, Phryne!' exclaimed the young man. 'There he is, walking along there with all those children. Oh, no...' he groaned, as Phryne saw what was happening and moved without thinking.

A ring of grubby children were dancing around an elderly man who was standing still, as though they had trapped him in a magic circle. They looked positively Pixie O'Harris, if you could not hear what they were saying, thought Phryne, as she crossed the road at her fastest run and grabbed the biggest assailant by the ear.

'Yid, yid, yid.' The chant stopped abruptly.

'And just what are you doing?' she snarled at the largest child, suspending him painfully by the lobe.

'He's a yid,' he protested.

'Very clever. So he is. Is that a reason for tormenting him?'

'It's only what Dad says,' offered one child, biting her plait.

'What does Dad say?'

'That they're yids.'

'Then your dad is a bigoted idiot and you'll grow up the same.' Phryne was furious. The child she had by the ear began to cry.

'We didn't know it was wrong, Miss,' he pleaded.

'Well, you know now,' snapped Phryne. 'Now get home, you horrible little ratbags, and if I catch you doing such a thing again I shall take you all home to your mothers and order the biggest belting—you won't sit down for a month. Is that clear?' She thrust her face close to the terrified blubbering countenance, and he nodded.

'Go away right now,' said Phryne, dropping him and dusting her hands together. The children ran for their lives.

'You should not have done that, Miss,' said the old man softly.

'Why not?' Phryne was not noticeably softened.

'It will cause more trouble.'

'If people of goodwill do not act against evil, then they assent to evil,' said Phryne sententiously.

The quotation from Maimonides stopped the old man in his tracks. Phryne looked up into his face.

He was tall and painfully thin, and he moved as though his bones hurt. The gaberdine was shiny black with age and inconspicuously patched, and his shoes were broken. His hat had seen better years and his hair was white. But his eyes were remarkable, bright, penetrating and deep.

'Who *are* you?' he asked abruptly.

'Phryne Fisher.' She did not offer her hand. 'I am trying to find a murderer. I need your help.'

'I cannot help you.' He turned and began to walk away.

'Shall I follow you down the street quoting Maimonides?' she asked, keeping pace with him. 'This is an evil thing, a young man dead, and I am responsible for getting a woman out of prison, which means I have to find the killer. Strychnine, it's a nasty death.'

'The dead are with God,' said Rabbi Elijah, not turning his head.

'But the concerns of the living are with the living.' She turned the quotation back on him. She had not spent three hours' hard reading for nothing. 'He who saves one man saves a nation. I cannot bring back Shimeon Mikhael, but I will save Miss Lee from the gallows. And I need your help.'

'How can I help?' At least he had stopped and was looking at her again. 'I go nowhere, see only my students.'

'I have some papers, found on the dead man.' She thrust them at him. 'No one can read them. It is thought that you might. They must contain a clue.'

He cast a glance over the red and gold parchments, shaking his head, then his attention was riveted by a line of Hebrew.

'This, maybe, I can read. Where did you find this?'

'In the pocket of a man called Simon Michaels, Shimeon Ben Mikhael.'

'Shimeon is *dead*?' murmured Rabbi Elijah.

'Shimeon is murdered, don't you read the papers?'

'The papers? No,' he said absently. 'We can sit in my study, Mrs. Rabinowitz will come in. This way, Miss...'

'Fisher. Phryne Fisher.'

Phryne walked beside Rabbi Elijah. He was looking at the Hebrew and speaking under his breath in an unknown tongue, a harsh and authoritative language, whatever it was. Phryne was amazed at the success of her tactic. But she wondered about the old man. He changed moods abruptly and his character seemed to flicker. He seemed close to the edge of sanity, perhaps senility. However, nothing to do but go on with the task.

They came into the lobby of a block of apartments, and he knocked on the second door.

The staircase smelt of urine; poverty reeked from the dilapidated building.

'Coming, coming,' yelled someone behind the blistered door. 'Oh, it's you, Rabbi, what can I do for you? Did you like the latkes I left for you last night?'

Mrs. Rabinowitz was small and would have been stout if she had been properly fed. She was wiping her wet hands on her skirt as she came to the door. When she saw Phryne she stared in astonishment. The Rabbi waved a hand at her.

'This is Miss…Miss…it is of no importance. She has a translation task for me; can you come and sit with her? I must consult my books.'

Mrs. Rabinowitz tugged off her apron, put her door key in her pocket, and picked up a covered plate. She accompanied the scholar and Phryne on a long climb. The old man was short of breath, and stopped to pant at every landing. Phryne, trying not to shame him with her own health and strength, fell behind with Mrs. Rabinowitz.

'There isn't any trouble, is there, Miss?' asked the older woman in a whisper. 'He's a holy man, no one to care for him; if it wasn't for his students he'd have nothing but his books, he'd be a great teacher if he would take more than a few pupils, but he won't. And he forgets to eat, so I bring him a little something when I can. You're not looking for…magic, are you Miss? Fortune telling, is it?'

'No, I need him to read some mysterious papers for me. Does he tell fortunes?'

'Everyone knows he can see the future. But telling fortunes, that's against the law. He never tells fortunes,' emphasized Mrs. Rabinowitz, making Phryne certain that occasionally the Rabbi did tell fortunes. 'He's studied all his life, never eats meat or drinks wine. But here he is, no one to care for him since his wife died last year—she was an angel, that woman.

Eventually they reached the Rabbi's door, and then had to wait while he searched all of his pockets for his keys. Phryne heard babies crying and smelt old boiled cabbage and ancient ghosts of long dead fried suppers. Her miserable childhood came back with a rush. Young Phryne had played up and down steps like these, cold dirty cement. She had lived in a flat like this, so old and grimy that it could never be made clean. Her scalp itched as she remembered filth and headlice, and she was glad when the rabbi finally managed to open his door and she could go in.

It was bare and poor and dusty, but it smelt of old books. On a kitchen table stained with ink was piled a treasury of leather-bound ancient volumes, and there were more on the floor, stacked up, open at illustrations of dragons and lions. She saw the Tree of the Kabala again in a folio tome on which a scatter of pages lay. 'Please sit down,' said Rabbi Elijah, in a rusty social manner. There didn't seem to be anywhere to sit, so Phryne stood and watched as the old man sorted the leaves and laid them out in piles. His hands were long and fine, with pale knob-knuckles which spoke of arthritis. His skin seemed untouched by any sun. His fingernails were clean and cut slightly long.

'These,' he said, pushing one stack over, 'are illuminations from a medieval textbook on alchemy, and I cannot decipher them, except to say that they show various stages in the composition of the philosopher's stone. The ancients believed that it rendered all things perfect.'

'I thought it turned base metal into gold,' commented Phryne.

'Certainly. Gold is the perfect metal. Therefore the *lapis philosophorum* would make lead into gold. It was also believed—' Phryne noted with glee that Rabbi Elijah, a teacher, could not refrain from teaching, even though his auditor was a *shiksa* and probably unclean—'that it could cure all diseases and make men immortal.'

'By raising them to their perfect state.'

'Good.' He raised his eyes, saw Phryne, and blinked when he realized to whom he was talking. But it was too late for him to slip back into his shell, so he continued. 'They described it as being as fine as oil and solid as glass, and no one has ever managed to make it. A dream, but men must have dreams.'

Phryne wondered what dreams the old man had dreamed, to bring him to Australia, and how they coincided with this poor drab place.

'Alchemy has always been connected with the study of the Holy Kabala, and these writings use a system of numbers which is derived from a reading of the Torah, the scriptures. If I can only find…here is *Zorah, Sepher Yetzirah, Akiba's Alphabet*, yes, and *Shuir Komah*, which states that the measurement of the body of man is the measure of being and of the nature of God. Hmm, surely I didn't lend it to Shimeon?' He lifted books with difficulty singing his litany of titles, searching for a particular text. Phryne did not offer to help. Who knew if her gentile touch might make his most precious books unclean? 'If you will excuse me, I must find the *Book of Razael*,' said the Rabbi, and dived back into the volumes.

Mrs. Rabinowitz was in the kitchen, clattering crockery. Phryne went that way, as the old man did not require her presence.

The kitchen contained one tray, one teapot, two cups and saucers and plates. It was dusty and unused. Clearly the Rabbi didn't do any cooking.

'Look at this!' exclaimed the older woman. 'Not one of my good pancakes eaten. It was different when Sarah was here, Sarah was his wife. But the boys are coming tonight and they'll bring food; they always do, the ones who can't afford to pay him. And that's all of them.'

'Will he let me give him money for this translation?' asked Phryne. Mrs. Rabinowitz's workworn countenance seemed to shrink.

'If he could give me a little towards the rent—that collector has no manners, he shouts at the old man—but if I could catch him in the stairway, he doesn't like climbing all them stairs…'

Phryne handed over a note, which vanished at the speed of light.

'Miss…Miss…er…I have it,' called the scholar, and Phryne swapped a grin with Mrs. Rabinowitz. She saw the old scholar on his feet, his white locks flying, a book open over one hand, reminding Phryne of the denouncing God over the church door in Ravenna. She hoped that he wasn't overstraining his heart.

'Yes, Rabbi?'

'It is a number code, using the most obscure system,' said Rabbi Elijah, looking as though he might combust with some emotion—rage? fear?

'Indeed?'

'He has based it on the name of *Adam Kadmon.* That such learning should be used for such a purpose—shameful. Shameful! I had not thought it of Shimeon.'

He was waving the papers around, and Phryne recaptured them before they flew from his trembling grasp.

'Shimeon is dead,' she reminded him. 'Is this the translation?'

'It is. What it means—' he waved a hand. 'But that such a thing should be!'

'Was Shimeon one of your students?'

'He was.'

'A good student?'

'Very good, a devoted young man. I cannot believe that he would have used this holy text for some mundane purpose. It must have been very important to Shimeon. We must sit *shivah* for him, say Kaddish. We were his only friends. I will speak to the others.'

'Who was his particular friend?'

'Kaplan, the oldest Kaplan boy.' The Rabbi was calming down.

'And Yossi Liebermann?'

'He is. What is Yossi to you, a…' He could not find a term which would not be insulting, so he left the end of the sentence to droop under its own weight.

'He lives at the house of my friend Mrs. Grossman,' said Phryne, and the old man almost smiled. '*Such* a woman,' he said approvingly. 'She feeds the hungry. Her price is above rubies. Her husband was a good man.'

'Her son Saul is also learned and almost at his bar mitzvah,' commented Phryne.

'The knowledge of the Torah is the beginning of all wisdom,' quoted Rabbi Elijah approvingly.

'Do your students study the Torah?' she asked artlessly, and Rabbi Elijah twitched, seemingly just becoming aware to whom he was talking.

'Always the Torah, and also the Holy Kabala. Not this…abomination. I do not know what this is, Miss Er, but I hope that it helps you. The murderer of my Shimeon should not go unpunished by the law, though surely God knows and will repay.'

'I'll do my best. Is there anything you can tell me which might help?'

Phryne saw that the old man was about to tell her something. Words were hovering on his lips. But then he flickered again, looking at Phryne's fashionable clothes and her undoubted gentility, shook his head and decided against it.

'No.'

'And your fee, Rabbi?'

'Feed the widow and orphan, give shelter to the fatherless,' said the Rabbi, then opened a book and began to read, dismissing her from his mind entirely.

Mrs. Rabinowitz took her to the door.

'No trouble, Miss, but I heard you asking about Shimeon. He was Yossi's friend, and David Kaplan and his brothers. And…' her hand crept out, cupped. Phryne produced another note which joined the first in its secret destination. Mrs. Rabinowitz breathed, 'He was mad for Zionism, that's why the rabbi was angry with him. Rabbi Elijah says that Israel is meant to be an exile, and until the coming of the Messiah should have no home. *Oy*, he's calling you.'

Surprised, Phryne turned and looked back through the doorway. The Rabbi's face was blank, like an ink sketch which had been crumpled and thrown away. He said 'Woman,' again in a voice which came from somewhere deep in his chest.

'He's having a vision. Go on.' Mrs. Rabinowitz pushed Phryne back into the scholar's room.

'Beware of the dark tunnel,' said the Rabbi. 'Under the ground,' he added. 'There is murder under the ground, death and weeping; greed caused it.'

He seemed dazed or tranced. The scholar's face was whiter than old linen, the sculptured bones visible under the tight-stretched old man's skin. The room seemed to have grown darker. Across the pages of the books, red-clad and black-clad letters seemed to crawl. Phryne smelt a scent like oranges and dust. Under the ground. Beware of the tunnels. She shuddered strongly. The old man's eyes were open but perfectly unseeing, like the eyes of a corpse. He looked like a patriarch, mummifed in some desert tomb.

Phryne smelt a blessedly familiar sour smell of soap as Mrs. Rabinowitz pulled her by the shoulder and conducted her to the door.

She didn't draw an easy breath until she was out in the comfortingly grubby St. Kilda street and Simon Abrahams was excitedly demanding to know what had happened.

'I really don't know,' she said, truthfully.

But she stopped the car on the way home to stuff a handful of paper money into the surprised tambourine of a Salvation Army lassie on the Esplanade.

That should feed the widow and orphan. And the puppy was certainly fatherless.

On arrival at her own house, Phryne collapsed into the leather sofa in the sea-green and sea-blue parlour, calling feebly for a cocktail and a light for her cigarette.

Simon supplied the flame for her gasper. Mr. Butler obliged with a mixture of orange juice, gin and Cointreau which he ventured to think that Miss Fisher might find refreshing. She did.

Simon accepted a cup of tea and asked, 'Phryne, do tell! What did that terrible old man do to you?'

'Tell me—is the Rabbi Elijah mad, or senile, or just possessed by something?' asked Phryne, blowing out a plume of smoke and taking another sip of the cocktail. She felt shaken. There had been power in the old man's eyes, and his trance or foreshadowing or whatever it was had made her feel extremely uneasy. Phryne did not like tunnels overmuch, or any close confined spaces.

'I've heard him called all of those things, and a miracle worker as well. Every now and again Judaism is swept by a Messiah fever, and quite sensible people are caught up in it.'

'Tell me about it later. Right now I have to change for lunch—can you stay, Simon?—and brief my two comrades about the Eastern Market. I'm sure that there is something there, and I want someone on the spot. I'll need to get them a job, though.'

'Uncle Chaim will arrange it,' said Simon. 'I'll mention it this afternoon.'

'Your uncle seems pleasant,' Phryne said idly. 'It's hard to get an impression of what he is like, you know, amongst all you vivid people.'

'Oh, he's a good chap. No talent for business on his own—no vision, or rather too many visions, my father says. He was on the verge of bankruptcy when Father came to Australia with the Michelangelo money. He had tried all manner of things, all rather good ideas, but under-capitalized, and anyway he lost interest after the first couple of months. He had a gem cutter's that failed because of an unwise investment in some smuggled diamonds, only they were white sapphires when he got them. His staff went on to join the best jeweller's in town, then he took up making knives, a good idea, no one can have enough good knives, but the market was flooded with Sheffield ware and he could not compete. Then he started the shoemaking business, that's the one my father rescued. Uncle Chaim was just about failing when Papa arrived on a white horse. Not that Chaim is not clever, but he doesn't know how to run a business. For instance, he had his premises scattered all over the suburbs and he was paying for cartage, also his leather was not the best and he was asking the best prices. My father went out to the abattoirs where they strip the skins, and chose them before they were cured. His shoes are the best ready made ones which can be found in Melbourne.'

'So I see, if you are wearing specimens. Is your uncle married?'

'No, well, it's a sort of family matter, Phryne, if you wouldn't mind not mentioning it? Uncle Chaim was in love with my mother, when she and my father first met. For awhile she thought about which brother she wanted, and she picked my father. And Chaim never really got over it—it's sad, over the years Mama has brought him all the eligible women in Melbourne and he will not look at them. But he is grateful to my father for rescuing him, and he's very useful to Papa. He handles all the day-to-day arranging: the social things and the dates, you know, anniversaries, that sort of thing. He's my father's secretary, and they get on well. But he is a bit self-effacing, Uncle Chaim.'

'Your mother is really delightful.'

'Did you like her?' Simon blushed. 'I'm so glad. She was a little worried about…about you and…'

'Yes, dear boy, but that is all sorted out. Only took three sentences and we were like sisters. Where does she stand on the Messiah and Rabbi Elijah?'

'Difficult,' said Simon, and Phryne extinguished a giggle in her high-octane drink. 'Naturally we all admire him, a man of such scholarship, such austerity. But he won't take more than a few pupils, all as fanatical as he is, and he lives in that dreadful flat as poor as a…'

'Church mouse?' suggested Phryne.

'I've always wondered about that. You'd think, in a church, that there'd be candles to munch on…where was I? Phryne, shall I tell you that I love you?' He took her hand and kissed it.

'Yes, I am always pleased to hear this, but not now, not when we have guests for lunch.' Phryne leaned forward and kissed Simon full on the mouth—he tasted of tea, an ordinary taste on a silky mouth—and effectively took his breath away. 'So despite my private feeling that one should only talk about important matters in bed, we shall stay here and converse about Rabbi Elijah and your father and many other interesting things.'

Simon nodded, gathering his wits, but kept one hand on Phryne's knee as he continued. 'Father tried to give him a nice place to live and a little money—maybe to hire someone to look after him—but he completely refused. Such a scene! The Rabbi denouncing Papa for being no better than a heathen because he does not spend all his time studying, Papa getting upset because he was trying to help a great scholar, Mama just stopping herself from denouncing the Rabbi right back for saying such awful things about Papa, who was only trying to save the old man from starvation, Uncle Chaim trying to stop Mama from yelling, and then the Rabbi just walked out, quite humbly, not angry at all any more. Possibly he is dotty. But Yossi and the others kiss the hem of his garment and say he is the holiest of holy men. Is the flat really dreadful?'

'Pretty dreadful, but he doesn't seem to notice. If your father still wants to help the ungrateful old person, he might give a little money to a Mrs. Rabinowitz, she seems to be looking after him as far as she can. And she could at least pay his rent for him.'

'I'll tell Uncle Chaim. He'll arrange something,' said the young man, sliding the hand up Phryne's thigh. She caught her breath and stood resolutely up, leaning on the mantelpiece and smiling into the imploring brown eyes.

'Later,' she promised. The doorbell rang.

Chapter Eight

I ever conceived that in metalls there were great secrets provided that they are first reduced by a proper Dissolvent, but to seek that Dissolvent or the matter whereof it is made in Metalls is not only Error but Madness.

—Thomas Vaughan, *Euphrates*

Phryne remembered the translation, took a brief look at it, saw nothing but a few lines of numbers and letters, and put the papers in her safe deposit as she changed for lunch. Bert and Cec were not likely to be able to help her with such things and she dismissed it, for the moment, from her mind. She was more willing to do so because she really did not want to think about the Rabbi Elijah.

Who was difficult. Truer word was never spoken, yet she could not account for the effect he had managed to produce in her level-headed self. She dressed quickly in a light shift patterned with wisteria, anxious to rid herself of black. The day was warm and heading towards hot. She was easing her feet into green sandals when her room was augmented by two girls in identical heliotrope smocks, Ember the black cat and one small puppy, which dived instantly for Phryne's discarded shoe and worried it ferociously, pinning down the unresisting pump with one tiny paw and obviously intending to teach it something—probably, Phryne thought, how not to be a shoe.

'No, Molly, we don't eat shoes. No,' chided Ruth, removing it before the puppy's milk teeth could scar the black kid. To her amazement, the puppy relinquished its prey, put its ears on alert, and appeared to obey. It was, Phryne realized, waiting for something. Ruth gave it a very small bit of dog biscuit and it licked her hand.

'That's very good,' said Phryne.

'She has to live with us,' explained Ruth earnestly. 'So she can't make a mess of our things.'

'And you've given her a name,' said Phryne, putting both shoes into the rack out of temptation's way. Even puppies who were resolved to be good could be distracted from the way by a really luscious kid upper.

'Jane named her.'

'Why "Molly", Jane?' asked Phryne, watching in fascination as Ember corralled the small dog and washed its face.

'She looks like a Molly,' said Jane positively. 'We came to ask, can we go to Rebecca Levin's house today? She's invited us for afternoon tea.'

'Yes, and pay attention to anything said about Zionism, the Messiah, an old man called Rabbi Elijah, or the murder in the Eastern Market. Are you lunching with me? Bert and Cec are coming.'

'Yes, Miss Phryne,' they choroused. Then, observing a certain contemplative look on Molly's face, the two girls rushed the puppy downstairs into the garden, with Ember streaking after via the bannister. He had found out how to do this by accident, slipping down fast, all paws together and tail outstretched for balance, and Phryne suspected that he was showing off.

Obscurely cheered by their undemanding company, Phryne finished dressing and descended to the dining room where, by the sound of masculine conversation, Albert and Cecil had arrived.

Phryne liked Bert and Cec more than most people she had ever met. They were, of course, red raggers, but they did not espouse any particular figurehead or warlord, being neither Marxists or Leninists or Trotskyites. They were IWW—Industrial Workers of the World, called Wobblies. Their main aim appeared to be the establishment of the perfect Communist State, and although their philosophy would seem to encompass the mass slaughter of all capitalists, they kindly did not include Phryne in this category, and she looked forward to their stout defence of her person when The Day arrived and she was about to be strung up to a lamp post. 'Nah, she's a good sheila,' Bert would drawl. Cec would say, 'Too right,' and the rope would be removed from around her neck by the respectful Comrades....

This fantasy amused Phryne as she entered her drawing room.

Bert—short and balding and becoming stout—was drinking beer, as was his custom, and Cec—tall and lanky and blond— had a small glass of arak, a drink he had encountered at Gallipoli. Simon had accepted a glass of white wine and Phryne took another cocktail—two before lunch! she reproved herself. Then she forgave herself instantly. It had been a long morning. The girls were exhibiting Molly to the assembly. Phryne marvelled at their ease in company. That had been the hardest thing for the newly ennobled Phryne to learn, and she still had no taste for idle chat, but Jane and Ruth could have been taken into any drawing room in Melbourne without disgracing themselves. Phryne was proud of them.

Cec had the puppy cupped in his big hands and was examining her points. Molly, like all creatures, trusted him instantly and chewed unceasingly at his thumb as he said slowly, 'I reckon she's part sheep dog, eh, Bert?'

'Yair, maybe,' agreed Bert, not wanting to hurt anyone's feelings. 'The inside part. Maybe a touch of whippet, too. Got that deep chest.'

'Reckon,' agreed Cec, detaching the teeth from his thumb and giving the puppy back to Jane. Ember wreathed himself around Cec's ankles, and the tall man bent down to stroke him.

'Ember thinks that Molly is his kitten,' said Jane.

'Well, that's fine,' said Cec. 'Cats are good mothers.'

'But Ember is a boy cat,' Jane pointed out. Bert said something like 'Not any more,' took a gulp of beer, and caught Simon's shy smile. He grinned at the young man. Mr. Butler struck the gong—a custom on which he insisted—and they went into lunch.

In deference to the weather, there were small egg and bacon tarts, a couple of cold chickens and a whole salmon on a bed of torn lettuce, lovingly enveloped in a mayonnaise cloak. It sat next to a neatly carved ham and a profusion of salads. Phryne, who loved beetroot, observed that it was in aspic and thus she might preserve her dress unstained. There was something about the nature of beetroot which made it fly as for refuge to the most expensive cloth available. Only the Chinese laundries could really remove beetroot stains.

'Spinach salad and boiled eggs,' said Mr. Butler. 'Asparagus vinaigrette, Miss Fisher. Cucumber and onion. I hope all is to your satisfaction, Miss? Can I help you to some salmon?'

'Oh, you can,' said Phryne, suddenly ravenous. Mrs. Butler's mayonnaise was not made with condensed milk and mustard. It was an alchemical combination of oil and egg and, since it was to be for the salmon, lemon juice. It was delicious. So was the salmon, the scales and fins of which evidently had been the magnet which had drawn Ember that morning to disembowel the dustbin. Phryne had heard Mr. Butler grumbling about it in the yard. Ember was a cat with expensive tastes.

The rest of the company was obviously as hungry as Phryne, and there was a clatter of cutlery as each diner marked down a dish as his or her own. Their tastes, luckily, were different. Simon took cold chicken and cucumber. Bert tucked into salmon mayonnaise as though he hadn't been born in Fitzroy and had only seen them in tins. Cec had ham and salade Russe. He liked beetroot, too. Dot, who loved onions and sharp tastes, feasted on cucumber in vinegar, spinach and bread and butter. Jane preferred egg and bacon tart and Ruth a taste of everything on the table. Ruth had been hungry all her life until Phryne had rescued her, and still found such a variety and amount of food astonishing. If she struck a taste which did not please her, she swallowed it anyway and moved on to the next. Mr. Butler was quietly pleased. Mrs. B had been worried about the salmon. Cooking such a huge fish whole was a task requiring split second timing. One moment it was still grey and raw in the middle, the next falling off the bone and overdone. The kitchen had been tense all morning. Now he could tell her that it had gone down a treat. He might even get a taste of it himself. And tonight Mrs. B would be calm enough to appreciate the pictures. There was a new Norma Shearer, *The Student Prince*. It sounded good. Mr. Butler thought that Norma Shearer was a bit of all right.

After about ten minutes, Phryne put down her fork and sighed. Nothing like food to centre the spirit and steady the nerves. The asparagus, particularly, had almost reconciled her to Rabbi Elijah. She sipped a little more of the new hock coming out of South Australia—quite good, if a little young to leave its mother—and said, 'Ladies, gentlemen. We have a case.'

'Yair?' asked Bert. 'I suspicioned as much, but since you invited us to such a bonzer lunch me and Cec'll listen to whatever you want to say.'

'Good. This is the Eastern Market murder; you've read about it?' The company nodded. 'Well, then, this is what happened.' Phryne ran through the sequence of events as seen by Miss Lee. 'I'm investigating the papers found in his pocket. They seem to have a Jewish connection. Dot, I want you to go to the Eastern Market and talk to the stallholders around Miss Lee's shop. Someone must have noticed who came in and out that morning, and you might be able to find someone who knew the customers.'

'Someone ought to have noticed that hat,' agreed Dot. 'Even Miss Lee remembered it real well.'

'See what you can find out, Dot. And you Bert dear, I want you and Cec to take a job at the market, and see what there is to be seen.'

'You don't have nothing to go on,' protested Bert.

'Quite right. It's pure intuition. Something is afoot and I want to know what it is. Just exist there and see what information drifts your way. Usual rates?'

The two men looked at each other.

'How long?' asked Bert. 'Only we can't leave the taxi business for more'n say a week tops—Cec's saving up to get married end of next year.'

'Oh, congratulations!' said Phryne. Phryne's first case had involved her with a rapist and abortionist. One of his pitiful victims had been Alice Greenham, the girl of Cec's heart, but she had hitherto put off his suit until she felt that he had had enough time to change his mind. His dogged refusal to do so had at last, it seemed, paid off. Cec grinned.

'Champagne with dessert, if you please, Mr. Butler,' said Phryne. 'Can you tell Mrs. B with my congratulations that we could not have had a better lunch at the Ritz in London? It was superb. Especially the salmon mayonnaise,' added Phryne, who had been aware of a certain amount of plate-flinging while it was cooking. Mr. Butler bowed and withdrew to get the champagne glasses and tell his wife the good news.

'All right, Miss, we'll do it,' conceded Bert, 'but it ain't going to be easy if you don't know what we're looking for.'

'I know. Give it a try. I'm gambling on a feeling—that's never reliable as a cause of action but it often works, eh?'

Bert agreed and took some more chicken.

'What about us?' asked Ruth, taking up an asparagus spear and sliding it into her mouth. She wasn't sure how to eat them until she had seen Phryne do the same. The taste was new and she savoured it. Phryne was watching. Was Ruth to be pro-or anti-asparagus? She liked feeding her adopted daughters new things; their reactions were different. Jane decided right away if a taste was good or not. Ruth was willing to give even boiled pumpkin ten or more tries before she decided that she loathed it. Ruth reached for another piece. Asparagus was definitely on her menu.

'You're going to afternoon tea with the Levin family. Just watch and listen. Customs will not be different, or not noticeably. If it's a kosher house you won't get milk with your tea if there are meat sandwiches. Talk to Simon about it—he'll brief you. Now, this afternoon I will see the autopsy report on the poor young man, and we'll go from there.'

'But, Miss Fisher,' protested the scion of the Abrahams fortune, 'you haven't given me a task! I'm part of this team, too, aren't I?'

'I have a task for you,' said Phryne, with such deep meaning that Simon blushed and took a sip of wine the wrong way.

When he had finished coughing, the conversation turned to the Eastern Market and the changing face of the city. Dessert was fruit salad with a little cointreau. Jane and Ruth stayed to toast Cec's coming nuptials in a little champagne before they went for their briefing with Simon on Jewish Customs and How Not To Outrage Them.

He found them disconcerting. They sat either side of him on the couch, looking sweet and very young, and asked acute questions which indicated that they had not only heard everything he had said but had analysed it.

'So the kosher laws are derived from Leviticus,' mused Jane. 'Cloven-hoofed mammals that chew the cud. Would that include giraffe?' she asked.

'I don't know,' said Simon.

'What about whale?'

'I don't know,' he repeated. 'A whale isn't a fish, is it?'

'No,' replied Jane patiently, 'it's a cetacean, but in the bible the whale that swallows Jonah is called "a great fish" so the desert fathers probably thought a whale was a fish, and it certainly has bones. Unlike a shark, which is cartilaginous.'

'Well, we cannot eat flake.' Simon was delighted to have something to offer.

'Hmm. I can see that I should have talked to Rebecca about her customs before. They are really interesting,' said Jane. She collected Ruth and they left the room to find the Bible and read Leviticus in preparation.

Simon hoped that the Levins were better informed about the laws than he was.

Detective Inspector Robinson was tired. He hated arresting women for murder, especially real ladies like Miss Lee, and he was no further along in his case. His chief was getting testy and when he got real testy, bulls with sore feet were kindergarten children compared to him. He hated the heat, and the papers were saying that the next day was going to be stinking. Phryne waited as he put down a large buff folder on the table, ostentatiously turned his back on it, and was conducted to a small table laid with an embroidered cloth. It depicted a garland of native slipper orchids and maidenhair fern. Phryne had ordered it made especially for him. He liked it; the orchids were botanically correct. He slumped down into a comfortable chair and was supplied by Mr. Butler with a cup of very strong, very sweet tea. On the table reposed an array of scones, strawberry jam and cream, and a copy of *The Hawklet*, a pink periodical emanating from Little Lonsdale Street which was guaranteed to elevate and amuse a tired police officer.

'Adultery and Divorce!' screamed the headline. 'Hotel Maid's Evidence!'

The Detective Inspector split a scone, slathered it with jam and cream, sighed happily and began to read.

Phryne took the buff folder and extracted the autopsy report on one Shimeon Ben Mikhael otherwise known as Simon Michaels, native of Salonika. As she read she made notes, and tried not to think of a dark young man dissected on a cold marble table. Much better to just think of him as a body.

Observations: a tall young man somewhat underweight, bearded, recently washed and healthy. Some bruises on the right knee and hip, as though he had recently fallen, probably sustained in the spasm which had also cracked his spine. Small transverse cut on the ball of the right index finger. A clean cut, probably from a razor or from the edge of a piece of paper. The pathologist paid no further attention to it or to the bruises. No tattoos, scars, or identifying marks and he had all his own teeth. His wisdom teeth had not fully erupted so his age was estimated at between sixteen and twenty-five. Cause of death: strychnine poisoning. Contents of stomach: a starchy scented fluid composed of bread and black tea. Subject died about one hour after eating this austere last meal. Fingernails and contact traces: substance under the nails referred for chemical analysis. Phryne leafed through the folder and found another report. It was found to be common glue, such as is used by carpenters and shoemakers. Chemical burns on the hands.

To the sound of a Detective Inspector slurping his way through a second cup of tea, Phryne reviewed her notes. There was no doubt that he had died of the effects of strychnine. The pathologist had made a note:

'No strychnine found in the stomach contents, but it passes into the bloodstream quickly, being one of the most fast-acting poisons.'

Phryne replaced all the pages, ordered them quickly, and closed the folder. She replaced it exactly as it had been, laid her notebook on the hall table, and came in saying brightly, 'Well, Jack dear, how nice to see you! Is Mr. Butler looking after you? No, really, I couldn't eat another thing, Mr. B, not after that wonderful lunch.'

'Miss Fisher,' said the policeman, standing up and swallowing a mouthful of scone. 'Nice of you to ask me to tea. No one has a hand with scones like Mrs. Butler.'

He wasn't adverting to the report which he had carelessly left on the table where any passing nosy woman could read it, so Phryne didn't mention it either. She sat down at the tea table. 'Any news?'

'No, no one seems to have seen anything. However, I've got hopes of something breaking soon. Has to be soon, or the case'll go stale and my chief'll go spare. You got anything?'

'Not really, but you shall have it as soon as any of it makes sense. You know Miss Lee didn't do it, Jack, don't you?'

'We haven't got a lot of evidence, certainly,' admitted the policeman. 'But have you found anyone else who fits as well?'

'I'll meet the rest of his friends tonight,' said Phryne. 'At Kadimah, in Drummond Street. Then we shall see what we shall see, and hear what we shall hear. There's some secret element in this, Jack. I've had those papers translated. They were in a code, and they translate into another code. The pictures are all the stages making the philosopher's stone.'

'Like Johnson's play, *The Alchemist*?' asked the policeman. He had been to a night course in Elizabethan drama and had never regretted it. Shakespeare was now his constant companion.

'Yes, like that,' answered Phryne, a little taken aback. 'I'll find out more when I have time to read the texts. I've even got Elias Ashmole's *Theatrum Chemicum Brittanicum*. Miss Lee found it in a French auction and bought it for the dead man. Poor thing. Never even saw it. However, I don't know if it will help. The Rabbi had a lot of books, but they were all in Hebrew and he said that he knew nothing about alchemy.'

'Rabbi?'

'Rabbi Elijah. Simon Michaels was his student. He lives in St. Kilda. If you are going to talk to him, Jack, I have to tell you that he's…difficult.' She smiled at her choice of words.

'Difficult?'

'Really difficult,' Phryne emphasized.

'Well, must be going,' said Jack Robinson reluctantly. He had, however, cleared the plate of scones. 'I'm afraid that you may have taken on an impossible task, Miss Fisher. I don't see how you're going to find this murderer when the resources of the police force can't track him down.'

'But the resources of the police force aren't trying to track him down,' Phryne pointed out reasonably. 'You don't believe he, she or they exist. I do. So I have the advantage,' she said, escorting him to the door.

'About the only advantage I have,' she added, as the door shut on Jack Robinson and the buff folder.

She poured herself a cup of the cooling tea and thought. She had sent Dot to the market to look for the customers, Bert and Cec to the understorey to find out whatever it was that was making her feelers twitch. The girls were still with Rebecca Levin, having studied up on Leviticus. Mr. and Mrs. Butler had a free evening tonight, and Phryne needed to read some alchemy so that she would have a sporting chance of understanding Kadimah's conversation on the topic.

She took her notebook up to her own room, scribbled for a while, then sat down to attempt to acquire some grasp of alchemy and of the Holy Kabala, which she felt was a big task for one rather somnolent afternoon.

She laid out Waite's *The Holy Quabbalah*, the *Theatrum*, Thomas Vaughan's *Lumen de Lumine* and *Euphrates*, the *Secreta Secretorum* by Roger Bacon and Dee's *Monas Heiroglyphica*. *The Emerald Tablet Explain'd* by an anonymous Elizabethan lay open on her bed.

She read solidly for an hour, swore, lit a cigarette and rolled over onto her back with *Secreta Secretorum* balanced on her stomach. The black letter Elizabethan printing was easy to read but it made very little sense, and as for the Holy Quabbalah, she had grasped only the very first of the first principles; that is, that it needed a lifetime's study.

'And I don't have a lifetime,' she said aloud. Thomas Vaughan the Brecon man was the easiest alchemist to follow, and by far the most charming.

> On the same day my deare wife sickened, being a Friday, and at the same time of day, namely in the evening, my gracious God did put into my head the Secret of extracting Oyle of Halcali, which I had once, accidently, found at Pinner in Wakefield in the dayes of my deare wife. But it was againe taken from me by wonderful judgement of God for I could never remember how I did it, but made an hundred attempts in vaine. And now my Glorious God (whose name be praysed forever) hath brought it again into my mind and on the same day as my deare wife sick-

ened; and on the Saturday following, which was the daye she dyed on, I extracted it by former practice.

And how his wife felt about it, left to die without her husband, was another matter of course. Phryne resisted the urge to fling the books out of the window and began again.

What was alchemy? An attempt, the difficult rabbi had said, to raise matter to its perfect state. Good. That meant base metal into gold and men into immortal bodies. And how did one go about this task?

One first acquired a patron with a lot of money, and purchased or made a lot of equipment. Phryne wondered whether to tell Mrs. Butler that her *bain marie* which kept the soup warm was an alchemical vessel invented by Miriam, sister of Moses—later called Maria Prophetissa in case Miriam seemed too Jewish—who had founded *alchimia practica*. Previously it had been a theory. Miriam seems to have actually tried to do it, thought Phryne, wondering if she had succeeded. The first principle was *solve et coagula*, that is, to dissolve and to recombine. Thomas Vaughan told her 'in this matter is all the essential principles, or ingredients of the elixir, are already shut up in Nature and wee must not presume to add anything to this matter…for the stone excludes all extractions, but what distill immediately from their own chrystalline universal Minera'. Keeping that in mind, one began to make the first mixture, the so-called gold yeast. Everyone was vague on what else went into it except for gold in fine powder and a lot of mercury metal. Then, knowing that there are three elements—salt, sulphur and mercury—one cooked this gold yeast with some other ingredient, called *Terra Adamae*—Adam's earth, the material of the first creation. Phryne noted that since one could not just send down to the grocer's for half a pound of Adam's earth, that there must be a recipe for that also, but could not find one.

The first stage was reached when the material turned black. The illumination from Simon Michaels' books showed it: the head of a crow, beak open. This *melanosis* was also, in the

Emerald Tablet, called Adam's earth. Phryne stopped trying to reconcile the varying accounts and continued with her list.

Adding some other liquid, variously described as 'womanseed' or more bluntly 'monthly blood', to the black mixture and heating it again with orpiment and borax made it turn white: the *leukosis* or albedo stage, the purifying or purgation of the mixture. The picture fluttered onto the satin bedspread: a white dove.

Distilled in an alembic, the funnel-shaped vessel, the matter was sublimated by high heat and the gas trapped in a coil of pipe. This was *conjunctio*, the mystic marriage where the red king lay with the white queen. The two entwined crowned figures joined the other pictures and Phryne scribbled busily.

Then, if one was really lucky, *xanthosis* or yellowing would take place with the addition of unslaked lime, ground bones and more mercury. It occurred to Phryne that with the amount of mercury vapour that these wise men were breathing, it was no wonder that they saw visions of Hermes Thrice Great. In due course they would also have seen rhinoceroses on scaling ladders.

Finally, after the work of years—the mixture buried in fresh horse dung to be heated to just the right temperature—the watcher would see the span of colours called the peacock's tail and would achieve *rubedo* and *iosis*, completion. The red king would be enthroned and the *lapis philosophorum* would elevate the alchemist to heights of knowledge such as other men would never share.

> Thou shalt see…a shining carbuncle most temperate splendour, whose most subtile and depurated parts are inseparably united into one with a concordial mixture, exceedingly equal, transparent like crystal, compact and most ponderous, easily fusible in fire, like resin or wax yet flowing like smoke; entering into solid bodies and penetrating them like oil through paper; friable like glass, in powder like saffron, but in whole Mass shining like a ruby.

His life would be crowned. He would be untouchable, immortal. He would not seek riches, as Elias Ashmole said, 'And certaynly he to whom the whole of nature lies open, rejoyceth not so much that he can make Gold and Silver, or the Divells to become Subject to him, as that he sees the Heavens open, the Angells of God Ascending and Descending, and that his own name is fairely written in the Book of Life.' He would live forever in his dark robes, wrapped in his ecstatic visions, and his lamp would never go out, for it would be fuelled by Oil of Eternity.

Phryne closed her books and glanced out the window. It was darkening towards dusk. She heard the tree branches scrape the glass. The wind must have changed. I am getting uncommonly jumpy, she told herself.

Surely no one was really trying to make a philosopher's stone in 1928? It sounded both ridiculous and impossible. The instructions and recipes were all vague and where, exceptionally, they weren't vague, they were all different. If Ashmole said that one used mercury, bole ammoniack and saltpeter and Robert Fludd said that the same operation was achieved using slaked lime, verdigris and oil of tartare, then how could the chemical result be the same?

Phryne, in common with all girls at her school, had learned a little chemistry, known with a jolly laugh as 'stinks'. She recalled watching as the teacher poured mercury into a chamber and heated it. Phryne had seen it oxidize into a red powder, then she had watched in amazement as the powder had been heated again and little beads of silvery metal had popped up out of the oxide. That was alchemy, Phryne thought.

She got up and washed her face. She was losing her sense of proportion.

But if he wasn't trying to make a philosopher's stone, why did Simon Michaels have those parchments in his pocket, and why did an honest shoemaker like Yossi Liebermann burn his landlady's table with chemical experiments?

It promised to be an interesting evening.

Chapter Nine

Air: this is no Element, but a certain mirac-
ulous Hermaphrodite, the Caement of two
worlds, and a Medley of Extremes... in this
are innumerable magicall Forms of Men and
Beasts, Fish and Fowle, Trees, Herbs, and all
creeping things.

— Thomas Vaughan, *Euphrates*

Dot was not enjoying her attempts to extract information from Miss Lee's neighbours.

She had started at the nearest poulterers, and had waked what was clearly a long-standing feud.

'I'm investigating the murder in the bookshop,' she said to the boy behind the counter. He stared at her, momentarily forgetting the large chicken which he had under his arm. It also stared at Dot, and clucked.

'You know, two days ago. A young man was poisoned,' she encouraged. The boy gaped. Dot, who was nervous and shy, reflected crossly that she might get more answers out of the chook, and tried again. 'Is Mr. Lane in?'

For answer, the poultry-bearer shuffled to the door and yelled 'Boss!' Then he seemed to feel that he had fulfilled his obligations and returned to his duties, which appeared to consist of staring out the window at passing girls and sucking his teeth. Mr. Lane was stout and worried. He wore a bloodstained apron.

'This is too much,' he exclaimed before Dot could open her mouth. 'That bloke has gone too far this time. I'll have the law on him. I'll call the cops if he says one more word! It's slander, that's what it is. And libel,' he added, hedging his bets.

'Sorry?' said Dot, utterly fogged and a little taken aback by his vehemence.

'Don't I work hard?' demanded Mr. Lane. 'Don't I put in all the hours God gave to support my wife and little ones and run my business?'

'Mr. Lane,' Dot began.

'If he's sent you here about the chicken, I tell you, it was all right and if anyone says any different I'll do something, I tell you, starting with going round and knocking Gunn's block off!'

'Hello?' said Dot loudly. 'Mr. Lane? I don't know what you're talking about. I came from Miss Lee, and I'm trying to find out about the dead man in her shop.'

'Oh.' The red face lost a little of its pre-apopleptic colour. 'Miss Lee, eh? Nice lady. Sorry, Miss. It's just that Gunn is getting on my nerves. He says one of my chooks was off, and I swear, my chooks eat the same feed as his and they're all in the pink of condition. Look at that now.' He held up a limp plucked corpse for Dot to examine. She did so, pinching the breast and manipulating the feet to see if it was fresh.

'Perfectly good,' she pronounced. 'Fit to be served to the Queen.'

The poulterer relaxed and mopped his brow with a red handkerchief.

'Sorry to go crook at you. Thanks, Miss. Now, what can I do for you? It's terrible about Miss Lee, though trade's been up since it happened I'd rather it was for a different reason, if you see what I mean.'

'I need to find the customers who were in Miss Lee's shop before the murder happened.'

'You don't reckon she done him in?'

'No, I don't, and my employer, Miss Fisher, she doesn't think so either. Did you see anyone you knew in the market on Friday?'

'Yes, plenty of people. Most of my customers are regulars, though they won't be much longer if Gunn keeps on telling 'em my chooks are poisoned. I'll have the law on him if he opens his gob again. But no one I know went into the bookshop, Miss. No one came in here carrying a book, not that I noticed. My boy might know more, but he's a bit light on for brains. A few kangaroos loose in the top paddock, you know?' Mr. Lane tapped his forehead. 'Not that he isn't good with the chooks, though. They've got a lot in common. Billy, c'mere. Do you remember anyone coming into the shop on Friday carrying a book?'

The boy looked frightened. Dot tried a gentle approach.

'I'm sure you're a good boy, Billy, and you like the chooks, don't you?' Billy nodded. 'And you remember Friday?'

'Man dead,' said Billy.

'That's right. Before the man was dead, did anyone come in here with a book?'

'No, but there was a lady.'

'You spend too much time looking at sheilas,' growled his boss, and Billy gaped again, losing whatever concentration he possessed.

'Tell me about the lady,' coaxed Dot.

'Lady with a chook on her hat,' said Billy importantly. 'Nice hat. It had a white chook on it. And shells.'

'Did she buy anything?'

'Two chooks,' said Billy.

'So she did. Why, does that mean something to you, Miss?' asked Mr. Lane.

'It certainly does,' said Dot. 'I really want to find that lady. There can't be two hats like that in one market.'

'Well, if you really need to find her,' said Mr. Lane slowly, 'I might be able to help.'

'How?' asked Dot.

'Well, she didn't want to carry two chooks and a dozen fresh eggs home in her hand, did she?'

'Do you deliver, Mr. Lane?' asked Dot, reaching for her notebook.

'I do, Miss. But it doesn't seem right to give away a customer's address.'

Dot knew what was happening. Mr. Lane was waiting for a bribe and Dot was momentarily at a loss. How do you bribe someone? Miss Fisher had not covered this in her briefing. She took out a ten shilling note and laid it on the counter. 'For your trouble,' she mumbled.

It was easier than she had thought. The note vanished with speed and Mr. Lane seemed unaware that it had ever been there. He consulted his ledger.

'Delivery…now where is it? Two chooks and a dozen…yes. Here we are, Miss.' He jotted down the address and name on the corner of a piece of white wrapping paper. 'There you are, Miss. Good luck. Miss Lee's a real nice lady.'

Dot left the shop, vowing never to buy any of his produce. If he thought Miss Lee was a real nice lady, why did he need a financial inducement to give Dot the address? His chickens probably were poisoned, thought Dot, and went into the bird dealer's shop. So far, she was doing very well.

The air was full of twittering. Cages lined three of the walls. A profusion of rainbow-coloured finches, canaries and budgies occupied the smaller cages. Dot was bending to look into an elaborate wrought-iron construction when a gruff voice remarked, 'Pretty girl.'

Dot jumped. There did not seem to be anyone else in the small room. She looked around.

'Pretty girl,' said the voice again.

Dot heard a discordant whistle and then the jingle of a chain.

'Polly wants,' said the speaker, shuffling into sight.

It was the biggest white cockatoo that Dot had ever seen, sulphur-crested, with a beak which looked capable of opening tins. It was secured by one leg to a fine chain fixed to the perch, which allowed it considerable freedom of movement. It eyed Dot with its ancient cynical gaze and said again, 'Polly wants....'

'Polly wants?' asked Dot. 'What does Polly want?'

'That's the trouble with that bird. He can't make up his mind,' observed another disembodied voice.

Dot began to feel that it was going to be a very strange afternoon.

From under the counter a small man arose. He was dressed in what had been a respectable blue suit, but he was liberally scattered with bird seed, and he had hay in his thick fair hair.

'Sorry, I was just sweeping up some feed,' he said. 'What can I do for you, Miss? A nice budgie? Pair of lovebirds? How about a canary, I've got some fine singers.'

Dot explained her errand. Mr. Gunn scratched his head, looking oddly reminiscent of the cockatoo. His fair hair spread like a crest, shedding bird seed.

'I didn't notice anyone carrying a book, not on Friday. I remember the day because the police came and took statements from all of us. I was upset because that b...man Lane had poisoned some of my birds.'

'How do you know?' asked Dot, practically.

Mr. Gunn blushed. 'It was the end of the week, and I was out of sunflower seeds, see, and he has an open sack of them, so I borrowed a couple of handfuls—I would have put them back at the end of the next week when I get my delivery. It was for the one cage of zebra finches. They're seed eaters, Miss. I saw Lane throw a handful to a couple of penned chickens. Then, in the morning, I found my finches dead, and I saw his boy plucking a pair of chickens. They hadn't been killed in the usual way. Their necks weren't broken. He was selling poisoned chickens to the public, and I'll keep telling people that. It's not right.'

'What was wrong with the sunflower seeds? Did you ask him?'

'Well, no. I couldn't, could I? But those finches were healthy the night before and dead the next day and so were his chickens. I'm partial to a sunflower seed or two myself,' said Mr. Gunn, looking more avian by the moment. 'Bl…very lucky I didn't eat any myself. Some ant poison or something must have got into the feed.'

Dot debated whether to tell him that Mr. Lane was thinking of suing him for libel, or slander, but decided that it was not her argument and took her leave politely of both Mr. Gunn and the parrot.

'Polly wants…' it temporized as she shut the door.

'Make up your bloody mind,' said Mr. Gunn, irritated.

By the time Dot reached Mrs. Johnson's teashop she was ready for a nice cuppa and a sit down. She had drawn blanks in all the other businesses on this side of the market. Fred Marryat had shouted over the thud of his press that he hadn't seen anyone with a book, and had offered her a special deal on personal cards, no rubbish, printed in the most elegant type and in the best style. Dot knew that visiting cards have to be engraved, not printed, and refused politely. Anthony Martin the chiropodist noticed only feet, though he was an encyclopedia of information on his special subject.

'People all walk differently,' he told Dot, who had sat down in his chair. His shop was hung with photographs of feet and posters which enjoined the reader to wear properly fitted shoes. An articulated skeletal foot occupied the counter. 'That's why second-hand shoes are always likely to pinch. You wear your shoe into the shape of your foot. Now you,' he looked at Dot's stockinged feet, 'you walk like you're in a hurry, lots to do, must get on. You wear your shoes on the ball of the foot. Nice straight wear though, not pigeon-toed or crooked. No bunions. Last you a lifetime, those feet. Got a good grip on the earth.'

Dot was pleased and bought a tin of foot powder, guaranteed to soothe and refresh.

Mrs. Johnson was blonde, pretty and slightly harried.

'I'll do my best to help,' she declared. 'Imagine, arresting Miss Lee for murdering someone; it's absurd. All the traders think so. Mr. Johnson nearly got himself arrested, calling the police a gang of Bolsheviks. Of course, he is hot tempered,' Mrs.

Johnson said admiringly. 'He wasn't a bit scared. Told them right to their faces that Miss Lee couldn't do a thing like that. And I told them too. But they arrested her anyway. Is there anything she needs, Miss Williams? And is she all right?'

'She's got books and comforts and things like that,' said Dot. 'She's brave. She's bearing up. But I'll tell her that you were asking after her; that'll cheer her up. Now, I'm trying to find the customers for that morning. Did you notice anyone?'

'Oh, dear, well, I saw a woman in the most absurd hat. And I think Mr. Doherty's young men came in for a cup of coffee, they had a book. Something about horse-racing, I think it was.'

Dot took out her notebook. 'Who's Mr. Doherty?' she asked.

'He runs a garage and a livery stable—not much livery now but he shoes the dray horses; we still have some drays. He has an interest in the grain and feed shop two doors up. Nice young men.'

'Do you know their names?' asked Dot.

'The tall one's called Smith—they call him Smithy. And the other one must be called Miller, because they call him Dusty. Does that help, Miss Williams?'

'Yes,' said Dot, hoping that it did. 'You didn't see anyone else?'

'I was busy that day,' said Mrs. Johnson. 'That silly girl of mine got herself married, and now she's in the family way, and she's sick. I was run off my feet. I didn't poke my nose out of my own door until Miss Lee came in and said that the young man was dead. White as a sheet, she was, poor girl. I really must go, tell her I was asking after her, will you?'

Dot continued her walk to the grain and feed shop. It had a number of sacks outside. Each one had its cat, couchant. Dot wondered if the hay cat always sat on hay, or whether it swapped with the corn cat, the wheat cat and the chicken food cat. They were well fed and sleepy, and moved obligingly when the merchant came to measure out his produce with a tin scoop. Dot, fascinated, noticed that as soon as the man was finished, the cat leapt back and settled down again. Clearly everyone in this shop was well adjusted to their roles.

'Yes, Miss?' asked a burly man. Dot explained her mission.

'Miss Lee, eh? Never believed she done it. You want the boys? Dusty! Smithy!' he bellowed, in a huge voice which shook the walls. 'You talk to the lady,' he ordered, as two young men came skidding into the shop. One was still carrying a tally.

'We're short a sack of sunflower seed,' said one. Dot refrained from comment. Crime appeared to be endemic in the Eastern Market. She explained what she wanted for what felt like the thousandth time, and the shorter young man nodded intelligently.

'You're trying to eliminate the innocent, eh? That's what Sexton Blake does, eliminate the innocent. Me and Smithy went to the shop about oh, I don't know, tennish? On our smoko. We wanted a book on how to win on the gees, because we ain't been doing too flash lately. Miss Lee sold us one, and we'll be millionaires when Smithy works out his system, eh Smithy?'

Smithy nodded uneasily.

'Was there anyone in the shop when you came in?'

'This weird female in a hat with a bird on it who was giving Miss Lee h…, er, having an argument about what an atlas was. I mean, everyone knows what an atlas is! And someone had just delivered a big box full of books—I stubbed my toe on it. Anyway, we looked around a bit, and then the hat went away, we bought our book, had a cup of coffee at Mrs. Johnson's, and came back here. Then we had to take a horse to the farrier's so we missed all the excitement.' Mr. Miller sounded rather disappointed.

'System,' said their boss with infinite scorn. 'Youse'll both be in Queer Street with Smithy's system. If there was such a thing, bookies'd be begging in the street, and yer don't see that happening, do yer? Well, then.'

'Yes, Boss,' murmured his subordinates, not very convinced.

'And I want that quid back that I lent you out of me own kick. If that's what you're spending it on.'

'Aw, Boss, don't be a Jew…' wheedled one of the young men.

Dot took her leave. She stood at the door, caressing the corn cat, which was a tortoiseshell, while she considered what to do next. It angled its jaw into her fingers and purred.

'Nice kitty,' said Dot. 'Now, I'm going well. Only the clerk to find. We can get the carter from the dispatch note, it will be in Miss Lee's ledger. No, I can't see any line of enquiry which might lead me to the clerk. I wonder if Miss Phryne has thought about an advertisement? With a reward. That might bring him out of the woodwork.'

She looked down at a sharp hiss. The wheat cat had decided that if there was any patting going it wanted some too, and the corn cat was objecting to this intrusion into her territory. Dot stroked both, then drew the piece of butcher's paper from her purse.

The lady in the hat was called Mrs. Katz, and she lived in Carlton. Dot walked around the corner of the market into Bourke Street, past tailors and mercers and Rob't Fulton, Chemist down the hill to Swanston Street, where she caught the number 11 tram.

Miss Lee paused in the construing of a difficult verb in *The Gallic Wars* to remember with a desperate pang that she was captive and in danger of death. The fact hit her like a physical pain and she clutched at her breast, feeling her heart knife.

Then she returned her gaze to the page, and the prison guard heard her murmuring 'Rego, regis, oh, Lord, protect me, God have mercy on me, regis…'

That one wouldn't have to be dragged screaming to the gallows, thought the guard approvingly. She wouldn't give any trouble to her executioners.

Simon Abrahams was sulking.

Here he was, witty, handsome and young, possessed at last of a lover, a beautiful woman who had lain in his arms and ravished his senses, and she had deserted him. She had basely sent him away while she studied alchemy (of all things), enjoining him to be a good boy and not bother her while she was trying to make sense of a lot of medieval writings in illiterate Latin and middle English. There he could not help, not having studied at a university, as her other lovers doubtless had. He kicked at an inoffensive wainscot. How dare it lurk there, being blessedly insensitive wood, while his heart was bleeding?

His mother called out to him not to kick the furniture. He gave the wainscot another boot, careful to make less noise. It was no use complaining about Miss Fisher to Mama. Phryne had made a splendid impression on Mama, who had insisted on telling all the old stories about life in Paris when she and Papa had been so poor. They weren't poor now and Simon was desperately ashamed of those stories.

Papa was visiting the shoe workshops, which he did at least once a week, to talk to the staff and the managers. But there was someone who always had time to listen to the sorrows of the young Simon. Someone who had always been the repository of all Simon's secrets and had never told. Someone who shared his enthusiasms, though he would never publicly disagree with Papa.

Simon stopped assaulting the skirtingboard and went to find Uncle Chaim.

◇◇◇

Bert and Cec followed Matt Rosenbloom, the foreman, down the steps to the undercroft of the Eastern Market and into a wide, echoing space. It was harshly lit with strung electric bulbs, which augmented the obsolete gaslight but left pools of black shadow in between. The footing was treacherous and uneven, and the patched shadow and glare made it hard to see any pits or holes. It was full of boxes, bales and sacks and smelt of so many scents that Bert gave up trying to analyse them, deciding that the essence could be sold to the public as *Eau de Trade*.

'Tomorrow you can work in the main cellar,' observed Mr. Rosenbloom, who had been told to employ these men for as long as they liked, and was constitutionally incurious. He was required to see that the shoeshop was supplied, that the boxes delivered to the market contained the correct boots in the correct sizes, and he wasn't employed even to resent the way his Australian employees called him Rosybum. In a way it was probably a compliment, he thought. He had come a long way from Stuttgart to Poland and then Rome, and reserved his passions for Mrs. Rosenbloom and birdwatching. That reminded him that he had time for a chat with that nice Mr. Gunn of the birdshop, and he left Bert and Cec to deal with a severe young woman with a ledger. She was standing in the middle of a heap of shoes, all spilled out of their boxes.

'This delivery is wrong,' she declared. 'I definitely ordered ten pairs of the brown glacé kid court with a Louis heel. Look at this.' She held up an offending shoe. 'Does that look like a Louis heel to you?'

'Me, Miss?' Bert was all innocence. 'We're just here for the heavy work, Miss. Now if it came to beer, now, that's different. Cec can identify eight different types with his eyes shut. Which they mostly are after eight beers, eh mate?'

'Too right,' said Cec.

The severe young woman unbent. She knew real ignorance when she heard it.

'I'll have to catch Rosybum when he comes back. I'll get him at Gunn's, that's where he's gone, he lives for the day when he can teach that cockatoo to finish a sentence. Can you pack them back into boxes, please?' Cec fetched a handcart. Miss Harrison of Harrison's Shoes knelt next to the shorter and stouter of the new labourers. Bert, she observed, could find the sizes and the boxes and match them almost quicker than she could, and she was impressed.

'Just load them all up and bring them through to the shop. I'll sort them out with him later. It's a good deal, they're excellent shoes at that price. After all,' she said philosophically, preceding them up the ramp, the shoes piled on the handcart, 'perhaps the customers would prefer a court heel. What do you think?'

'Too right,' agreed Cec.

He resolved to ask Miss Fisher, when he next saw her, what a Louis heel was. Maybe Alice would like Louis heels for the wedding. And she was wearing white. Miss Fisher, when appealed to for a decision, had agreed that white was the only possibility. So what if she'd had a little slip? So had Cec and no one was trying to debar him from his own wedding because he wasn't a virgin. In fact he'd gone to considerable trouble and expense to make *sure* he wasn't a virgin.

No, white it was to be, and Dot Williams had very kindly agreed to go with Alice to the first fitting, in case she was nervous. No one in her family wanted her to marry. She was earning good money at the grocer's shop, and her dad was a soak. But she had made up her mind. She was marrying him, and her dad couldn't say nothing about it.

Cec allowed his train of thought to wander even further, until he was brought back to the present by his mate Bert nudging him and advising him that he was grinning like a loon and asking whether he had taken leave of his senses?

'Here you are with a soppy smirk on your dial, and we're supposed to be paying attention,' scolded Bert.

'All right, mate, here I am,' said Cec soothingly. Bert was a good bloke, but he was prone to go crook when he was nervous.

And Bert was nervous because he didn't know what to look for in this big bustling market. Neither did Cec, but his Scandinavian ancestors had bequeathed him some Viking fatalism. If they were meant to find out, they'd find out.

They delivered the shoes for Miss Harrison, and she was so mollified that she offered them a tip, which they took graciously.

'Now what?' asked Bert.

'I reckon we stroll around to the birdshop and see what Mr. Rosybum wants us to do next,' said Cec. 'And we get an idea of what this place looks like. He'll be with his birds for half an hour. What's up the stairs?'

They climbed, to be greeted with a wave of scents, all manner of flowers and wet stone. The top floor was full of florists—John Lane and several Irelands. They noticed Tintons Glass and China Repairer, Albert Fox, Fruiterer. Strolling by they saw through his window a man in titanic struggle with a pineapple, which was resisting having its crown chopped off. His language was most restrained. It reminded Bert of a book of Realist posters someone had sent Miss Fisher. He mentioned it to Cec. 'They could make a bloody huge bronze out of it and call it "Spirit of Fruit" or "Man Conquering Nature",' he suggested.

Cec chuckled. They stopped at Miss Ivy Brown, Pastrycook, and bought a pie and sauce. The rest of the top floor was inhabited by a couple of fancy goods shops, a music seller and a maker of the sort of solid leather trunks which can stand by themselves and house a modest family of three, and their dog.

'Wouldn't want to get a bodgy cargo net under that,' said Cec consideringly. 'Make a bloody big hole in the dock,' agreed Bert through his pie. 'Good pies, these. Right, now what about the next floor down? Just a quiet stroll, mate.'

'Too right.' Cec was relieved. It looked like Bert was getting the feel of the place. He always liked to do that. In the trenches at Poziéres, Bert had often suggested a little recce into No Man's Land. He said it relieved the monotony.

They walked into Exhibition Street in time to hear a scream. 'Murder!'

Chapter Ten

Whole Dispositions, vertues and naturall
motions depend on the Activitie of the heav-
enly motions and Influences.

—John Dee, *Mathematicall Praeface*

Dot wasn't sure what to do next. Here she was at the correct address in Carlton. It was a workman's house, of light and dark stone with a slate roof, very dark and uninhabited-looking. She had unlatched the wrought-iron gate, tripped over the statutory misplaced brick and rung the doorbell. It had made a ratchety broken sort of noise, a strangled clockwork grunt.

Dot knocked firmly with one gloved hand and the front door swung open.

So she stood in the dark doorway, wondering what to do. It was clearly unsafe to leave one's front door open. No one would have done so unless they were at home. If it had been someone whom Dot had previously met she would not have hesitated. But there was something so intrusive about entering a house where she had not been introduced....

While she was thinking about it, she listened. The house, as far as she could see, was of the usual Carlton cottage design. Two rooms beside a central corridor, leading into a main parlour which had the kitchen and the bathroom behind it. All the blinds were closed, even though the day was not hot. The house smelt of furniture polish and burning; something had been left unattended on the stove.

That decided Dot. There was probably something wrong in a house where the front door was ajar, but there was definitely something wrong in a house where the front door was ajar and something had been left on the stove. Possibly the lady of the house had been called to an emergency and had neglected to take what Dot's nose told her was probably fish cakes off the gas, but if that was the case she would not be offended if a stranger came in and, with the best of motives, prevented her house from catching fire.

Dot hurried down the hall, through a disordered parlour and into the kitchen, where she found a gagged woman in a heap on the floor and a pan well alight on the stove.

Dot opened the back door. Then she grabbed a teatowel, wadded it up and carried the flaming pan out into the yard. She laid it down and smothered it with earth. The pan had been burning for some time. It fumed unpleasantly. Then Dot returned to the woman.

She wasn't dead, Dot was pleased to note. She was already trying to sit up, hindered by being attached to a chair by what Dot judged were probably stockings.

'Mrs. Katz?' Dot asked. 'Don't struggle, I'll try and get the knots undone.' Dot first stood the chair up and then removed the gag, another teatowel.

'*Wasser*,' croaked the woman. Dot spoke only English but this was clear enough.

'Water?' she asked. The woman nodded. Dot brought her a glass of water and held it as she gulped, then knelt to try and undo the knotted stockings.

Mrs. Katz, who appreciated a rescuer who knew how expensive stockings were and did not immediately dive for a knife to cut them, coughed and said, '*Oy gevalt*, such a thing to happen!'

'What did happen?' asked Dot, managing to release the bonds on Mrs. Katz's ankles. Her wrists had been tied more tightly, or perhaps she had struggled. Her hands, which were veined, had swollen alarmingly. 'I think I've got this knot; stay still for a bit.'

Years of housework had given Dot strong fingers, and a child-hood spent untangling her little brother's fishing line had made her supernaturally good at knots. It was a matter of allowing the line to unravel itself from what she had heard Phryne·call a *point d'appui*. Dot found the central hitch in Mrs. Katz's bind-ings and the stocking unwound itself from around the arm of the wooden chair.

'*I* should know?' demanded Mrs. Katz. She stood up, shedding stockings, rubbing her mistreated wrists. '*I* should *understand*? I am about to cook a few fish cakes for my lunch, I just lay them in the pan, and suddenly there they are, screaming at me, where is the paper? I tell them what are you doing in my house, is this Russia, anyway, what paper, I don't know nothing about no paper. Then they grab me—see, what bruises!—and tie me here, and then I hear such noises, everything they must be turning over, breaking, stealing, and then the tall one comes back says, nothing there, and they're gone, I hear the door slam, leaving the pan on the stove which they should have known would burn, I sit here, I struggle, the house it will burn down, Maxie when he comes home will find nothing but smoking ruin, I can't get free because they tie me so tight, *oy*, bandits, *gonifs*, what have they taken?'

'I don't know,' said Dot. 'We'd better call the police.'

'No!' Mrs. Katz seized Dot's sleeve, a surprisingly strong grip for those reddened claws. 'No, please, lady, not the police. Anyway,' she demanded, 'thank you for rescuing me, don't think I'm not grateful, wonderful you should come in nick of time, but, Miss, who are you?'

'My name is Dorothy Williams,' replied Dot, rather relieved to be able to declare herself. 'I came because you were in the bookshop the other day, just before the young man died there.'

'I was?' asked Mrs. Katz evasively. Dot nodded.

'Your hat was there,' she said. 'I saw it in the hall. It's a very distinctive hat.'

'Is good, yes?' said Mrs. Katz, giving up her attempt to avoid admitting that she had been in Miss Lee's shop. 'I like it. Max says it is too big, but I don't like the sun. Max says I look like mushroom. He's got no style. *Oy*, Maxie, what will Max say about this? And my good fish cakes is all burned. Miss, do you know what those *gonifs* wanted? Do you know what this is all about?'

'No,' admitted Dot. 'Not really. But I'm sure that Miss Fisher will. Why won't you let me call the police, Mrs. Katz?'

'We're in new country,' muttered Mrs. Katz. 'We don't want no trouble. No old country trouble.'

'Old country? What do you mean?'

Mrs. Katz shut up like an oyster. Dot considered her. She was perhaps fifty, dressed in an art silk dress with rather too many brooches. Her hair was dyed an unconvincing shade of gold and she was made up with pancake and lipstick, but the effect was oddly attractive and innocent, as though a child had amused itself with her mother's cosmetics. Her wrist bore a heavy gold bracelet and there were small gold rings in her ears. Robbery had not been the motive for this incursion into a respectable Carlton household.

'Perhaps I can give you a hand with the tidying up,' Dot offered, giving up on the police.

'No, no, you put the kettle on if you will be so kind, we'll have some tea, how can I explain to Max what happened, maybe he'll understand, he's got a better *kopf* than me, he'll be home by three, *oy*, what a terrible thing....'

Mrs. Katz pottered off into the parlour and Dot put the kettle on and then followed. She found her hostess on her knees, picking up the sad fragments of what had been a fine plate, red and blue china embossed with gold.

'With me I brought it,' she said, breaking into tears. 'Such a long way I brought it.'

Dot realized then that Mrs. Katz had not cried during her ordeal. She had courage, or perhaps felt that she had no reason to fear the robbers. But now she was weeping desolately. Her make-up was being eroded into runnels by her tears, and Dot offered her a handkerchief.

'Perhaps it can be mended,' said Dot.

'No, it's *kaput*,' said Mrs. Katz. But she gathered up the pieces nonetheless. She and Dot stood the furniture up again, and they surveyed the room. Books had been emptied out of a bookcase, shaken and flung down. A small table and two easy chairs had been upturned and the springs were now showing in the chairs where the undersides had been ripped.

'They were looking for something,' said Dot.

'Something small,' agreed Mrs. Katz, drying her eyes. '*Ai*, such a silly woman I am, to cry over a plate when we are all alive, but my mother it belonged to. Apart from her Sabbath silver it was all I could bring…but the silver is still here,' she said with relief, setting up a beautiful nine-branched candlestick on the mantel and counting out spoons and forks into their wrappings of tissue. Dot shook out and refolded a much-darned white damask tablecloth, and Mrs. Katz replaced it in a wooden chest with the silver and the candlestick.

'It is a *Menorah*,' she said unexpectedly to Dot. 'We are Jews.'

'Yes,' agreed Dot, re-shelving books. Mrs. Katz appeared to be waiting for her to say something. 'That's what this case is about,' she added. 'Mr. Abrahams asked Miss Phryne to look into the murder in the bookshop.'

'Abrahams asked her? Benjamin Abrahams? And she agreed?'

'Yes, she's a detective,' said Dot, and blushed slightly. Detective never seemed like a really respectable profession to Dot and she still wasn't entirely used to it.

'Mr. Abrahams, he is respected man,' commented Mrs. Katz, after a pause. 'Abrahams is a *mensch*, that's what Max says. See, this—I am glad this is not broken. This belonged to my grandfather, who made such things.'

She turned a brass key, and then lifted the lid of a small, intricately carved wooden box. It began to play a Strauss waltz, very tinkly and pretty, and in the box a small clockwork bird opened and closed its beak. Dot exclaimed, delighted, and Mrs. Katz smiled.

'Such a pretty thing. Now we have a look at the other rooms, and then tea, yes?'

When they came to examine the front room, they found it in the same *schemozzl* as the parlour. It took the two of them to heave the mattress back onto the spring base and to remake the bed. Everything in the room had been roughly and hastily searched. All the drawers from a bureau had been torn out and emptied and turned over, then tossed onto the heap of bedding. But nothing had been taken, not even Mr. Katz's best watch, which had been hidden in between the mattress and the base.

The other room contained some furniture which was in the process of being mended. It smelt strongly of wood glue. Even here all the pieces of a large bedstead had been moved, and some of the glued joints had been broken.

It took Dot and Mrs. Katz an hour to put everything to rights, and by the end of it they were friends.

'You see,' explained Mrs. Katz over another cup of straw-coloured tea flavoured with lemon, 'I thought it old country matter because they were speaking Yiddish. "Find it," they say many times. There were two of them, dark men, young, one taller than other, and they were angry. But me they never told for what they were looking, just a paper. What paper, maybe your Miss Fisher knows. But they don't found it here.'

'Why not?' asked Dot.

'Why not?' Mrs. Katz cried. 'Because *here* it was never hidden.'

'Have you ever seen them before, Mrs. Katz?'

'That I can't answer, it was sudden, I didn't see them too good, but no, I don't think so.'

'In the bookshop, Mrs. Katz, what did you see in the book-shop?'

'I don't see nothing, I went there, the lady is very nice, my Max wants a book of maps, we talk for a while about an atlas, I never hear the word before. Then I go home. That's all.'

'Did anyone else come in while you were there?'

'Two young men, maybe they work at the market. They wait while the lady talks to me about the atlas—what a word, I'll never learn all the English words.'

'Was there anyone there when you came in?'

'Just a man with a box. The lady signs a paper and gives it to him and he goes away. I never hear him speak, even.'

'Can you describe him?'

'A drayman or a carter,' Mrs. Katz shrugged fluidly. 'Strong, in overalls, gloves, a cap pulled down over his eyes. But wait....' She sipped more tea, thinking hard. 'There was something about him, maybe. No, nothing,' she decided.

'Tell me,' urged Dot.

'It's nothing, just that I thought he walk wrong for a labourer. Men like that, even when they're not young, they walk like they own the world, you know.' Mrs. Katz got up and mimed the shoulder-heavy walk of a muscular man, hands lightly clenched by his sides. She looked strangely convincing and for a moment Dot could see the standover man she was mimicking. 'Like gorilla, *nu*? Or gunfighter. This one, he was different. Like he was shy, no, not shy....' She shook her head, unable to find the right word to convey what she meant. Dot reflected that it must be terribly hard to come to another place when one was no longer a child and try to learn a new language.

'Never mind, I know what you mean,' she said. 'Now, I'd better go. You're sure you're all right?'

'Sure,' agreed Mrs. Katz. 'Max, he can talk to Mr. Abrahams about this? He'll want to know.'

'Yes,' said Dot.

She used the journey home on two trams to make careful notes of everything Mrs. Katz had said. Because she was constitutionally exact, she also included a description of the red, blue and gold plate which the robbers had broken.

The plate made Dot very angry.

'Well, that's more like service,' commented Bert.

'Too right,' agreed Cec.

They ran lightly down the stairs to the street. The cry of 'Murder!' had been repeated and was even then attracting the attention of a beat cop. He was a mountain of a man in blue serge and helmet, and Bert doused a small flame of alarm when he saw this bastion of the law approaching. Constable Clarke, the biggest policeman in Melbourne. Bert reminded himself that he and Cec were now firmly on the side of law and order, not to mention goodness and righteousness.

The crier was a middle-aged man who had evidently just arisen from a haystack. He was kneeling over a man in an apron, who was not struggling, probably because the smaller man had his foot poised over a very delicate area. But he was spluttering denials. The crowd was enjoying this after-lunch floor show.

The person who wasn't enjoying it was Mr. Rosenbloom, who was on his hands and knees, vomiting into the gutter. Bert noticed that every now and then he would give a twitch, convulsively rising up and then sinking down again.

'Now, then,' said the policeman. Bert held his breath. Was he going to actually say it? Was he going to say 'What's all this then?' and preserve the dramatic unities?

'What's going on here?' asked the policeman, and Bert was disappointed.

'Murder!' screamed Mr. Gunn. 'He poisoned Mr. Rosenbloom!'

'That coot's crazy!' yelled Mr. Lane. 'I didn't poison nobody. Lemme up and I'll knock your block off!' he added to Mr. Gunn, who did not move.

'You let him up,' ordered Constable Clarke. 'You two come into the shop. You and you,' he pointed to Bert and Cec, 'see what you can do for the victim. You,' he pointed to a boy, 'run for Dr. Stein, tell him we need him quick. All the rest of you, on your way, please. Nothing more to see here.'

The crowd, which was anticipating lots of distractions to come, stayed put. The constable blew his whistle for assistance.

'Mate,' said Bert, 'I reckon we need some water. I reckon he's taken strychnine and I reckon that Miss Phryne's going to want to know all about this.'

'Too right,' said Cec. The stricken man was panting with effort, but the tremors which ran through all his muscles would not allow him rest. Cec removed his coat and wrapped it around him.

'You'll be all right, mate,' he soothed. 'Try and sit up a little, now. That's the ticket. Boy's gone for the doctor.'

Mr. Rosenbloom's teeth gnashed together as he tried to speak. 'Pain,' he grunted.

Bert, who knew no harm of the tubby foreman, said, 'Where's that bloody doctor?'

A youngish man with a permanently worried face came through the Eastern Market escorted by a proud boy, and dropped unaffectedly to his knees on the pavement.

'We need to get him inside—can you carry him?' he asked Bert and Cec, who lifted Mr. Rosenbloom with some effort. They hauled him into the printer's shop and deposited him in the room's only chair.

'Sit him down here, good, now, I am going to give you something to drink, and then an injection for the convulsions, and soon you will sleep,' said the doctor. Such was the conviction in his quiet voice that Bert instantly believed him, and so did the stricken Mr. Rosenbloom.

'Come next door,' he nodded to Cec.

The birdshop was loud with denunciations. Bert drew the policeman aside by one sleeve.

'I reckon you'd better call Detective Inspector Robinson,' he informed the blue serge land mass which was Constable Clarke.

'Oh, do you? And who're you?' asked the constable, unimpressed.

'Just call him. He's been looking for the poison what done in that bloke in the bookshop. Strychnine, it was. This is the same stuff.'

The constable glared at Bert and Bert glared back. There was a long interval when neither man lowered his gaze. After a minute,

Clarke stepped to the door and called one of the others who had come in answer to his whistle. Three officers were occupied in keeping the crowd back.

'Call Detective Inspector Robinson, Cadet Richards,' he ordered. 'I think that this has a bearing on his murder case.'

Bert grinned at him. The recriminations in the shop rose again.

'Shut up!' roared the constable. The walls shook and bird seed fell like brightness from the air. Sheer surprise produced silence. The constable took out his notebook and his pencil.

'Now, I want your names,' he began.

Bert and Cec listened as the two men identified themselves.

'Now what's all this about murder?'

'He poisoned his chooks and my finches, and then he tried to poison Mr. Rosenbloom!' declared Mr. Gunn.

'He's cuckoo,' said Mr. Lane pityingly. 'All I did was offer Mr. Rosenbloom a handful of sunflower seeds—he's foreign, he likes eating them.'

'And Mr. Rosenbloom then became ill?'

'Keeled right over,' said Mr. Lane. 'But I didn't poison him.'

'Show us these sunflower seeds,' said the policeman. Mr. Lane led the way into the back of his shop. A small sack of seeds stood on top of a table, next to a couple of penned chickens. A boy looked up from a huge ham sandwich and allowed his mouth to fall open. Bert tipped it shut with a careful forefinger.

'We'll have to wait until Dr. Stein tells us what came over Mr. Rosenbloom,' said the policeman. 'Where did you get these sunflower seeds, Mr. Lane?'

'I…er…bought them.'

'Yes,' said the constable, pencil poised. 'Who from?'

'My usual supplier is Doherty's,' said Mr. Lane.

'Did these come from Doherty's, then?' The constable knew an evasion when he heard it.

'Well, in a manner of speaking, yes.' Mr. Lane wiped his upper lip. 'These were a special sale, just the once.'

'Who sold them to you?'

'A mate of mine,' said Lane. 'I don't want to get him into trouble.'

'You'll be in trouble if you don't tell me what I want to know right now. A man could be dying out there,' said Clarke.

'All right, all right, it was one of the boys, Dusty Miller. He's pushed for cash and so he sold me some seeds.'

'Did you have reason to believe that these seeds had been stolen or unlawfully obtained?' asked Clarke heavily.

'No, I was sure it was all on the level, he's square, Dusty is. Good sort of young lad.'

'Oh yes,' said Constable Clarke. 'And why did you say that Mr. Lane had poisoned your finches, Mr. Gunn?'

'Oh, well, it was nothing, I just…er…borrowed a handful of sunflower seeds for my finches, I would have put them back…'

'You been pinching my feed!' yelled Mr. Lane, thankful that the black spot of legal attention appeared to have passed from him. 'You thief!'

'That's enough,' said Clarke.

'He knew the seeds were poisonous; he sold two chooks which had died of poisoning, I saw his boy plucking them!' Mr. Gunn was not going to let go of his grievance.

'Dead in the pen,' agreed the boy. At a glare from his master, he corked his mouth with sandwich again.

'See?' demanded Mr. Gunn.

'All right, all right,' said Constable Clarke. 'That's enough. From both of you.'

Bert, who had been looking at the sunflower seeds, caught a glimpse of something in the sack which had no business being there.

'There's a stain on the left side of this sack,' he commented. 'And I reckon…', he probed the seeds with a stick, '…yes, there,' he said with satisfaction, as a small uncorked glass bottle emerged from the black and white striped shells. It still had a few white crystals in the bottom. 'That's done you a bit of good with Jack Robinson,' he said to Constable Clarke. 'I reckon you've found his missing bottle of strychnine.'

Chapter Eleven

Mercury and Sulphur, Sun and Moon, agent and patient, matter and form are the oposites. When the virgin or feminine earth is thoroughly purified and purged from all superfluity, you must give it a husband meet for it: for when male and female are joined together by means of the sperm, a generation must take place in the menstruum.

—Edward Kelley,
The Theatre of Terrestrial Astronomy

Phryne received reports as she was dressing for dinner. The girls had enjoyed their afternoon with the Levin family, which had been lavish as well as informative.

'We're coming up to the fast of Yom Kippur,' Jane told Phryne, sitting on her bed and watching her select a flame red dress, shake her head and return it to the wardrobe. 'On the twenty-fourth of September. That's the holiest day of the year. The Day of Atonement,' said Jane.

'I like the sea green better,' obseryed Ruth. 'It's just the same colour as lettuce. What are they atoning for?'

'Everything,' said Jane. 'They can't eat or drink for the whole day, from dawn to dusk. Everyone, though not sick people or women who are expecting. Rebecca says she's going to be allowed to do the whole fast this year. She says it's to teach her what it's like to starve and thirst.'

'I know that already,' said Ruth soberly. Jane and Ruth exchanged glances. They were considering their school mates, who had certainly never been hungry for more than ten minutes in their well-padded lives.

'I think it's a good sort of thing to do,' decided Ruth.

'So do I,' agreed Phryne, who also knew all that she needed to know about privation.

'And I found out about giraffes,' said Jane. 'I asked Mr. Levin. He says it is kosher for the same reason that camel isn't. Giraffes have hoofs, but camels have hard feet. But he said that the Talmudic teachers say that if it is a choice between eating non-kosher food and starving, one is required to live, so one could eat camel if the alternative was death. He pinched my cheek and laughed,' said Jane philosophically, who could take the rough with the smooth in pursuit of knowledge.

Phryne chuckled. 'What shall I wear? I'm going to dinner and then to the Kadimah, which may be anything from an anarchists' den to a Sunday School—well, no, not precisely that, perhaps.'

'Where are you dining?' asked Jane.

'The Society.'

'You must really like this one,' commented Ruth. The Society was one of Phryne's favourite restaurants. She only took people she really liked to the Society.

'I do,' said Phryne. 'What do you think, Dot, the green or the red? Or maybe the tunic and Poitou trousers?'

'Are you going to be doing anything active?' asked Dot, who had divulged her story about Mrs. Katz and the broken plate. 'I mean, not climbing around anything in the dark or that?'

'No, mostly sitting, with a little quiet elegant dining and some driving.'

'I'd wear the green and a fillet,' said Dot.

The girls nodded in unison. Phryne therefore dressed in a cocktail length dark green dress of figured satin, with black shoes and stockings and a long, long necklace of amber-coloured glass beads which winked and twinkled halfway to her knees. She found an amber cigarette holder, fitted a gasper into it, and allowed Dot to place a gold fillet with a black panache made of one curled ostrich feather on her sleek sable head.

Ember levitated onto the bed and thence onto the dressing table and batted at the beads.

'Where's your puppy, Ember?' asked Phryne, removing the string from his strong claws.

'Shut in the kitchen until she gets used to the house. Puppies take a long time to get used to the idea,' said Jane. 'It only took Ember one day—didn't it, precious?'

Ember snuggled up to the caressing hand, radiating consciousness of being a cat (and therefore naturally superior) and Jane cooed.

Bert and Cec, come to report, found the scene touching, if a trifle over-feminine.

Phryne sat them down in her parlour and supplied them with beer.

'We found your bottle of strychnine,' said Bert. 'Detective Inspector Jack Robinson himself came down and looked at it. It was in the sunflower seeds.'

'I thought there was something odd about them sunflower seeds,' exclaimed Dot. 'Everyone was pinching them from everyone else!'

'Unlucky for poor old Rosenbloom, but the doc says that he only got a small dose and he'll be all right.'

Phryne begged Bert for footnotes, and he obliged. Phryne took out her notebook.

'So the sunflower seeds were stored—where?'

'In the undercroft, in old man Doherty's bins. Because he don't buy as much as say wheat or corn, the sunflower seeds are in little sacks. Doherty's boy Miller admitted pinching one bag and selling it to Hughes to finance his system on the horses, and did his boss go crook! Nearly sacked him on the spot, but let him stay provided he promises never to put another bet on a horse.

Might be the making of him. Betting systems buy more bookies Rolls Royces than anything else. Silly cow. Where was I?'

'Undercroft,' said Cec. Phryne wondered if he talked less because it allowed him to drink more, but decided that this was unfair. Cec didn't drink very much more than Bert, who was now approaching his point with relish.

'But this is the important bit. These particular sunflower seeds was in the front because the bag was busted, and Doherty was going to throw them away. He says if he can't guarantee hand on heart that they're good feed, he won't sell 'em, and that's probably why the Miller boy thought it'd be sort of all right to take it. So they were next to the rubbish bin. Doherty's store is on the main way through the storage area, and the cop reckons that the murderer threw the bottle at the bin and missed. It went into the seeds, the stopper fell out—it was in the bag too—the dope spilled and wet the sack, and the remains dried up inside. They're taking them for testing, but I reckon its strychnine all right.'

'Where are the conveniences in the Eastern Market?' asked Phryne, who hadn't noticed them.

'On the ground floor, nearest Exhibition Street,' answered Dot, who had.

'So Miss Lee wouldn't need to pass the storage bins to go there?'

'No,' agreed Bert. 'She would have had to go downstairs, for starters.'

'Bert, she wasn't out of sight of someone all morning except for that brief visit to the Ladies'. How could she have thrown a bottle into the sunflower seeds?' asked Phryne.

'I put that to the cop,' Bert said uncomfortably. 'But he says she must have had an accomplice.'

'Does he,' said Phryne, heavily ironic. 'The plot keeps changing, doesn't it? First there was Miss Lee as a lone maddened spinster killing the young man who done her wrong—or refused to do her wrong, perhaps. Now there's Miss Lee as a woman scorned with an accomplice who can't throw straight. Very convincing, I don't think.'

'That's silly,' said Jane, with conviction.

'I'm with you there, Janie,' said Bert. 'You want us to stay in the market, Miss?'

'Yes. Dot will give you the name of the agent who sent the books. I want to find that carter. He might have seen something. There's more to learn and there is some sort of dirty work at the crossroads, Bert dear, I'm positive of it.'

'Female intuition?' asked Bert.

'Absolutely.'

Dot gave Bert the carbon of the dispatch note, which had *Wm Gibson, Cartage* and an address in Carlton on it over the blotted contents. The room emptied. Bert and Cec were escorted to the door by Jane and Ruth. Ember stalked after them, scenting cold meat in the kitchen. The Butlers were going out for the evening and sometimes Mrs. Butler forgot to lock the pantry. Phryne allowed Dot to put her into a loose velvet coat which had cost a prince's ransom and picked up a pouchy handbag on a string. Phryne had had enough of trying to hang onto a coat with one hand and a bag with the other and use a putative third hand for useful things, like opening doors, stroking beautiful young men and holding her cigarette.

'Have we got enough to go on with, or not?' sighed Phryne. 'More questions, not fewer. Who were the two thugs, speaking Yiddish, who tied up poor Mrs. Katz and broke her plate and ransacked her house? What paper were they looking for, and if it was the piece of paper I showed to Rabbi Difficult, what use is it? Even decoded, it doesn't mean anything. Who killed Shimeon Ben Mikhael? If that bottle contained the strychnine he was poisoned with, who gave it to him and when? Not Miss Lee and not, presumably, in her shop. Can we trace his movements? Have we got anywhere with the clerk?'

'No, Miss, and not likely to, unless we advertise,' replied Dot.

'Well, we have done very well for one day. Bert and Cec have found the strychnine and they can look for the carter. Strange that he hasn't come forward with all this publicity, but perhaps he doesn't read the newspapers or he was on some fiddle or frolic of his own. And you have found Mrs. Katz. Excellent work, Dot dear. Expect a bonus. Are you going out?'

'Me and the girls are going to the pictures. Hugh's taking us.' Dot blushed, though a more blameless way of meeting one's beloved than by taking two adolescents to see the new Douglas Fairbanks was hard to imagine, Phryne thought. 'I hope you have a lovely time. Don't wait up for me,' said Phryne, and went out in a wave of Jicky.

Simon was waiting in the parlour. Phryne descended the stairs, making her entrance, and he was gratifyingly struck by her elegance.

'Where are you taking me?' he asked, wonderingly, a question which could mean many things. Phryne chose the practical answer.

'To the Society for dinner and then to Kadimah, where I expect to hear many interesting things from all your friends. Come along,' she extended a hand, and he went willingly.

'I didn't know there was anything really good at this end of town,' he remarked, as Phryne stopped the car in Bourke Street, almost to the Treasury.

'Once,' Phryne said, 'there was a man who was just stopping off on his way from Italy to his home in the Argentine, but as has happened to a lot of people, he liked it here so he stayed. He set up a meeting place for Italians in Little Bourke Street. He makes real coffee,' said Phryne, a confirmed caffeine addict. 'He was successful so he moved to a bigger place. It's just a simple restaurant but I expect that he will flourish. You'll like him. His name's Guiseppe Codognotto and he's a superb chef. Oh, I hadn't thought. Can you eat his food?'

'Yes, of course,' replied Simon, a little nettled. 'But I will have my coffee black.'

'The only way,' agreed Phryne, and opened the door.

The Society was bright and warm and they went in on a gust of air scented with basil. Robby the waiter, fair haired and elegant, appeared to take Phryne's coat and murmur admiration of the green dress, and suddenly Simon felt as though he had been coming to this place for years. He sat down and beamed.

'Very nice,' said Robby ambiguously, looking at Phryne and then at Simon. 'Nice to see you again, Miss Fisher. You match the decorations.' Phryne's green satin was indeed much the same shade as the green pines in the mural of Capri behind her.

'Thank you Robby dear, I don't need a menu. The gentleman is Jewish and I'm starving. Feed us,' said Phryne, and leaned back in her comfortable chair.

Robby returned with a bottle of wicker-clad chianti, which he opened with an ease which spoke of long practice. Simon looked at it dubiously.

'Isn't that the stuff that tastes of red ink?'

'Generally, yes, but this won't,' promised Phryne. Simon was delighted to find that it didn't. It was a light vintage tasting of crushed grapes. He watched Phryne sipping, noticing the way that the red wine was matched by her ruby mouth, how she passed her tongue neatly over her wet lower lip.

'This wine is the colour of your mouth,' he said. 'You don't really want to go to Kadimah and listen to a lot of people talking, do you?'

'Yes,' said Phryne uncompromisingly. 'I do.' She slid one fingernail over the back of his hand, and he shivered. 'But I haven't forgotten you,' she added.

'I haven't forgotten you,' he replied. 'I love you.'

'No, you don't,' said Phryne gently. 'You love the idea of me. You love the femaleness of me. I told your mother that I was just borrowing you, and that I'd give you back. I have had that conversation before,' she added, remembering Lin Chung's alarming grandmother. 'But I'll love you while I have you, dear Simon.'

Robby, who had been waiting for a break in the conversation, put down two plates of pasta with a thin red sauce.

'*Fettucine puttanesca*,' he said, grinning at Phryne, who grinned back. Fettucine in the manner of whores, eh? Phryne resolved to clip Robby's ears for him when she got him alone.

'Now pay attention, because this is the best pasta you will ever have,' she instructed.

Simon found that spaghetti, which he had only previously experienced as white gluey worms in a tinned tomato sauce, could melt in the mouth. The sauce was sharp, almost sweet, and strongly garlicky. He was glad that Phryne was eating the same thing. It was so delicious that he put off his further declarations of eternal passion until he had wiped his plate with a piece of bread, as he saw Phryne doing. It would have been a sin to waste any of that sauce, anyway.

'Tell me about Zionism,' she said, as Robby filled her glass. He had the talent of being always there when needed and impalpable and invisible when not needed. Phryne had noticed this admirable quality before and wondered if he had any will o' the wisp in his family.

'Zion has always been the hope of the Jews,' said Simon. His face lit with a fervour almost as strong as his passion for Phryne. She was pleased with the success of the question. She had distracted him from making any more unwise speeches, and she needed to know about Zionism. 'Every year when the youngest child asks the questions, he asks, "Why is this night different from all the other nights?" And he is told that it was the night that God chose us and brought us out of Egypt and bondage. But we pray "Next year in Jerusalem". Next year in Zion. One day it *will* be next year in Zion.'

'Palestine. Your father says it is desert and swamp.'

'It will bloom,' said Simon confidently. 'We just need the will.'

'Tell me about this movement, then. Is it a political party?'

'No, not at all—well, yes.' Simon explained. He started again. 'It used to be wholly religious until late last century, when Herzl, Theodore Herzl, didn't actually found but crystallized Zionism as a political movement at the first Zionist Congress in 1897. People went to Palestine and started farms, businesses, bought land from the Turks; they owned it then. Later we bought land from the Arabs. Baron Rothschild has poured money into it, although patronage has its own problems, but everything has problems. Herzl said we had to find political support or we would never survive, but no one likes Jews, and although some of the most anti-Semitic countries supported a homeland—they want to get rid of us—Herzl was in favour of Uganda and we cannot have that. Who is to say that Africa would be safer than anywhere else? And there must be a place which is ours—ours alone.'

'Africa, certainly, would not seem to be a good choice. It's just a little unstable—but surely, so is Palestine?' Phryne was interested. She saw his point.

'Herzl died in 1904, I think it was. Then there was a terrible quarrel which led to some people leaving—the ultra religious, for instance, who believe that only God can restore us and wait for a Messiah. We divided into Practical Zionism and Theoretical Zionism, which was eventually resolved in 1911 into Synthetic Zionism, largely due to Chaim Weizmann arguing everybody into a reasonable frame of mind; a *mensch*, that Weizmann. The Zionists kept the faith through the Great War....'

'*Pesce*,' said Robby, who was worried that the food would get unacceptably chilled if he waited for a break in this discourse. 'Grilled mullet, steamed celery and boiled potatoes. Eat it while it's hot,' he chided. Simon, startled, picked up his fork without thinking.

'You sound like my mother,' he said to Robby, who smiled mysteriously and wafted off in his will o' the wisp fashion.

The fish Phryne was eating was soaked in butter, but that given to her escort was brushed lightly with olive oil. Phryne was immensely impressed. Her faith in the Society had not been misplaced. The fish flaked away from the fork, perfectly cooked, perfectly delicious.

'Simple cuisine is the hardest to manage,' said Phryne, trying not to gobble. 'There are no rich sauces to mask overdone food or disguise something not quite fresh.'

'Certainly,' agreed Simon, through a mouthful.

A respectful interval followed. When Robby had cleared the plates and poured the last of the wine, Simon continued. 'Then there was the Balfour Declaration. 1917. Weizmann had managed to get the British Government to declare that Palestine ought to be a Jewish State. Sokolow had persuaded several European powers to agree—France and Italy, for example. And the Americans had brought in President Wilson. He died soon after, it was sad. But then the British, who have Palestine as a Protectorate, restricted immigration to avoid offending the Arabs. Zionism now is bending all its efforts to promoting immigration and arguing with the British.'

'Are you getting anywhere?'

'It's hard to tell. They said we couldn't be farmers—my father says that Jews cannot be farmers—but we are farmers now. We have a university at Jaffa which teaches agriculture as well as all the other subjects. And General Allenby even lifted the quarantine on trade with Trieste to provide myrtles for the Feast of Tabernacles. It will work. It has to work!'

'Your father does not think so,' commented Phryne. Simon was too full of an excellent dinner to lose his temper, but his voice rose a notch.

'Father is too comfortable. He does not care about the rest of the world. His family, his factory, that is all. But Sokolow reported on the rise of anti-Semitism in the world. A scoundrel called Hitler in Germany published *Mein Kampf* in 1924, a long rant about the Jews, a declaration of war against us. He is a gangster, but some people will always listen to such scum. Germany, some fear, will rise again after the war reparations are paid, and Germany has never been our friend. Mussolini in Italy is anti-Semitic. Hungary and Rumania and Poland are no safe places for Jews, and Russia is allowing pogroms. The Revolution does not include the Chosen people. We make the ideal scapegoat. The world will go hungry again. Whose fault is it? The Jews. The world will have plagues. Who causes plagues? The Jews. The Jews of Spain were fat and rich, but they walked over the mountains and died in the journey when Isabella and Ferdinand needed the Church on their side. The Jews here think they are safe, too. But they are not. One cannot find safety by assimilating, until there is no Jewishness left in us. How many of those

Spanish Jews thought of themselves as Spanish first and Jewish second? They died all the same, and it was their neighbours who stoked their fires and looted their houses.'

'And what is happening now in Palestine?' asked Phryne, shaken by Simon's passionate sincerity.

'We are building and learning and persisting,' said Simon. 'We have patience. Except that I don't have enough of it,' he admitted, relaxing a little and drinking more wine.

'So no one in your family shares your views?'

'Uncle Chaim does, but he would never say so. He does not want to quarrel with my father. But I can talk to him, when the other fellows are at work.'

'The other fellows?'

'You've met them, they'll be at Kadimah tonight. Mrs. Grossman's lodgers. The Kaplans, Yossi Liebermann and Isaac Cohen. It's a pity about Uncle Chaim. He has really good ideas. He did a degree to become a pharmaceutical chemist, except that he didn't finish it, and he had a really good scheme to make artificial silk, but he couldn't get capital and when he did someone else had already invented it.'

'Oh?' Phryne was wondering what Robby was intending to bring for dessert.

'That's definitely the way the world is going, you know, Phryne. Artificial things. Like art silk, much cheaper than real silk and you can wash it—are your stockings art silk?'

'Certainly not,' said Phryne, brushing away a hand which was, of course, only attempting to gauge the reality or superficiality of her underclothing.

'Artificial wood, that chap and his Bakelite—Uncle Chaim had an idea about that, too. And artificial rubber, except that no one's managed to do that yet. Rubber must be more difficult than it looks. And….'

'Indeed,' agreed Phryne. 'This, however, is real.'

Robby put down a bowl piled with a strange fluffy yellow substance which smelt of egg, marsala and sugar.

'*Zabaglione*,' he said triumphantly. He poured her a glass of Chateau Yquem Sauterne, fragrant and grapey. Phryne sipped, smiled, and picked up her spoon.

Over *café negro*, black as night and sweet as sin, Simon returned to his previous subject.

'Tonight?' he pleaded. Phryne touched his lips with one forefinger.

'Perhaps,' she whispered.

Robby, manifesting himself at her left shoulder with a light for her cigarette, did not voice his own opinion aloud.

'Half your luck!'

Kadimah was as ordinary as a church hall, and as extraordinary as a landing of Well's Martians. It was as sane as porridge and as lunatic as singing mice.

There was a row of them, over to one side. They were singing a Yiddish song about—perhaps—cheese, or the dangers of mousetraps. 'There is no such thing as a free munch', possibly. Phryne was a little overwhelmed. She followed the willowy form of her lover to the set of tables and chairs farthest from the door, where the singing mice were somewhat muted by distance.

Nearby was an English language class, patiently repeating 'Am, is, are, was, were, be, been,' in the charge of a tired young woman with seamstress' hands. The students and revolutionaries were seated in a group, with one teapot per person, one cup and one ashtray should anyone have tobacco. Only one person was smoking; a pipe evidently loaded with old rope.

A play was rehearsing next to the singing mice—whose ears, now Phryne had recovered enough to look, were made of stiff paper and whose whiskers were definitely glued on.

'The Young Judeans,' said Simon. 'They're doing the 1928 Follies. Should be a very funny show. It's at Monash House on the third of October and there's a dance afterwards. Would you accompany me?' he asked, and Phryne nodded. She could not pass up an offer like that.

An urn occupied a table near the students, flanked with cups and pots. A very plump, very pretty young woman in a jazz dress carried a large tray piled with little sandwiches and biscuits—the remains of supper—to the brooding young men and smiled at them. The ones whose attention was not on the table or a fierce discussion in an undertone smiled in return, and all hands, even those of the most absorbed, reached instantly for the food.

'They should be finished with their rehearsal soon,' said Simon hopefully. 'Then we only have Louis, and you'll like Louis.'

'I will?'

Simon pointed to a frail-looking boy with glasses. He was sitting perfectly still, his bony knees bare and his knobbly wrists revealed by a too-short, too-tight jumper, reading a massive folio which Phryne realized was an orchestral score. Occasionally he raised one hand and wiggled his fingers in the air. He was completely self-absorbed. His only claims to beauty were his thick black hair, which had been home-cut by an amateur hand, and the pure Middle Eastern line of his forehead, nose and chin. His profile could have belonged to a Pharaoh. One of the Children of Israel had been seduced, Phryne was sure, to lie down in a Princess' arms. What Louis would be like when he grew into his limbs left Phryne feeling a trifle breathless. At the moment, however, he was both gawky and spotty.

The players were packing up, promising to meet again next week. The singing mice detached their whiskers and ears. The room emptied of the scented, highly coloured throng and left it to the students and the English class, which was also putting its notebooks away and returning its cups. Soon the room was relatively quiet.

'This is Miss Fisher,' Simon introduced her. 'You've met her before. This is David Kaplan, this is his brother Solly and his brother Abe, this is Isaac Cohen and this is Yossi Liebermann—you going to run away again, Yossi?' Yossi ducked his head at Phryne and muttered something which no one could hear. He got up abruptly and went out.

Phryne sat down, careful of her stockings on the scratchy wooden chair. Simon supplied her with a cup and one of the Kaplans poured

her some thin tea. Phryne did not look for milk or sugar. She opened
her cigarette case and offered the company a gasper.

They all accepted.

'I've been hearing about Zionism,' she began.

'From Simon?' asked David Kaplan incredulously. '*You've*
been *hearing* about Zionism from Simon? You've been *hearing*
about *Zionism* from *Simon?*'

'Why not?' asked Phryne. 'Doesn't he know about it?'

'Simon is a theorist,' scoffed Solly Kaplan.

'And you're not?' Phryne decided that this was going to be
one of those robust debates and returned the ball briskly.

'We are for Practical Zionism. These governments—they will
not listen to us. The best argument is force,' snarled Isaac Cohen.

'Force? Hasn't enough blood been shed? Besides, the armies
of Zion, whoever heard of such a thing? Jews do not fight,'
objected Simon.

'No, we just die,' snapped Abraham Kaplan. 'What do you
mean, Jews do not fight? Have we not been in armies? Have
we not won the Croix de Guerre and the Iron Cross and the
Victoria Cross?'

'Not all at once. There will always be brave men. But you are
not talking about a country, with a government and an army and
borders on a map. We have no country,' said Simon.

'We should take one, then.' Isaac Cohen was thin and his
liquid eyes seemed designed for love-making, not war.

'You are still of the opinion that we should declare war on
the Arabs and take the land?' asked Simon.

'I am. And if we reach the medicine of metals, we shall win
a country of our own where no Jew need cower.'

'That's the *lapis philosophorum*,' said Phryne, who recalled the
phrase. 'You're talking about finding the universal solvent.'

Five pairs of eyes looked at her. She looked back.

'What do you know of such matters?' asked Solly Kaplan.

' "Tis a stone and not",' quoted Phryne with Ben Jonson.
' "A stone; a spirit, a soul, and a body. If you coagulate it, it is
coagulated. If you make it flie, it flieth." '

Silence fell. Finally Isaac Cohen asked, 'Simon, who *is* she?'

'She's The Honourable Miss Phryne Fisher. She's a student of the Great Art. She's my lover,' replied Simon, allowing them to choose which definition they pleased.

'*She* is a Zionist?' demanded Abe, incredulously.

'She's a friend to Zionism. And she saved Rabbi Elijah from being tormented by some children.'

'She knows the rabbi?' asked Solly.

'Certainly,' said Phryne. She did not like being discussed while she was present in this way. 'He gave me a vision. Beware of the dark, he said, dark tunnels under the ground. "There is murder under the ground, death and weeping; greed caused it". That's what he said.'

The others exchanged glances.

'Now there is this,' said Phryne, laying her cards on the table. 'Shimeon Ben Mikhael is dead, murdered, in the bookshop. He was a friend of yours, wasn't he?'

'Poor Shimeon,' murmured Solly, lowering his eyes.

'And Miss Lee is taken for his murder and is in jail, and unless I come up with something, she will hang. And she didn't do it, did she? You know how Simon Michaels died.'

'No!' Isaac Cohen leapt to his feet. 'We don't know. All night we talked about it, and accused each other, and we don't know. You have to believe it, lady. We liked him, we mourn him, we will say kaddish for him, such a *miesse meshina*, an ugly fate…'

'All right, you don't know how he died or who killed him, but you know something, that is plain. I want you to help me. I will go over there and you can talk about it. I will not insult you by offering a reward, but you know that Mr. Abrahams is rich and he will not be unappreciative. I want to know what you and that difficult old man have been doing. I want to know what causes Yossi to burn his landlady's table with chemical experiments. You can't really be expecting to find the philosopher's stone, not in this day and age. I don't believe it. I want to know what you are doing. If it does not bear on my investigation, I don't have to tell anyone, and I won't.'

Phryne walked away across the empty hall as the argument bloomed behind her. Voices were raised. Phryne could not understand Yiddish, which was probably what they were speaking.

Phryne felt alien and isolated. As Solly leapt to his feet to pound the table, the gawky boy Louis opened a violin case, tucked the instrument under his chin, and began to play.

Not a popular tune, but Bach. Not a Jewish song, but the Ave Maria. His skill was partly constrained by the cheap instrument, but each note was perfect, full and round. Phryne, who had been about to go into Drummond Street out of the sound of the quarrel, sat down. Louis did not see her or notice her appreciation. His eyes were shut. His strong fingers shifted and pinned each note to its pitch. It was not the over-emotional rendering expected of a boy, a sob in every string, but a mature performance good enough for the Albert Hall.

He completed the work, sighed, then opened his eyes, propped his score open at *Violin Concerto in A Minor: allegro assai* and began to play phrases, trying them one way and then another.

'Bach is difficult,' offered Phryne, wanting to hear Louis' voice.

'Nah,' said the boy, as if he was speaking to himself. His accent was pure Carlton. 'Bach's controlled. It's the wild ones that are crook for me. Tchaikowsky. The Brahmns gypsy dances. Ravel's flamin' *Bolero*. Bach's simple,' he said, and tried the phrase again, now faster, now slower.

He was a pleasure to listen to, so Phryne listened.

Louis had worked his way through the whole of the *Violin Concerto in A* and was well into the *Concerto for Two Violins and Strings in D Minor* when Phryne heard the ordinarily placid Simon shout '*Zoll zein shah!*'

This brought almost instant silence.

'Enough!' He pounded the table in turn, so that one of the cups dropped and smashed. 'Make up your minds! Either we tell the lady or we don't! I can't stand any more of this endless arguing, round and round and *round* in circles!'

'We tell her some,' decided David Kaplan. 'And we apologize for the noise.'

Phryne came back to her place at the table, crunching over fragments of thick white china. David Kaplan took her hand and kissed it.

'You like Louis' playing, eh? He's good? He lives in a room with his father and he can't play there. He's auditioning for the orchestra as soon as he's old enough.'

'He's a *mazik*, that Louis. He'll go far,' opined Phryne, who had had a Yiddish lesson from Mrs. Abrahams. She was pleased with the goggle she elicited from the students.

'We study the Torah, lady. With Rabbi Elijah. And the Holy Kabala. There are ways of reading the Torah, you see, different ways.'

'Notarikon, Temurah and Gematria,' said Phryne, composedly.

'Er…yes. Temurah is about anagrams, words spelt backwards or scrambled. Notarikon relates to the abbreviation of Hebrew words, you see, we do not have vowels. Gematria is about numbers turned into letters, and letters to numbers. It is the perfect way to hide a code, say, or a string of figures. *The Book of Splendour* tells us that we must look always for hidden meanings, the emanations of the Divine, what the Christians call Thrones, Dominations and Powers. So when we got interested in alchemy, Yossi here was reading Paracelsus and he began looking under the surface of the experiments in the *Occulta Philosophica*, and…'

Solly Kaplan took up the tale. 'Paracelsus was the first great chemist, as well as an alchemist. He knew how to transmute mercury, for instance, into oxide and back into metal. He had a recipe for the philosopher's stone, so we tried it, and we got nowhere, Miss, as you would expect. Then Yossi began to work on glues and…'

'Do not tell,' warned Isaac.

Solly looked hurt. 'Not about the experiment, no, but no harm in the other things, is there? Then there was Zion, you see. We need guns. It will only be a matter of time before Palestine is attacked and we need to fight. Because of Yossi's work we had something to sell, but we are not fools. We needed to exchange information with an intermediary without him knowing who we were. So we left the notes in Miss Lee's shop, because we know that she will never sell the books in the corner. Shimeon must have tried to retrieve the paper. Someone killed him for it. It is lost,' he said desolately.

'But it is not gone forever, while you still have Yossi,' said Phryne.

There was another silence, in which Louis mastered another phrase of the adagio of his violin concerto.

'He can't remember what he did,' wailed Solly suddenly, clutching at his forehead. 'Once, he got it to work *once*, and he noted down all the proportions, but he tried to repeat it and it doesn't work. And now Shimeon is dead and someone has the compound!'

'Tell him to keep trying,' urged Phryne. 'Tell him to repeat the experiment and vary the ingredients. I don't suppose you feel like telling me either what you were selling or to whom you were selling it?'

They shook their heads.

'So Shimeon went to deposit the paper and he died. And you haven't seen the paper since?'

'No,' David replied.

'All right. Tell Yossi to keep working. Remember also that it might be better to register the patent the usual way. When you get the money, you can always buy guns for Palestine with the proceeds. Now, I want to see all of your shoes.'

'Our shoes?' asked Isaac, bewildered. 'You want to look at our *shoes*?'

'If you please,' said Phryne, quietly determined.

One by one they removed their shoes and Phryne inspected them. Leather soles retained particles of white china, such as studded her own soles from the broken cup. But not one of the shoes she was shown, from Simon's immaculate Oxfords to Isaac's broken and unpolished ex-army boots, showed a crumb of red, blue or gold from Mrs. Katz's plate.

She returned their footwear and stood up.

'If you decide to tell me more,' she informed the group, 'you can always find me at this address.' She gave David Kaplan her card.

He was still staring at it as Louis played Phryne and Simon out with the first strains of Ravel's flamin' *Bolero*.

Chapter Twelve

Water: This is the first Element...the most Ancient principles, and the Mother of all things amongst Visibles. Without the mediation of this, Earth can receive no blessing at all, for the moysture is the proper cause of mixture and Fusion...The Common Element of Water is not altogether contemptible, for there are hidden treasures in it.

—Thomas Vaughan, *Magia Adamica*

'All right,' said Simon, as Phryne started the engine and the Hispano-Suiza purred into life. 'The chemistry I sort of understand. The argument about Zion, that has been going on for a long time. At least since Bar Kochba. But the shoes, Phryne darling, *I* should understand the *shoes?*'

'I thought of it when I walked on the bits of that cup you smashed in the heat of discussion. Broken china sticks in the soles. Someone invaded the house of a Mrs. Katz today, and searched it for "the paper". In the process they shattered a very old and distinctive plate. There was no trace of it in your friends' shoes, though Yossi left before I could examine his. Therefore those present did not break into Mrs. Katz's house.'

'Katz? In Carlton? She's Max Katz's wife. Is she all right? How does she come into it? Why did you think that we might have done it?'

'Because she was in the bookshop, the lady in the awful hat. Now what paper could they be looking for, hmm?'

'Yossi's compound,' said Simon.

'I should have looked at it more closely. It was just a string of letters and numbers, but that's what a chemical formula is. Like H_2O or O_2. Water and oxygen. Do you know any chemistry, Simon?'

'Me? I'm a shoemaker. I wonder what Yossi was working on? A new glue, perhaps? In shoemaker's glue, there's a lot to improve. You have to keep it hot, it's very inconvenient. And carpenters use the same stuff.'

'Possibly. In any case, we know that it probably wasn't your friends who were searching Mrs. Katz's house for the paper. There is someone else in this, some other party.'

'The buyer. He hasn't got the formula,' said Simon. 'Because we've got it.'

'And he's looking for it,' said Phryne. 'He knows it's not with the Katzes. I hope Bert and Cec can find that carter tomorrow. He might be in danger.'

'Oh, danger, Phryne, please!' scoffed Simon.

'They broke into a house and tied an old woman to a chair. They left a pan on the stove. The house could have burned down; that would have been murder,' Phryne reminded him.

Simon did not speak until the big car was rolling off the road onto the grass. 'Where are we going?' he asked. 'You're going to drive into the sea?'

'What time is it?' asked Phryne.

Simon consulted his watch. 'Nearly midnight.'

'It's a hot night and there's no moon,' said Phryne softly. 'We can leave the car here and no one will see us. I'm going swimming.' She stopped the engine and pulled off her shoes and stockings. Simon heard the clatter of her beads as she dropped them, and could see a flash of milk-white flank and thigh as she stood up to take off her dress and then her cami-knickers.

He caught his breath. She was naked: even her head was bare of the ostrich feather fillet. In one smooth movement she vaulted out of the car onto the prickly grass, and was running towards the sea.

He tore at his buttons with shaking fingers.

He caught her by sound in the darkness. The air was heavy and thick, and the sea kissed his naked flesh; a city's ocean, which slapped ashore and made genteel little waves which ran whispering down the sand. Behind him St. Kilda went on with its late night life. There weary painted women solicited for trade in beery streets where the six o'clock drinkers had swilled and vomited. He had yearned after the whores once, desperately curious about the sexuality of women. He had envisaged seduction, the urgent plea and the concession which allowed him access to the flesh he desired.

But not even in tangled sweaty sheets at three in the morning, despairing of ever finding a lover, had he imagined anyone like Phryne.

She was wet and her skin was cold, but under his hands it was scalding. Arms wreathed around his neck and a mouth met his, opening, salty and soft. She pulled him down into the embrace of the water, sliding around and under him like a fish, so that he ducked and dived, grabbing for her as she eluded him, laughing and then coughing as he breathed ocean.

She was as fast and sleek as a seal. The distant street light showed him her head as she emerged, a frill of foam around her neck, her black hair plastered to her head like a depraved Pierrot.

'Such a beautiful boy,' she crooned, slipping forward with the wave and kissing him hard. 'Come, come to me.'

He grabbed again and this time she allowed herself to be caught; she yielded to his embrace, clinging to him in the salt water which bore them both up.

'Oh, my nymph,' he gasped. 'Nereid, I'm yours.'

She moved again so that he was on the shingle, lying just above the backwash of the waves, supine, astonished, wholly at her mercy. Her mouth and hands caressed him, then she was astride him, just visible in the distant light as she sank down onto him and moved as though she was riding Thetis' horses of the sea. He thought of *conjunctio*, the crowning alchemical mystery, as his hands found her breasts, and then he lost capacity for thought altogether. He did not know how long it was until he groaned, and heard Phryne cry aloud like a seabird.

Late, sandy and incompletely dressed, Phryne parked her car and brought Simon into the house. She led him up the stairs and into her apartment.

'A shower,' she said, pulling off the green dress. Under it she was naked. She dropped stockings, shoes, underclothes and jewellery on the floor. Simon began to remove his hastily donned garments, wondering why fly buttons were so prone to desertion. He had lost two. Phryne flung him a gown and he pulled it on, still astounded at the ferocity of her passion.

She showered thoroughly, rinsing the salt off her skin and the sand from her hair, then yielded her place to the young man. Such a beautiful boy, she thought, observing that he was somewhat abraded around buttock and back by the shingle. Prior experience had taught Phryne that it was wise not to be underneath if making love on sand.

'Oh, Phryne,' sighed Simon, 'that was…'

'Astonishing?' asked Phryne, towelling her hair. 'Yes. Lovely.'

He was a little disappointed by her response. After all, he had given her all he had to give. She leaned past the fall of water and kissed him gently.

'You are quite delightful,' she said, and went into her bed-room.

He heard her exclaim, 'Jesus wept!' and he got out of the shower and draped the gown over his wet body. He would dry quickly enough in the hot night, no matter what his mother said about catching cold. Phryne was looking at a room which had been comprehensively ransacked.

'The others,' she said, and ran for the stairs, her black kimono billowing behind her.

Downstairs was silent. Simon was behind her as she opened the girls' door and exclaimed with relief when she heard them breathing peacefully. He followed her to the kitchen where she opened the Butlers' door and listened for Mr. Butler's snore and Mrs. Butler's whuffle. Both present and correct. Beside the combustion stove, which had not been lit, there was a faint noise. But it was only Ember rising from beside his puppy and suggesting politely that although it appeared to be the middle of the night, if Phryne thought it was breakfast time then he was ready to graciously fall in with her wishes.

She stroked the cat and told him that he must wait until a reasonable hour.

They returned to Phryne's rooms, where she let out a great breath which she had not known she was holding. Then, to Simon's surprise, she threw herself into his arms and hugged him hard for almost a minute, her wet head on his silk-clad shoulder.

'Dear Simon,' she said softly. He held her close, feeling her heart beating fast against his own. Then she pulled away and surveyed the damage.

'What a mess, but nothing is too badly damaged,' she commented. 'Help me,' she said, and he grabbed the end of the mattress.

Half an hour later, and Phryne's boudoir was in its accustomed state.

'There's nothing missing, and fortunately for them they didn't disturb the rest of the house or I would have had their blood,' said Phryne matter-of-factly. 'This definitely excludes you and your friends, Simon. It must have happened while we were at Kadimah. This must have been one of the dark young men who robbed Mrs. Katz. Erk. I hate to think of him being in my room, handling my things. Though what he made of all those silk cami-knickers he fumbled through I'd like to know.'

'Excludes *me*?' asked Simon. '*I* needed to be excluded?'

'Don't be offended, old thing. It's part of being a detective. You have to suspect everyone, it's one of those rules. But they didn't find my safe deposit,' she said in satisfaction.

'They didn't? But *everywhere* they looked!' protested Simon.

Phryne smiled the smile of a canary-fed cat. 'Not everywhere. They just thought that they looked everywhere. They got the alchemical paintings, though. I left them on my dressing table. But the paper and the translation—no.'

'How can you tell?' asked Simon. 'You haven't checked.'

'Yes, I have. Now, I think we should open a bottle of champagne, which is still cooling in the bucket over there just as Mr. Butler left it. The burglar had no taste for good wine, fortunately. There are glasses in the cupboard underneath, and he's learned from Mrs. Rose's. He didn't break one of them.'

'Phryne,' Simon begged. 'Please!'

'No one ever died of curiosity, Simon dear, and I'd rather you didn't know. What you don't know cannot be persuaded or forced from you.'

'You're serious, aren't you?'

Phryne lit a cigarette and drew in the smoke hungrily.

'Certainly. Consider: to get into this room, someone had to climb the tree and then the roof, a dangerous climb with no holds. I have felt as though someone was watching me for the last few nights, he must have been waiting until we were all out. The person took a huge risk of being seen by anyone passing by in the street or being caught by either of the two groups who returned at a more decorous time than we did. I expect that the girls were home by ten, and Dot would not have let Hugh stay beyond eleven. And the Butlers would have come home about then, possibly a little later depending on the running of the last tram. Our burglar really wanted to get in. It must have taken fully half an hour to search as comprehensively as he did. No, this is serious, Simon, and I am getting a better latch on that window tomorrow. Not even my insurance company thought that a window in an upper floor needed a lock. And you know how constitutionally suspicious insurance companies are. Thank you,' she said, gulping thirstily.

'All right, it's serious. But if it wasn't me, and *I've* known it wasn't me all along,' said Simon severely, 'then who was it?'

'Agents or minions of the buyer,' replied Phryne. 'See if you can persuade your friends to tell you who it is. I understand that they want to buy guns to start a patriotic war in Palestine, but they can do that just as illegally by selling this compound of Yossi's on the open market. There is some sort of elaborate mind in this: the same mind that managed to kill poor Simeon in Miss Lee's shop. A scheming mind.'

'I'll ask them, but I don't think they'll tell me,' said Simon.

'No, I expect we'll have to find it by ourselves.'

'About this hiding place,' Simon teased. 'I can show you a really good one.'

'Oh, indeed?'

'If you'll show me yours.'

'No,' said Phryne, and drank some more champagne.

'Oh, well.' Simon took up the *Occulta Philosophica*, a leather-bound folio. 'Now, where would you hide something in a book?'

'At page thirty-five,' said Phryne, lighting another gasper from the butt of the first.

'You're chain smoking,' reproved Simon. 'Just folding it into the pages, that's not safe. Anyone comes along and shakes the book, your secret is revealed.'

'Stop *nudzing* me, I'm a victim of crime and I'm a bit shaken. Where, then, do I hide my paper in a book?' asked Phryne, irritated.

'Here.' Simon laid the book down, spine upward, and opened it. The leather binding gaped, revealing a tunnel between the spine and the cover.

'See, you fold your paper into a spill and slip it down here. Then to get it out you just pick up the book, open it like you are reading it, and then feel down that gap for…Phryne! Are you all right?'

'Oh, my God, he had a cut on his finger,' said Phryne. 'What did I say about an elaborate mind?'

Simon, alarmed at her sudden pallor, quoted, 'You said that whoever did this had…'

'An elaborate, scheming, evil, murderous mind,' said Phryne, fanning herself with one hand. 'A really nasty mind. I'm looking forward to meeting him.'

'Phryne, would you like to tell me what you are talking about?' asked Simon.

'Not tonight. Bring the bottle. Come and lie down with me,' she said faintly, stubbing out her cigarette. 'What with one thing and another, Simon, darling, I don't want to sleep alone.'

Morning brought Greek coffee and Dot, looking rather severe.

'There's things all out of order,' she reproved. 'All the soaps have been moved and someone's dropped a bottle of them expensive French bath salts. And the towels have all been unfolded and bundled back anyhow. What were you looking for, Miss? I left your things out on the dressing table like I always do.'

Phryne, sitting up reluctantly, shoved her hair out of her eyes and shook the smooth shoulder of the sleeping boy.

'Wake up, Simon, it's morning. That wasn't me, Dot dear, we had a burglar. He didn't take anything. Ring that nice carpenter, I forget his name, and get him to put a lock with a key on my windows, will you? Not bars. I don't want to be kept imprisoned by my own security. But a nice solid lock.'

'A burglar?' Dot put down the coffee and boggled. 'What, a burglar in the house, here, when we were all asleep?'

'Dot, if you say "We might have all been murdered in our beds", I'll scream,' said Phryne, who had woken up cross. 'We weren't touched and that's fortunate for the burglar. Otherwise I'd have his guts for garters. Curse the horrible little hoodlum.'

'You might say, "May beets grow out of his stomach",' suggested Simon, sleepy with satiated desires, lapped in more luxury than he had ever imagined. 'That was one of *zayde*'s, my grandfather. He was good at curses. His favourite was "May a fire burn in his belly to boil his brains." Wicked tongue, my grandfather, *alav ha-sholom*.'

'Amen,' agreed Phryne. 'It's all right, Dot, don't worry. If it would make you feel better, why not ask Hugh to sleep in the spare room for the next couple of nights? This should be over soon.'

'Oh?' asked Dot, uneasily.

'Yes,' said Phryne. 'After a suitable interval for ablutions and breakfast, I am taking Jack Robinson to the bookshop to show him the murder weapon, and shortly thereafter I expect to get Miss Lee out of quod.'

'The murder weapon?' asked Simon, after looking at Dot for guidance and realizing that she was as ignorant as he was. 'It's still in the shop?'

'I hope so,' said Phryne, and refused to say any more.

Miss Lee had moved onto the fourth declension. She wondered, occasionally, sleepless at three in the morning, if she would master the whole lexicon before they hanged her, which seemed to be a terrible waste of an education.

But one must not give way. Because she was on remand, she was allowed to receive gifts. Every day fresh flowers arrived, and chocolates, books and cigarettes. The last bunch was red roses, from Mr. Abrahams.

Someone still believed that she was innocent. And the remarkable Phryne Fisher was still investigating.

'*Manus, manus, manum,*' sang Miss Lee. '*Manus, manui, manu.*'

'What's a man gotta do to get an answer?' asked Bert of Cec, as they stood before a gate which was not only closed but had two braces nailed across it.

'I don't reckon we're gonna get an answer, mate,' opined Cec.

'Yair, looks like Wm. Gibson, Carter, has cashed it in and gone to the South Sea Isles, all right. You should be able to see over the fence if I can give you a bit of a boost.'

Bert bent and Cec rose. He held on to the shaky grey timber and reported, 'Nothing in the yard, mate. Let me down. No truck. There's a busted-looking old dray, and that's all. Not even a cat.'

'Well, that's torn it,' said Bert, removing his hat and scratching his bald spot. Working for Miss Fisher, he reckoned, was hard on a bloke's hair. His had already been appreciably thinned by some of her cases. It was going to be hot. The streets already had the faint, glazed look which spoke of pavements just about to soften and shimmer.

'P'raps the neighbours'd know,' suggested Cec, diffidently.

'You take that side of the street,' sighed Bert, 'and I'll take this.'

They split up and began knocking on doors. Bert began to long for the good old days of ferrying drunks from one side of the city to the other. More than that, he could do with a good cold beer.

Phryne, policemen in tow, opened the door of Miss Lee's shop. The little bell rang tinnily. The room was clean, but already a slight film of dust was settling on the polished desk. It felt shabby and desolate. Jack Robinson was not in the mood for excitable females, though he was vaguely wondering why she was carrying a craft knife and a pair of thick gloves.

'Well, Miss Fisher?'

'Now, Jack, is the shop the same? No one has been here?'

'It looks the same,' he said warily.

'I've told you all about Yossi's formula. I have told you about Mrs. Katz and the burglary of my own house. Now there's something I have to conjecture. Part of the fun of being a conspiracy is the ridiculous mumbo-jumbo which men so enjoy. Passwords, you know, and secret handshakes and all that sort of thing. It must be something endowed with the male hormone we hear so much about in these glandular days. Anyway, like schoolboys playing catch with trinitrotoluene, those unworldy scholars used to pass their information to each other by putting it in one of the unread books in Miss Lee's shop. Shimeon the go-between put the formula into a book.'

'No, he didn't,' objected the policeman. 'We've had all those books out and shaken. There wasn't anything hidden in them.'

'That's what you think. I was talking to these poor bunnies last night and they told me that Shimeon had hidden the formula in a book. I thought as you did, and then Simon showed me how to conceal something in a book so that no casual search will ever find it.'

Phryne walked to the bookcase which concealed the Great Unread. 'Now, I don't know which of these it is. I remember Dot saying that—now what was it? Unfortunately we can't use the dust as a guide, now they are all dusty. We'll try the leather-bound folios. What have we here?' She laid them on the counter with a thump. '*The Letters of Sir Walter Scott*. Volume 9 of Hansard for 1911. *Sermons in Stones* by the Rev. Walters. Now, which is the most deadly?'

'Probably Hansard,' opined Detective Inspector Robinson, who did not admire politicians.

'We'll try that first. The way this must have worked is that Shimeon put his message in one book, and picked it up from another. God knows why. Gimme the knife, Simon.'

Phryne put on the gloves and slit the binding of the folio from one end to the other.

'No, nothing in Hansard,' she commented. 'What about Sir Walter?'

The leather and stiffening peeled away from the blade.

'Miss Fisher, if you've dragged me here to watch you mutilate books...' began Jack Robinson, who had other things to do. Phryne bit her lip. She turned the sermons so that light fell on the spine, and slit the binding for the third time.

'See?' she said.

'What am I looking at?' asked Robinson.

'A murder weapon,' said Phryne. 'No, don't touch. Not unless you want to join Shimeon. That's what killed him.'

'It's just a bit of sharp metal, part of a razor blade, embedded in the spine,' objected Jack Robinson.

'That's exactly what it is,' said Phryne. 'Simon, demonstrate how one would remove a message. Use another book,' she added hurriedly.

Simon hefted a large volume, opened it, and groped in the interstice. Robinson felt suddenly very ill. To cover this, he took out his pipe and made a great show of lighting it.

'Shimeon comes into the shop,' said Phryne. 'He is supposed to plant the formula first and then to collect his reward, perhaps a note which says that an arms dealer has been arranged for this war in Palestine, God help them. But he didn't do that. Perhaps he was cleverer than the others, or more suspicious. Perhaps that goes with being born in Salonika, where they know more about conspiracy than gentle innocent Australia. You can see how it happened, Jack. Exactly as Miss Lee says it happened. He opened the book, groped for the hiding place as Simon is doing, then his right index finger met the razor blade. A thin cut, like a paper cut. It was a trivial injury, so he didn't scream and draw attention to himself. But it was a fatal injury, because the blade was loaded with strychnine crystals. You can still see them. Someone has used paste to make the blade sticky. Then he turned to Miss Lee, falling, and held out his hand to her, to draw attention to the wound. He tried to speak to her, but he failed.'

Simon stared at the exhibit, still holding the book. He was as white as a sheet. The attendant constable noticed that he looked very sickly and moved towards him.

'They found no strychnine in the stomach,' said Robinson. 'There's a report from the toxicologist, too. It was pure strychnine, chemically pure. Not the mixture they use to poison rats. This is an awful thing,' he said slowly. 'A trap for the most unsuspecting. Just when he thought that he was going to get what he wanted.'

'A cruel thing,' said Phryne. 'The product of a cunning mind.'

'But whose mind?' demanded the policeman.

'Ah, that,' said Phryne, 'we have yet to ascertain. But I tell you one thing, Jack dear, it wasn't Miss Lee.'

'She could have been an accomplice,' said Robinson, without conviction.

'Have a heart,' begged Phryne.

'You're right. We'll release her this afternoon. All charges dropped and her release proceeding from sure and certain knowledge of her complete innocence,' said Robinson, heavily.

'There's a good policeman.' Phryne patted his arm.

'Someone set a trap for poor Shimeon,' whispered Simon. 'And killed him as coldly as you kill a mouse.'

'Yes, and with the same poison,' agreed Robinson absently.

There was a crash as the book hit the floor, but the alert constable managed to catch Simon.

The Detective Constable had no imagination, so he was not shocked by the murder weapon or the collapse of the dark boy, which he had expected. But he was horrified by the way Miss Fisher had called his chief 'Jack, dear'.

He had never thought of Detective Inspector Robinson in that light before.

As they left the shop, a woman in shabby clothes caught at Miss Fisher's arm. 'Excuse me, Miss, are these the jacks who are saying Miss Lee's a murderer?'

'They're the ones,' agreed Phryne. 'Who are you?'

'I'm Mrs. Price. I clean this shop and I'm here to tell them they're wrong. You the head cop? You're looking for the rat poison, ain't yer?'

Jack Robinson said 'Mind your language, Mrs. Price. Yes, I am looking for the rat poison. Do you know what happened to it?'

'Yair,' said the cleaning woman angrily. 'I spilled it and I threw it away. I been sick with the 'flu and I didn't know about all this till my son told me tonight. So that's where it went, right?'

'Right,' said Detective Inspector Robinson, humbly.

Chapter Thirteen

…there is in nature a certain Spirit which applies himself to the matter, and actuates in every Generation.

—Thomas Vaughan,
Anima Magica Abscondita

'Strewth,' Bert declared after two fruitless hours. 'What have you got, mate?'

'Not much,' said Cec. 'Well, something. Not many people live around here.'

'Lotta dogs, but,' said Bert, who had been bailed up in two different yards by hounds which Mr. Baskerville might have considered overdrawn.

'Yair. Met a few nice dogs,' said Cec, whom all animals instantly recognized as a friend of a different but related species.

'You'd get on like a blood brother with a tarantula,' snarled Bert, mopping his brow.

'Never met one of them,' said Cec, interested. 'But I had a pet huntsman. My landlady went crook, so I had to find him another home. Used to feed him flies.'

'What've you found?' asked Bert, who was a confirmed arachnophobe. He did not want to think about Cec's communion with his many-legged friends.

'Lady at the house over there says that Gibson's been gone for six months. Says he sold up his stuff and went to join his daughter in Queensland—so you were almost right about the South Sea Isles.'

'That can't be right,' objected Bert. 'The bloke delivered a box to Miss Lee's last week. We've got the dispatch note.'

'Can't have,' insisted Cec. 'The old lady was pretty clear about it. Said she missed him being there. She's crippled, and she liked watching his trucks go in and out. Poor old chook. But she's got a good dog to keep her company. A blue heeler called Sally.'

'I hope they'll both be very happy,' said Bert sarcastically. 'But we're at a dead end, then.'

'Yair, well, Mrs. Hebden told me that all Gibson's stuff went to a dealer, and she gave me his name. And she says his top cocky driver, bloke the name of Black Jack Alderton, practically lives at the Albion Hotel since his latest job folded. That's at the corner of Faraday Street and Lygon Street, isn't it? That's the next step.'

'Bloody beauty,' said Bert. 'I gotta get out of the sun, it's as hot as bloody Cairo.'

Miss Lee looked up from her book. The hard-faced warder was there.

'You're to pack up your things, Lee,' she said crisply. 'Governor's waiting.'

Miss Lee closed the book and reached for her bag. She had been moved from cell to cell over the last four days and was used to packing quickly. She laid the last garment in her case, clicked the latches, and asked, 'Where am I going?'

'Governor'll tell you,' said the guard. 'Off remand, anyway.'

That must mean that she was going to trial. Miss Lee followed the wardress through the corridors. The floors in the prison were scrubbed every morning by a special punishment detail; they were so clean that an unwary mouse might skid on them. The walls were an unrefreshing shade of mud. Miss Lee preceded the wardress at the proper distance. In that moment she realized that her body belonged to the State, that she would never be free, and that her days on earth had been numbered by men who would shortly judge her, condemn her and kill her. And that there was nothing at all she could do to affect her fate.

She would have run if there had been anywhere to run, but she was still Miss Lee, who prided herself on her control.

Inside her, someone was weeping hysterically.

The journey seemed to last for years. Miles of disinfected corridors were passed. They reached the Governor's office, and she stood at attention before it as the wardress negotiated entry. It was not until she smelt Nuit D'Amour perfume in the Governor's office that she began to hope. No one in prison smelt of anything but soap. The scent emanated from a small woman with Dutch-doll hair, a jewel-blue dress and cloche and a handful of papers. She was flanked by a plain young woman in beige linen and a policeman with a forgettable face.

'Miss Lee, I've come to take you home,' said Phryne.

'You've found the murderer?' Miss Lee fought down elation.

'We soon will. But the police know that it isn't you. Have you got everything? Good. Here is the order for release, here is Jack Robinson to confirm that there are no charges against you and that you are a pure and stainless soul, and here is my companion, Dot, who is going to stay with you for today. I know you would rather be alone, but we still have a few ends to tie up. This way, Miss Lee,' said Phryne.

Miss Lee found herself holding out her hand to the Governor, and almost thanked her for having her.

'Goodbye, Miss Lee,' said the thin woman, and smiled bleakly. 'Congratulations.'

'Thank you,' gasped Miss Lee, who had regained her honorific with her freedom.

It was not until the last set of prison doors shut behind her that she found herself wondering if she would ever get to the fifth declension—*res*, *fides* and *spes*.

'Well, you're out of that horrible place and you're a free woman again,' said Phryne. 'Anything you want, just name it.'

'I want a bath,' said Miss Lee promptly. 'A real bath with real soap. I want a boiled egg and some bread and butter and a cup of real tea. Then I want to go and walk around the city.'

'It's yours,' said Phryne. 'Dot will look after you. She will also tell you everything that has happened.'

'Where will you be?' asked Miss Lee, bewildered by the speed of events. An hour ago she had been a condemned prisoner. Now she was sitting in a very expensive red saloon car and the suburbs were speeding past.

'I have to go and talk to a chemist,' said Phryne.

Bert put down his empty glass and licked a little foam from his upper lip.

'That hit the spot, eh, mate?'

'Too right.'

The pub was filling rapidly as the temperature outside climbed. The Albion was a spacious pub, built in the days when a public house with any pretensions to gentility had to have fourteen foot ceilings, brass taps and a polished wooden bar you could skate down. It had no floor coverings, but the black and white tiles were cool in the heat. Bert, in his reflective moments, considered that if heaven didn't have a well-appointed pub where a man could sit down over a beer for a yarn with the other angels, then he didn't want to go there.

'Mate,' Cec nudged him. 'Looks like trouble.'

Even in Arcadia, thought Bert resignedly, and looked where Cec indicated. A bulky middle-aged man was raising his voice to carry over the hum of peaceful voices. His dark face was flushed with beer. He had been in the pub for a while. Five empty glasses were on his table and his ashtray was full of butts. The fact that these had not been cleared away spoke volumes of the Management's desire not to retain him as a customer.

'What I mean to say is the rotten cow shouldn't ha' sacked me just like that,' declared the drinker, sharing his grievance with the pub at large. 'Just because I lost his flamin' dustcoat. It was an old rag anyway. It's going against the dignity of the working man to make him wear a dustcoat.'

'That was six months ago,' said the barman resignedly. 'You gotta get over this, Jack.'

'I ain't had a job that lasted more than a few days since,' complained Jack. 'This country's going down the gurgler, that's where it's going. Things ain't been the same since the war—that's what done for us fighting men.'

'You weren't in the Great War,' said a nearby drinker. 'You spent your whole time in the bloody pay corps while we was sweatin' blood at Poziéres.'

'About now,' said Bert to Cec, and ordered another beer.

'How will it go?' asked Cec. Bert was never wrong about the progress of a fight.

'He'll scream at the digger that he was too in the fighting,' predicted Bert.

'I fought all right!' yelled Jack.

'Then some other coot will put his oar in...' said Bert.

'No, you bloody wasn't. Anyway, Alderton, what's happened to all that money you was flashing around? Lost it on the gees?' asked another drinker, evidently devoid of the sense of self-preservation so essential in tête-à-têtes in Australian hotels, or else fancying his chances.

'Then Alderton will stand up and offer to fight everyone...' said Bert.

'I'll fight any man in this pub!' howled Black Jack Alderton, pulling off his coat.

'And then someone will king-hit him,' said Bert.

The soldier from Poziéres rose to the challenge. He was small, with a gamecock walk and big hands, so pale that the inexperienced might have thought that he was afraid. But Bert knew that he was flooded with cold rage. His dad had always told him that the red-faced were blusterers, not to be taken seriously.

'But if you see a bloke who's pale and shaking, son,' Bert's father had instructed, 'then run like blazes, because he might flamin' kill you.' Bert watched with interest, hoping that he would not have to interfere.

Without any preparation or parley, the soldier walked up to the big man and hit him matter-of-factly on the point of the chin. A beautiful punch, thought Bert. Perfectly placed, delivered with just the right amount of force and exactly what was needed to restore the peace of the Albion. Mr. Alderton was jarred off his heels and went down with a crash.

'Silly coot,' someone remarked.

'That's our man,' said Bert to Cec.

'What do you want to do?'

'I reckon that the barman is about to assist Mr. Alderton into the street. Perhaps we can do it for him,' said Bert.

No one commented as they shouldered through the crowd, lifted Mr. Alderton by the heels and shoulders, and carried him out. The barman opened the door for them.

'What are you goin' ter do with him?' he asked, curiously.

'Sell him to the white slave trade,' grunted Bert, manoeuvring the body down the worn front steps.

'Well, I hope you get a good price for damaged goods,' said the barman. 'Don't bring him back, will yer?' he added, and closed the door.

Bert and Cec placed Mr. Alderton gently on the cobbles of the lane next to the hotel. The man was already beginning to stir and groan. Bert knew that he was also about to throw up. This looked like a good place to do it in—the lane had a suitable gutter running down the middle of it and water was available from a nearby tap.

'We want you to answer some questions,' he said.

'Jus' go away and let me die,' groaned the patient.

'Not yet,' said Bert. 'You get to die later. There might be a quid in it,' he hinted. One bloodshot eye peeled open.

'How much?'

An unpleasant interlude followed. The ex-driver was in such a bad way that Cec was forced to go into the pub and buy a hip flask of brandy to bring Black Jack up to his usual operating level, which was not very high.

'Now go over it for us,' said Bert patiently.

'More brandy.'

'Not yet, you'll be seein' snakes, and I want you with us. Do you remember delivering a box to the bookshop in the Eastern Market last Thursday?'

'No,' said Black Jack.

'Then you're no use to us,' said Bert, getting up and brushing the knees of his trousers. 'Or anyone else,' he added, looking down at the disgusting figure now sitting on the cobbles.

'No, wait,' said Alderton, grasping at Bert's knees. 'I didn't deliver it myself. But I know about it.'

'Yair?' asked Cec with strong disbelief. He had no time for drunks. 'What d'ya know?'

'I used to work for Gibson, but he sold up and moved out. I ain't found a decent job since then. But when I put on my driver's coat to take this box to the market, from Ballarat it was, bloody heavy.' Black Jack stopped, having lost his thread.

'You put on your driver's coat,' prompted Bert.

'Yair, I put it on and found that I had a pad of Gibson's old waybills in the pocket. I hadn't worn the coat for a while. I got to the market and I was unloading in the underneath part, you know, where the trucks go. See, the boss had just sacked me, that box was my last delivery, then I was goin' to be out on the street again, so long, son. I was crook on it.'

'Yair, life is tough for the working man,' agreed Bert. For the first time in his life, he was sympathizing with a capitalist. 'What happened in the undercroft?'

'This bloke came up to me, see, and said he was playing a joke on a friend. He wanted to borrow my dispatch book and my dustcoat and cap and gloves. He said he'd deliver the box. Well, what's a man to do when he's got a coot offerin' a pound for a simple little joke? I didn't see no harm in it. He scribbled a name on my own dispatch note, so the bloody boss couldn't say I was half-inchin' his delivery.'

'So what happened then?' asked Bert. He was revolted. He had no difficulty with or moral objection to most crime—some of his best friends were criminals, and property was theft after all—but he hated liars, and Black Jack Alderton wasn't even a very good liar. Didn't see any harm in it, indeed. Bert wondered if his dive into the bottle had anything to do with the murderous implications of this simple little joke.

'Why didn't he just take your dispatch book, then?'

'Dunno.' Mr. Alderton's face creased. Cec wondered how many brain cells he had left. He was reaching a working estimate—about six—when Bert asked, 'What did this bloke who liked expensive jokes look like?'

'Didn't see him clear,' replied Alderton. 'He had to be about the same size as me, I reckon, or me coat wouldn't have fitted him. I thought he talked sort of funny. I'd had a few,' he admitted. 'That's why the boss threw me out. They're always out to do down the honest man.'

'Yair,' said Bert. Cec was impressed with how much scorn Bert could pack into one syllable. 'Here's your quid,' he added, dropping it into Mr. Alderton's spattered lap. 'Don't drink it all at once.'

Phryne dropped Miss Lee at her own house. Dot, possessed of fellow feeling, insisted on the bath being the best available, and the best bath in Melbourne was certainly Miss Fisher's. The ex-prisoner's reserve was showing signs of cracking under Dot's practical sympathy—had she not herself been on the edge of murder when Phryne Fisher had swanned into her life? Dot knew how hard it was to be rescued.

Phryne told Dot not to spare the bath salts and to give Miss Lee some clothes if she needed them, and turned the car to Hawthorn, where Jack Robinson's chemist lived. She had expressed her need for absolute confidentiality to that admirable officer, and he had instantly come up with the name. Dr. Alexander Treasure, analytical chemist, was her man he said. Robinson had said that Treasure had no curiosity at all and had given him the highest recommendations for honour and integrity.

Phryne was anxious that Yossi's formula would not be stolen and patented by someone else. Such things had happened. She did not approve of what he and the others intended to do with the money, and she was still undecided as to whether they had other allies who might have robbed Mrs. Katz and Phryne herself. But it was Yossi's discovery, made while he could have been doing something which he considered fun rather than slaving over a hot test tube and enduring Mrs. Grossman's wrath at her burned table. Phryne made a mental note that if anyone connected with this Treasure of a chemist patented anything vaguely resembling Yossi's compound, she would be very cross and probably litigious.

Dr. Treasure lived in a nice house. It was a standard red-brick building which matched its neighbours, even down to the uniform height of the fences and the tree dahlias peering over them. This was a good sign. He did not practice chemistry for money. She rang the bell and presently a young woman with a baby on her hip opened it. She was trying to tuck back her straggling fair hair and button her dress at the front.

'I have an appointment with Dr. Treasure,' said Phryne.

'Oh, yes, Miss Fisher, is it? Come in. We're a bit at sixes and sevens, my girl hasn't come in and the baby's fretting. My husband's in the lab. This way,' said Mrs. Treasure, hefting her offspring. It was whining in a way that set Phryne's teeth on edge.

'Ssh,' she said to it. The baby was so surprised it shut up instantly and plugged its mouth with its none-too-clean thumb. The young woman said, 'I wish you'd teach me how to do that. I can't do a thing with him. Takes after his father.' She opened a door. 'I can't do a thing with him, either.' She knocked, then opened the door. Then she grinned ruefully at Phryne as the baby began to cry.

'Your spell's worn off,' she commented and bore the scion of the house away to continue his interrupted feed.

'Miss Fisher?' Dr. Treasure was tall, lanky and English. He had a mop of brown curls and a shy, endearing smile. He looked much younger than Phryne had expected.

'Detective Inspector Robinson told you about my qualifications, and you are thinking that I am too young,' he said, and sighed. 'I'm actually thirty-seven, but I can't even convince passport officials about that. Sit down, if you please, Miss Fisher. You aren't the Hon. are you? Duchy of Lancaster, eh? I believe that my father knows your father. Jack said you had a fascinating problem for me. Do tell.'

Phryne produced the translation, and Dr. Treasure spread it out on his bench. He was surrounded by a forest of glass tubes and retorts. Phryne wondered how many of them had derived from alchemy.

Dr. Treasure was groping for something, never taking his eyes off the string of letters and numbers. Phryne put a pencil into his hand. He began to scribble on a notepad, tore it off, screwed it up and threw it onto the floor, paused, scribbled again and laughed.

'By God, it's so simple,' he said.

'What is it? And I have to tell you, this is involved in a murder investigation and you cannot have it.'

'Not my field,' he said absently. 'Anyway, wouldn't think of it, old Jack'd have my skin drying on a fence—isn't that the expression? I think I've got butadiene, yes, but this uses styrene, got some potassium persulphate, mercaptan, yes, this is going to niff more than a trifle. Basically we just bubble a couple of gases through cold water and then add all the other things, stir slowly, and—*voila*. Or not, as it happens. Now, can we make it? No reason why not. Just a moment.

'We begin by bubbling this gas through nice clean distilled water,' he said, doing so. 'Then we add the soap and other things, and might I suggest you put on that mask?' He indicated with an unoccupied finger an ex-army gas mask. Phryne slipped the straps over her head and breathed in a scent of charcoal and rubber. Dr. Treasure beamed. 'Good. Mercaptan is the absolute essence of things which stink.'

Even through the mask Phryne could scent something reminiscent of old garbage, mixed with a strong overtone of sewers.

Dr. Treasure seemed immune to the stench. He mixed several other fluids and poured them into a large glass vessel over a very weak flame. He took up a stirrer.

'This is exciting, isn't it?' he remarked in his lilting Cambridge voice.

'What is it?'

'Don't know, quite. But don't worry about secrecy, Miss Fisher. I work for the police often, I give evidence in court. My integrity is exceptionally important to me. Hmm. I think we'll give this a bit more of a stir.'

'Dr. Treasure, what is this compound? All I can see is a clear fluid and a bit of paper with letters and numbers.'

'Ah, yes, well, how am I to explain this? Are you familiar with the term polymerization?'

'Never heard of it,' said Phryne firmly.

Dr. Treasure did not seem cast down by the lamentable ignorance of his visitor. In fact, he seemed pleased to have an auditor who really wanted to know the answer. Phryne reflected that his wife must be far too busy with the baby to pay proper attention to chemistry lectures and he was probably suffering from audience starvation. And, judging by the way he was now drinking in the sight of Phryne in her close-fitting blue dress, other sorts of deprivation as well.

'Well, let's start from the beginning. In nature, the polymer process is a biogenesis and we are not too clear about how it works. It's very complex, but it does not seem to induce polymerization by the manufacture of an isoprene monomer as such. Which is what this formula is endeavouring to do, I believe.'

'It is?' asked Phryne.

Dr. Treasure pushed his glasses up onto the bridge of his nose. 'Yes, you see, here—it says $-CH_2-C(Cl)=CH-CH_2$—times n, and there's an additional Cl, that makes it poly-chloroprene. Which is CR. Derived, as you know, from oil, though mine is made out of butyl alcohol, made of fermented grain. Much cleaner, don't you think? And it uses up all that surplus wheat. Yes, the formula is quite clear, though it's strange. Whoever wrote this, wrote it backwards.'

'The rabbi,' said Phryne, delighted to confuse this confusing man in her turn, 'is used to writing Hebrew, which goes from right to left.'

He gave her a puzzled look before he went on, 'The rest of the steps are expressed the same way. Dashed peculiar way of setting out a process but there you are, scientists are odd bods.' Then he started like a guilty thing surprised, and leapt to his feet. 'Oh, gosh, Miss Fisher, please excuse me. That's the doorbell. My wife will be feeding little Bobbie…back in a moment. Keep stirring. Don't let it boil!'

He was gone with a slam of the door and flourish of his lab coat, and Phryne was torn between extreme frustration and a serious fit of the giggles. She had never, not even when someone had insisted on explaining political economy to her, been so thoroughly informed without having the faintest idea of what was happening. But he understood the formula, which was good, and it was some sort of discovery, which was excellent. Yossi might get his guns for Zion after all, though he would not be able to buy them in Australia. And he might decide that violence was not a solution, and try and make peace with the inhabitants after all. Try as she might, Phryne could not imagine a Jewish State. What language would it speak? How would it live? And what would persuade people who had big houses and good jobs and flourishing businesses to move to the other side of the world where they were emphatically not welcome, and work breaking rocks in a desert, probably while being shot at?

Patently impossible.

The colourless fluids in the large vessel did not actually bubble, but something was happening in them. Before Phryne had time to worry about a) whether the scientist had been kidnapped or b) whether the laboratory was about to explode, the young man with the curly hair was back, bearing a tray of tea. There was a silver teapot, milk jug and sugar basin, but the

Royal Doulton cups were mismatched to bone china saucers. Dr. Treasure's household, Phryne thought, was not short of a shilling.

'Sorry it took so long, it was the chap next door wanting to talk about the rates, and when people around here talk about rates the conversation can get positively passionate. Will you be mother?'

Phryne, resigned to deferred explanation, poured the tea.

It was good tea and there was tea cake to go with it. Dr. Treasure informed Phryne that he had come to Australia because he had been in the Great War and couldn't bear Europe.

'The fields look green, but they are bloodsoaked: for the longest time men have been killing each other in Europe, and I was sick of it. So I came here. Australia has no history. I like that in a country.' He made a broad gesture, distributing cinnamon and sugar. 'It's spacious and it's civilized. They don't trust chaps like me here, and they have good reason. Look what science did in the war,' he said soberly. 'We found new and horrible ways to kill people. I decided that we had to be useful, or there was no excuse for us.'

Phryne murmured agreement. His fresh face and bright eyes were charming.

'Funny thing,' he said, 'I heard a rumour that someone had actually succeeded in doing this, but I discounted it. It's a philosopher's stone, you know, an impossible dream. Now, I have the other reagents, acid and a salt, and if I just pour them into the mixture very gently—' he did this without spilling a drop—'now all we have to do is wait. Shall we have some more tea?' he asked chattily.

'What are we waiting for?' asked Phryne, refilling his cup.

'Why, for polymerization. Should be visible any tick of the clock—if the formula works.'

'I can see something,' said Phryne.

'Yes, there's the little chap,' commented Dr. Treasure.

The mixture was thickening before Phryne's eyes. As the reagents mixed, they were forming some sort of compound. It was cooling and hardening, until there was perhaps half a pound of the substance.

Then Dr. Treasure siphoned off the remaining fluid and spilled the substance into a glass dish. It was as thick as cream and beige in colour.

'Not long now,' he told Phryne. 'Soon find out if it works.'

'What is it doing?'

'Coagulating, I hope.' Dr. Treasure picked up his tea cup. He was not calm, but excited. Phryne could hear his breathing quickening. He really wanted to know if this was going to work.

So did Phryne. She finished her tea and replaced the cups on the tray and put the tray out of reach of any wild gestures. She didn't think that Mrs. Treasure would view the advancement of science as any excuse for the loss of Royal Doulton china.

'Oh, yes,' whispered Dr. Treasure.

He reached into the glass dish and pulled off a piece of the compound, which was now almost solid, darkening a little as it hardened. He offered it to Phryne reverently, in both hands, like a priest handling the host.

It was soft, warm and gave when poked. It rolled easily into a ball. Somewhere Phryne had seen something like it. She racked her memory.

A twin of the object she was now holding had been found in dead Shimeon Ben Mikhael's pocket.

'Why, it's rubber,' she said. 'It's artificial rubber.'

'That's what it is,' Dr. Treasure affirmed. 'It's artificial rubber. And I just made it. I just made artificial rubber!'

He gathered Phryne into an embrace and kissed her.

Chapter Fourteen

*Cut that in three which Nature hath made
One Then strengthen hit, even by itself
alone, Werewith then cutte the poudred
Sonne in twayne, By lengthe of tyme, and
heale the wounde again.*

—John Dee, *Monas Heiroglyphica*

She was almost at her own door when someone grabbed for her handbag.

At first she thought that she had caught the strap on a rose-bush. Her neighbour loved roses beyond anything and was prone to forbid a blade to bruise a twig. But when she reached back to free it, she encountered a hand.

'Never drag, always yield,' her street fighting lessons came to mind. Therefore she did not pull against the grasp, which might have broken the strap, but threw herself unexpectedly backwards. She heard a grunt as her Louis heel impacted on an instep, and she spun, hands out, ready to kick or to flee.

The tall young man tripped, almost fell and ran across the road, stumbling through the traffic. He fell into a waiting car and was gone.

The whole incident had taken seconds.

Phryne opened her own gate, thinking deeply. It might have been an attempted handbag snatch—they were happening more frequently as unemployment began to bite and more and more people were rendered desperate. Phryne was certainly well dressed and the ordinary robber would be justified in thinking that her purse would be worth investigation. But there had been the car. The planned escape route.

And she had seen so little! She spat out a very rude word. Just a tall, moderately strong, moderately young man, face hidden by a scarf. He had not spoken. The car had been of some nondescript colour—black, maybe, or dark blue. She had not seen the numberplate. Nothing, in short, to go on.

'May beets grow out of their bellies,' cursed Phryne. She could really get to love Yiddish. It was a language made for situations like these.

No one but the Butlers were home. Dot had presumably taken Miss Lee for her walk about the city. The girls were out on a picnic. Phryne was passing the phone when it rang.

'Yes?'

'Miss Fisher, can you send my son home?' asked a heavily accented voice.

'Mrs. Abrahams?'

'You have someone else's *son*?' asked Julia Abrahams. 'Someone *else's* son you have *as well* as mine?'

'No, I haven't even got yours,' said Phryne. 'I haven't seen him since breakfast.'

'*Oy, gevalt.* Sons you have. Trouble you have!'

'He isn't home?' asked Phryne, wondering where Simon might have got to. He had wanted to come with her to set Miss Lee at liberty, and she had rather snubbed him. Probably the Abrahams boy was somewhere suitably depressing, eating worms.

'I expect he's just sulking,' she assured Julia Abrahams.

'You saw him this morning?'

'Yes, and I went out directly after breakfast. I thought he was going home to talk to his father.'

'Here, he hasn't come,' said Mrs. Abrahams. 'Where can my Simon be?'

'I'm sure he's somewhere. Where is Mr. Abrahams?'

'In the workshop. Always the workshop. I'll phone him. No, I'll send Chaim. Maybe Simon is there.'

'Listen, Mrs. Abrahams, if he isn't there, can you phone me again?'

'You're worried, *nu?*' Mrs. Abrahams' voice sharpened.

'I'm a little concerned,' temporized Phryne. 'But I'm sure he'll be all right.'

She replaced the receiver on another '*Oy!*'

Where was the boy?

Phryne requested strong coffee. She wanted to think.

In the bag which the robber had tried to steal was the rubber ball which Dr. Treasure had so triumphantly made. The formula was concealed inside Phryne's bust band. An obvious precaution. She had removed it that morning from its place in her packet of sanitary napkins. She had gambled on that not being searched. The subconscious male taboo on menstruation worked on customs officers, too. How desperate the buyer must be getting, to risk attacking Phryne in the street in broad daylight!

Phryne took up the phone and called Jack Robinson. The adorable Dr. Treasure and his family must be protected. Phryne had watched as he had poured out all the chemicals used in the making of Yossi's artificial rubber, and the rubber itself had been destroyed with acid and also poured away. Dr. Treasure, however, knew the formula. It might be tortured from him, especially if they had his wife or the fat noisy baby. And Phryne had enjoyed kissing him. People with that much osculatory skill cannot be wasted.

Detective Inspector Robinson agreed, though Phryne did not mention the kiss. There was no need, she considered, to tell policemen more than they needed to know.

◇◇◇

Miss Lee set about reclaiming her shop and her life with customary efficiency. Her interval in prison was now firmly behind her. She had bathed at length and most luxuriously in a huge sea-green tub, attended by Dot, who had supplied half an ocean of very hot water and pine bath salts. The soap had been of the finest milled castile, guaranteed to bring bloom to the complexion, and the bath sheet had been fluffy and exceptionally absorbent. Miss Lee had washed and rinsed her hair and was as clean as the soapmaker's art could make her. She was clad in new underclothes, which Phryne had donated and Dot had selected. Her stockings were of silk. She was wearing her own clothes, her sensible shoes and her beige linen dress with two horses embroidered on the bosom.

And she had talked, not about prison, which she was not intending to think about for some months, but about the shocking price of butter and why Miss Fisher's hens were not laying so that eggs had to be bought from that scoundrel of a grocer. She had eaten an egg boiled to perfection and very good bread and butter and drunk several slow cups of ambrosial strong fragrant tea. She had also inspected Mrs. Butler's orchids, had been greeted respectfully by two very nice schoolgirls, and had been licked by Molly the puppy and ignored by Ember the cat.

'Perhaps a little touch of sheep dog,' she suggested, as the girls held Molly up for her approval. Jane and Ruth, also, knew about being rescued. Possibly so did Molly, because she gave a small bark and began to gnaw Miss Lee's thumb. This was cheering. The real world was still there, it still contained puppies being puppies and cats being cats.

Then, accompanied by Dot, who talked or remained silent as she perceived her companion required, she took a tram to Flinders Street and walked through the city to the Eastern Market. Her natural pace was fast.

It was all still there, she thought. There was the bulk of the post office. Buckley and Nunn had not even changed their windows. The pallid mannequins were in the same pose, hung with the same jewellery, wearing the same dresses. Foy and Gibson's at the corner of Bourke Street was still advertising unparalleled cheapness in summer garments. Art silk dresses for nine and six!

The big advertising board told her that customers preferred Dunlop tyres.

Exercise was soothing Miss Lee's fears. Her stockings whispered as she walked, and she was pleasantly conscious of the silk underwear. The sun was beginning to bite, and her suitcase was getting heavier, loaded as it was with Latin books.

'I should go home first,' she commented to Dot. 'If I still have a home. My landlady keeps a respectable house. She may not want me back.'

'Oh, yes, Miss, I'm sure you still have a home,' said Dot. She was sure of this, because she had heard Miss Fisher talking to the landlady about the matter. Miss Fisher had been very firm, and when Phryne was firm even a boarding house landlady might quail.

Miss Lee led the way up the stairs to her apartment. Mrs. Smythe (with a y, please) met her on the landing with a pleasant smile.

'Miss Lee, glad to see you home,' she said. She had, of course, been intending to evict Miss Lee neck and crop—imagine, a woman accused of murder in her nice house! But her conversation with Miss Fisher had ameliorated her views. A woman who has been cleared of a murder charge which should never have been laid in the first place, and who moreover had aristocratic connections, was a different matter. Miss Lee smiled faintly and continued climbing.

'It all looks the same,' she said, as she opened her own door.

'I'll see you in an hour,' said Dot with tact, and withdrew.

Miss Lee unpacked her suitcase, put all of her prison garments in a bag to be washed, and sat down on her bed.

It was all still here. Her books piled on her bedside table. Her narrow bed, made up with clean sheets. On the table which she used as a pantry someone—Mrs. Smythe?—had put a fresh jug of milk and a brown paper bag of biscuits.

Miss Lee, with sacramental care, made tea and bit into a biscuit. It was the oatmeal and treacle mixture called an Anzac.

'I'm home,' she said to herself, recalled to reality. Nothing was more real than an Anzac. It seemed to leave no room for any other taste. 'I'm here in my own flat and I've got my life back, my shop and my city. I'll never leave you again,' she promised the room, and took another biscuit.

Dot met her at the door, coinciding with a huge bunch of flowers preceding Mr. Abrahams, and a babble of journalists.

'I don't know how they found out, Miss, but do you want to talk to them or shall I call the cops?' asked Dot, scowling at a mannerless young man with a notebook and a strong sense of the Freedom of the Press.

'I'll talk to one of them,' said Miss Lee, perfectly collected. 'Come in, Mr. Abrahams, what lovely flowers.' She scanned the assembled multitude and picked out a young woman who was being squashed. Cameras flashed and she blinked.

'You,' said Miss Lee, 'if you please. No, not you, the lady.' The journalist fought her way to the front with some fine hip and shoulder work doubtless learned from a childhood shared with bigger brothers. Miss Lee allowed her to enter, and shut the door on a groan of disappointment and more flashes.

Dot went to interview the landlady about a vase, Mr. Abrahams sat down in the boarder's parlour, and Miss Lee asked the journalist, 'What do you want to know?'

'How do you feel about being released?' gasped the girl, who was in possession of a scoop and was wondering how she had managed it. Her chief was going to eat his words. He said that women could not hold their own in the rough and tumble of journalism, and she had fought for this assignment. He had only sent her because all his male journalists were out.

'Very happy,' said Miss Lee.

'And…er…what are you intending to do now?'

'I shall go back to running my shop, of course.'

'You know that the police have said that they are confident of finding the real murderer? Have you read Jack Robinson's statement?'

She gave Miss Lee a cutting, and she read it and smiled.

'Very clear,' she approved. 'Detective Inspector Robinson has admitted his mistake like a gentleman.'

'Do you have a theory about the murder?'

'No,' said Miss Lee. 'I really don't know anything about it.'

'Is there anything you would like to say about it all?' asked the girl, sensing that she needed a quote.

'Many people have worked very hard to expose this mistake. Miss Fisher the detective and Mr. Abrahams, my landlord.'

'And what would you like to say to all the people who believed so firmly in your innocence?' asked the journalist.

'Thank you,' said Miss Lee, sitting down rather abruptly. 'Just thank you.'

'And that's all,' said Dot, returning with a vase full of red roses and a strong feeling that Miss Lee was not as calm as she sounded. Dot shoved the young woman into the street and shut the door with a slam.

'I do mean thank you,' said Miss Lee to Mr. Abrahams. He took her hand and kissed it.

'What else should I do?' he asked, gesturing with the other hand. 'I see a lady in trouble, falsely accused yet, I should *ignore* it? Believe me, it was nothing. So, now, I have to go. That son of mine should be coming to tell me the whole *megillah*. I just came to see you're all right. *Nu?*' he asked on a rising inflection.

'Yes,' said Miss Lee, realizing that this was the case. 'I'm all right.'

Phryne was mildly worried about Simon as the day wore on. His sulk seemed to be lasting a little too long. But spoiled young men will be spoiled young men and would come around in time. Or not.

Phryne had conducted a council of war with Bert, Cec and Jack Robinson. A plan of action was settled upon. Conclusive evidence was needed to make sure that no stain remained on Miss

Lee's character, not to mention to ensure the safety of Phryne, Dr. Treasure and the students.

'Someone is hunting for that formula,' said Phryne. 'He is so desperate now that he will follow up any hint or rumour. I intend to supply the hint and spread the rumour. The paper is in Miss Lee's shop, I will say. The student did as he was bid, and placed the paper in a book before he was murdered.'

'But he must know that we have the formula!' objected Robinson.

'This is a nasty twisty mind, Jack dear. If we have it, why hasn't he found it? He can't get to Dr. Treasure, I fervently hope.' Jack Robinson nodded. 'He can't get anything from me, either, not even outright assault worked. Miss Lee doesn't know anything, the students aren't telling, and he hasn't been able to get into the bookshop, has he? It was a goodish plan, if you like elaborate schemes,' said Phryne, who didn't. 'All he had to do was wait. The formula was hidden so that no one could find it. He just had to wait until he could walk into the shop and buy the volume. He didn't know that Miss Lee would be charged—he didn't care, may the fire in his stomach boil his brains. It works for him, either way. Either she is released and comes back to her shop tomorrow, or she is sold up and he buys the book from the sale.'

'So tomorrow he just has to go in and purchase it,' said Robinson. 'We can't arrest a man for buying a book—not that sort of book, anyway. He could just claim that he had a taste for Walter Scott or whichever it was. Or was missing Volume 9 from his 1911 Hansard.'

'Yes, that's the flaw. We need to precipitate the action.'

'And how do we do that?' asked Bert, with deep suspicion.

'We announce, in certain company, that Miss Lee has donated a big box of unsold books to the Fiji and Island Mission. She's a Methodist, you know. It's credible because she did exactly that two months ago, though what the South Sea Islanders are going to make of Volume 3 of *The Proceedings of The Royal Society* for 1896, Hansard, Walter Scott's *Letters* and the Rev. Walters' *Sermons* is more than she or I can imagine. She's packed it in the shop and stored it in the undercroft for the carrier, and it's going off to Tonga tomorrow.'

'And has this been done?' asked Jack Robinson. Phryne looked at Dot, who nodded.

'Yes, clearly marked and all sealed up, except for the one which had the poison, of course. The hard bit was getting her to agree to send them useless books, she said that wasn't charity but rubbish collection. But I talked her round by saying she could unpack it later and send some good ones instead.'

'Good. I suggest that my carters carry this box down to the undercroft before the market closes tonight. Then we wait,' said Phryne.

'Is this an endgame, Miss Fisher?' asked Robinson, detaching Molly from his shoe. She had relinquished her attack on leather, but was working her way through his shoelaces.

'No, not chess, Jack. It's more like snakes and ladders,' Phryne replied.

◇◇◇

Simon had left Phryne's house in a bad mood. He felt that he was being excluded from the action, which was about to get interesting. He also felt that his undoubted beauty was being insufficiently appreciated. He called on Yossi, but he was at work. He ended up, after some desultory wanderings, in the Kadimah, where there was always someone to talk to.

The Kaplans welcomed him gloomily and he filled his teapot and threw in a pinch of tea.

'It's terrible,' said David.

'*Oy*,' agreed Solly. 'Tell us something we don't know.'

'Yossi's work lost and the guns for Zion, where will we get them now?' asked Abe, drawing Hebrew letters in spilt tea.

'The rabbi's angry with us,' David informed Simon. 'He won't even see us.'

'Shut the door and yelled at us to go away and repent of our sins,' affirmed Abe.

'Because we were using holy text for secular purposes,' concluded Solly.

'*Oy*,' said Simon. 'And my lover threw me out this morning and told me to go away and play like a boy.'

'You *are* a boy,' Abe pointed out. 'And the pleasures of the flesh are a snare.'

'Far too young to have a lover. The strange woman's kiss goes down like wine, but her steps lead to perdition,' quoted David.

'*Shah*,' pleaded Simon. 'Enough.'

'What says the sage? "Deliver us from the woman, the strange woman who flatters with her words, for her house inclines to death, and her paths unto the dead," ' added Isaac Cohen.

Simon was struck with a vision of Phryne, white and predatory in the half-dark. He could feel her remembered nipples hardening under his hands. He shifted in his seat and decided that there were things to be said for the flattering woman, even if her paths did lead to death. But he had received his breakfast time orders from the same stranger, and if he carried them out he might get to spend another night in her bed.

'I know where Yossi's formula is,' said Simon.

'You know? You didn't tell us before? Where?' demanded David.

'It's in the book. Shimeon did as he was told, before he died.'

'But how can we get it?' asked Solly.

'I should know?' asked Simon, almost disliking his friends. They were all leaning forward with identical hungry expressions. Had one of them set that pitiless trap which had slaughtered poor Shimeon? Was one of them, *gottenyu*, a *murderer*?

Suddenly he wanted to be home, eating *kasha* and being scolded for not telling his mother where he was. But he would go on with his task. 'The lady who owns the shop, Miss Lee, she's giving the unread books away, to the Island Missions. They'll be packed up and in the undercroft of the market tonight. And that's all I could find out,' he said, forestalling further questions.

'Simon, *yeled tov*, good boy!' exclaimed Solly, clapping him on the back. 'So, we get the book, we find the formula, we give it to the people we know of, and…'

'Next year,' said David Kaplan, 'in Jerusalem.'

Simon still felt bad. He did not want to be thanked for his part in this trap which Miss Fisher was constructing at the Eastern Market. He wandered about a little, bought a bunch of cornflowers, his mother's favourite, and was waiting for a tram when a car pulled up beside him and a familiar voice invited, 'Get in.'

Simon and the cornflowers did as they were instructed.

'No, I don't know where he is,' Phryne told Mrs. Abrahams, now sounding shrill. 'I haven't seen him. Have you tried Kadimah?'

'The caretaker I sent down special to see if he was there,' said Julia Abrahams. 'Been there, the young men said, gone hours ago. Where can he be?'

'I'll find him,' Phryne assured her. 'And I'll send him home.'

'Is he all right?' wailed Mrs. Abrahams.

'I don't know, but I expect so.' Phryne was not at all sure. The young man should have surfaced from even the most monumental sulk by now. 'But I'll find him,' she promised.

'*Such* a clip I'll give him when he gets here,' said Mrs. Abrahams, and rang off, only slightly mollified.

Phryne dined early and well with her conspirators. Bert and Cec had borrowed suitable garments for moving large boxes. Phryne was dressed in men's clothes, suitable for whatever might happen. She had serge trousers, men's shoes and a soft dark shirt, and looked almost epicene to eyes unused to women in trousers.

There was a rumbling in the sky as they left. The air was close and very hot.

'Thunder tonight,' said Bert, looking at the sullen sky.

'There's going to be a storm,' agreed Robinson.

Chapter Fifteen

Surely in vain the net is spread in the sight of any bird. And they lay in wait for their own blood; they lurk privily for their own lives.

—The Holy Bible, Proverbs 1:17–18

The undercroft was darkening as one by one the glaring electric bulbs in their wire cages were switched off. It was hot and humid. The air was foul with exhaust fumes. The market stank of spoiling oranges from the fruiterer's pig bin, old peaches and mangoes past their prime.

Phryne Fisher had found a comfortable barrel to sit on, with a good view of the pile of packages and boxes which were stacked ready for the carrier's van on the morrow. She was shielded from casual view by the galvanized iron gate of Mr. Doherty's feed and grain store. She wondered if he had any sunflower seeds and stifled a high-tension chuckle. Next to her Detective Inspector Robinson sat and worried. His men were placed as carefully as in a chess game, but there were three entrances and he knew that he could not control them all if his pieces had to remain out of sight. He had a deal with Miss Fisher. No tricks, no denunciations, no pyrotechnics. He just wanted the murderer to come and claim the formula, and then he could be quietly arrested.

He had not been able to search every nook and cranny of the market, either, not without attracting attention which might warn the murderer off. He was fairly sure that no one was hidden there, but he was not certain, and he liked to be certain. Also, he was hot. There didn't seem to be a lot of air in the air.

Bert and Cec had done this sort of thing before. They were not fazed by darkness or heat or suspense. Cec wondered, sometimes, if they would ever be really astonished or really afraid ever again. They seemed to have worn such emotions out, at Gallipoli and in the mud of Poziéres. Still, it made no odds. He only wished this murderous bloke would make his move. He could do with a smoke.

He sank into dreams of his wedding, with only one whisker alert for action.

He'd already bought the ring.

Above, the Eastern Market closed. Phryne saw the last of the trucks leave. The returned soldiers parked their fruit barrows, covering their cargo against dust, and filed out into the street, talking and coughing. The last of the cleaners slid his or her big broom into its place. Rubbish bins were filled with the detritus of the day's trading. This enriched the already heavy air with an overlay of sweepings. Phryne suppressed a sneeze.

She also had things to think about. Where, for a start, was the irritating but beautiful Simon? His mother had not found him and he had not been seen since he had left Kadimah before lunch. It would be just like Simon, thought Phryne, to go to a deserted warehouse after dark and tell no one where he had gone, just because an anonymous note told him to. He would probably also burn the note. But surely no son of that remarkably durable couple, the Abrahams, would have entirely missed out on a certain inborn cunning? Surely he must have learned something from his parent's stories?

On the other hand, he could still be sulking. In which case, after his mother had scolded him Phryne would take him out to dinner.

She thought about Miss Lee, another remarkable woman. Straight out of bondage, she had handled the press with resource. The screaming headlines in *The Herald* with a female by-line—who would have thought it?—were evidence of her wisdom. 'Bookshop owner cleared of murder charges', it had said. 'Police apologize.' In much smaller letters which seemed to convey some scepticism, the front page added 'Police confident of early arrest'. Phryne hoped that this very public retraction and absolution would silence gossip, but knew that it would persist. But Miss Lee had handled confinement with aplomb. A woman who could concentrate on Latin declensions under such circumstances could handle gossip.

Phryne was just rehearsing her own knowledge of that language—*capio, capere, cepi, captum*—when she heard a creak.

The door into the undercroft from Exhibition Street was opening.

Phryne felt the tension level in the hot air rising. A slim dark figure was fumbling along the wall, looking for a light switch. There was a crash as he tripped over and a choked scream as he was apprehended by Robinson, who recognized him.

'Yossi Liebermann,' grunted the policeman. 'Now don't struggle, young man. We're after bigger game than you. You're small fry. Now sit still and don't say a word, and maybe I won't charge you with breaking and entering, for which you'll get six months. No, Constable, it's not the one,' he said to his offsider, who had run to his aid. 'Tell the others to stay where they are and keep mum. This is just a young fool and nothing's going to happen to him if he gives his word to be quiet.'

'I give my word.' Yossi, released, crouched by Phryne's side. She put down her hand and he grasped it urgently. His hand was hot and sweaty with fear and shock.

'Miss, please…my formula,' he pleaded, almost in a whisper.

'*Shah*,' said Phryne. 'Later.'

'How did you know that he wasn't the murderer?' asked Phryne of Robinson in an undertone.

'No one as clever as this bastard would come to burgle a dark cellar without a light,' grunted the policeman. Phryne nodded.

Silence fell again. Phryne began to suffer from the dark-induced illusion which caused so many sentries to pepper innocent shadows with shot during a long night. She thought she saw movement, then realized that it was her own eyes requiring some contrast to this black dark. The smell of rotten fruit enveloped the watchers, and the bitter city dust settled down on them.

Yossi, at Phryne's side, was kneeling on the hard floor, and Phryne could hear him as he rocked and swayed. '*Shema Yisroel*,' he began, very quietly. 'Hear O Israel, the Lord, the Lord is One.' It was the martyr's prayer, the last words of so many Jews tortured and murdered by so many people through the ages. Rabbi Akiva had died with those words on his lips. Phryne fidgeted, then folded her hands. She wondered how soldiers managed to stay alert and not become exhausted, and decided that they must be like cats. Ember could crouch, paws out, head up, like a sphinx before a mousehole for hours and hours, perfectly composed and utterly alert for the twitch of a mouse's nose through the gap. And he could control himself not to move until it had come all the way out of the hole, so that it would have to turn to retreat, before the clawed paw came thudding down, merciless and faster than sound.

What am I doing, playing games with lives? thought Phryne, as the night deepened outside, the air grew heavier and the trams clanged past.

She strove for the cat's resting trance, and achieved it so well that she heard Jack Robinson's hand move to touch her.

The door had creaked again.

A bright pinpoint of light flickered and moved over the walls and then the floor. A heavy tread. Phryne saw nothing of the incomer but the gleam of his shoes. He passed her hiding place and located the pile of boxes.

The torch was laid on the floor. The unseen person shoved the boxes aside until he found the one addressed in big black letters to the Mission to the Islands. A knife blade flashed as the paper was cut and the box opened.

The noise of breaking laths was loud in the hot darkness.

The unknown had not spoken, but now he muttered as he pulled out books and threw them to the floor. Finally he found what he wanted, opened the book and felt in the spine.

Yossi gave a convulsive jerk, and Phryne suppressed him with a heavy hand on his shoulder. The man examined the bit of paper by the light of the torch. He stowed it carefully in an inner pocket.

Then all the lights came on. There stood the murderer. Phryne at last met the cunning mind which had contrived a rat-poison death for Shimeon Ben Mikhael.

Uncle Chaim Abrahams turned and ran.

Phryne and Yossi sprang up, knowing that he could not get far. Here was the bulky man who had bought the disguise of a drunken carter and had been in Miss Lee's shop that morning, defacing a book. Here was the man who had flung the remains carelessly into the bin, and caused accusations of murder in the bird dealer's. Here was the man who was dealing for Yossi's compound, who listened to Simon talk about Zion and Palestine, who was so sympathetic to the aspirations of the young. Chaim who had no head for business, who had always failed, who had had to be humiliatingly rescued by his brother who had even married the woman Chaim loved.

The doors were guarded, but Chaim was not heading for the doors. He ran not along but up, clattering up the stairs into the market. Ten policemen, Bert and Cec, Yossi and Phryne raced after him.

They heard him pounding ahead as they reached the first gallery. They were close enough to hear his panting breath as he ran along the top storey. They ran him to earth by the flowershops, and then they stopped.

Uncle Chaim had a hostage, and he was holding a very sharp knife to his throat.

'Simon,' said Phryne. 'I might have known it.'

She turned to address a remark to Yossi Liebermann, but he had vanished.

'Chaim,' she said to the man. 'Let him go.'

'I should let him *go*?' demanded Chaim Abrahams. 'Never. You let *me* go and maybe I won't kill him.'

'Uncle,' said Simon. He was on his knees, his hands tied behind his back. His face was dirty and he had, perhaps, been crying. But his voice was soft and there was no thread of hysteria in it. 'Uncle, you can't kill me,' he said.

'I can,' said Chaim.

'Simon,' said Phryne, and the boy tried to smile.

'I'm all right. He hasn't hurt me, he's just tied me up.'

'Send for his brother,' said Phryne to Robinson in a low voice. Then she addressed the murderer cheerily, sounding in her own ears like a district visitor. 'Now, now, a respected gentleman like you, Mr. Abrahams, why are you making a scene like this? We've got you bang to rights, put down the knife.'

'Him, I've got,' said Chaim, between his teeth. He took a fistful of Simon's hair and shook it. 'You come any closer, he's dead.'

'Keep back,' ordered Robinson. He did not like the wild look in Chaim's eye. He turned from the scene and walked away out of Chaim's hearing. 'Go and get the boy's father, Constable, on the double. Keep a man at each door, keep the public out if any come along on a dirty night like this. And get me a marksman with a rifle. Station him out of sight if you can. He's to fire as soon as he's got a clear shot. Might save the boy's life.'

'Yes, sir. What are you going to do?'

'I'm going to wait,' said Detective Inspector Robinson grimly.

Thunder rolled. The storm was getting closer.

'I'm going to get a chair,' said Phryne conversationally. 'So tiring to stand on a night like this, don't you think?'

She sat down on a wrought-iron bench and regarded the tableau critically. It was rather sculptural. Chaim was standing behind the kneeling boy, and the knife was held firmly in his tremorless hand. Phryne greatly feared that Chaim was determined, and that if she didn't think of something very impressive the boy was going to die.

'Simon, how did he catch you?' she asked, sadly. 'Was it a note telling you to go down to the warehouse after dark and tell no one?'

'He picked me up in the car,' said Simon. 'I was going home. Then he drove me here and said that he had something he wanted to check—I thought it was the shoe shop—we came up here, and then he produced a knife and tied me up and gagged me and stowed me under the counter in there. I've been trying to get loose for hours.'

'Your mother was looking for you,' said Phryne meaningly.

'*Oy*, I'm in trouble,' said Simon, managing a creditable grin.

'Hey,' interjected Chaim, 'what about me?'

'What about you?' asked Phryne coldly. 'If you'll excuse me, this is a private conversation. Simon, I won't leave you,' she said.

'Tell me you love me,' he said. Phryne did not like being blackmailed but the circumstances were, she supposed, special.

'I love you,' she said obediently. 'And I'll take you to dinner at the Society again, and after that we will see.'

'Lady,' began Chaim Abrahams. 'Hey, lady!'

'Oh, did you want to say something?' Phryne's social manner was unassailable. 'Do please forgive me. I was just chatting to your charming nephew.'

'He's a fool. So is his father. All fools.'

'Oh? Tell us about it.'

Phryne lit a gasper and exhaled the smoke, leaning back in the bench. There was a small cold lump in her stomach. She began to fancy that she could smell blood.

'That compound is going to make me rich,' said Chaim. 'All my life I've been working, working, and always events were against me, even God was against me, *gevalt*! I toiled and I starved and I never got nowhere. Then, just when I've got a good shoe business going, comes my brother back from France, rich as Croesus, rich for life from just one deal, and what does he do? He takes it off me, he takes my shoe business for his own, and then what can I do? He's got the money. He's got the power.'

'It wasn't like that,' protested Simon, and subsided as the knife nicked his throat.

'A slave in his house, that's all I was.'

Phryne watched in horror as a thin trickle of blood slid down the young man's smooth throat and puddled in his collarbone. Murder under the ground, the Rabbi Elijah had said. Death and weeping. Greed caused it. Here was murder and greed. But Phryne could have coped much better with being threatened herself. Watching this madman murder her lover was as terrible an ordeal as she could imagine. Such a beautiful boy. She had to keep Chaim Abrahams distracted and talking.

'That must have been awful for you,' she prompted. 'Then what happened?'

'I heard of Yossi's work. A clever boy, that Yossi. Clever and poor and mad about Zion, that pipe dream! Palestine, what is there in Palestine but dust and camels and pogroms? Yossi wanted to sell the compound for guns, such a fool, he didn't realise what it was worth. For this formula he could have bought the British Protectorate and everything in it. Artificial rubber? The whole world wants it. He could have owned every yard of his precious Palestine! And he came to me, Yossi. To ask me to arrange a sale.'

'Why should he come to you?' asked Phryne, watching the trickle of blood overflow the collarbone and stain Simon's shirt.

'He thought I was sympathetic to his aims, what a *meshugenner*! No use talking to my so-clever brother, no, it was well known he was no Zionist. So he came to me! Of all people!' Chaim Abrahams laughed, a deep pleasant chuckle.

'I see,' encouraged Phryne.

'I knew people, I told him. Bring me the formula and I'll put you in touch with those who can deliver your guns. But I had to get rid of the go-between, see?'

'Not precisely,' said Phryne. 'Why didn't you just steal the formula?'

'Look how much you know,' sneered Chaim. 'Yossi would know when the Chaim Abrahams Rubber Plant started production. I thought that it was Yossi who would make the exchange, putting the formula in one book and getting his reward from another. So I took the place of the carter and delivered the box to the bookshop. Then, when Miss Lee was busy, I put the razor blade into the book and sprinkled on the poison which is crystals in office paste. Simple. Yossi dead from unknown causes and all I have to do is buy the book.'

'Except that it didn't work out like that, did it?' asked Phryne, sympathetically.

Chaim scowled. 'Who would have thought that it would be Shimeon who put his finger in the wrong place?' he asked rhetorically. 'Then the bookshop is closed and I cannot get to it; but I think, soon the woman will be hanged and the goods sold, and I will get it then. So I just wait.'

'You just wait?' asked Phryne. 'You don't go burgling houses?'

'Me, do I have the figure for burglary?' asked Chaim. 'Stay still,' he warned Simon, who had shifted on his knees. He must, Phryne thought, be in considerable pain. The cold lump was getting colder. She was running out of things to say.

Robinson rescued her. 'We've got men covering all the exits,' he informed Abrahams. 'You won't get away with this. Let the boy go. He hasn't done you any harm.'

'No harm?' screamed Chaim suddenly. 'No *harm* he's done me? If he hadn't been born, I would be the sole heir of my brother. All his life, he's been in my way.'

'Come on, Mr. Abrahams, you can see you can't get away,' said Jack Robinson, almost kindly. 'You're not going to inherit now, are you? Let him go.'

'Never!'

Silence fell again. Time passed. Simon shifted from knee to knee, grimacing at the stinging of the blade in the little wound. The air grew almost solid with rotten fruit and static electricity. Phryne heard the crack of thunder overhead.

Jack Robinson was taking Chaim through his actions again, and sympathizing with his troubles. Delay was all. Time was on their side. Chaim must get weary. The hand holding the knife must eventually cramp.

Then, possibly, Simon would die because Chaim was too tired to stand.

An hour, perhaps, had gone past. Bert had tried his hand at negotiation. Phryne could not think of anything to say, so she sent a constable for some water, which she intended to drink. Chaim must be thirsty by now. If he saw her drinking, he might be moved to bargain. A glass of water, for Simon's life?

There was a flurry of feet on the steps and a woman's voice screamed 'Simon!'

'Stay back, Julia,' warned Chaim. 'Don't come any closer.'

'Simon, you're hurt…' Julia came to a skidding halt next to Phryne. 'Chaim, what is this?'

'Julia, you are in time to watch your son die,' said the murderer.

'Why, Chaim, why?' she demanded, taking a step towards him. '*Bubelah*, are you all right?'

'I'm all right, Mama,' he said valiantly.

'You chose the wrong man,' said Chaim. 'You know it now. When you had to choose, in Paris, between two poor men, me and my brother, you chose wrong, Julia.'

'No,' she said faintly. 'I chose right.'

'Wrong,' he snarled, and Julia jumped back from his contorted face.

'All right, I was wrong, I was wrong, now let Simon go,' said Mrs. Abrahams. 'You let him go, Chaim, and I'll go away with you, I'll do anything you want. I'll lie down on this floor for you, let my son go!'

'Too late,' said Chaim. 'Once that would have made me happy, but not now. Come closer if you want him dead,' he added.

'Phryne,' whispered Julia Abrahams, 'do something!'

'I'm thinking,' said Phryne.

The police marksman would be in position by now. If she could get Simon away for only a second he would have a clear target and would fire, and police marksmen seldom missed. But Chaim was strong on his legs, had Simon in what looked like an unbreakable grip, and had more grievances to air. She doubted that he would kill Simon while he had a captive audience and further envy, malice and all uncharitableness to spill. Phryne pushed Mr. Abrahams forward.

'You talk to him,' she urged. 'Get him to tell you how much he hates you.'

'Chaim?' asked Mr. Abrahams. 'What are you doing, brother?'

'Brother?' snarled Chaim. 'What brother were you to me? You married the woman I loved, you stole my business, and you made me your slave. Find this, Chaim, fix this, Chaim, oh, Chaim will do it! He's got no head for business, Chaim, too visionary, a *luftmensch*, but good on the day-to-day details, keep the diary, arrange the appointments!' His mockery was merciless and instantly recognizable.

'Chaim,' said Benjamin Abrahams, 'Chaim, please, we're *mispocheh*! We're family!'

'Bennie, we're not related,' snapped Chaim.

'Then give me a great gift, stranger.' Benjamin Abrahams sank down onto his knees, eye to eye with his son. 'Give me this life.'

'I want you to mourn.' Chaim's voice was inhumanly gleeful, and Phryne shivered. '"Oh, Absalom, my son, my son! Would that I had died for thee," that's what I want for you, Bennie, I want you to mourn.'

'I will mourn,' agreed Benjamin Abrahams. 'I will mourn the loss of my son. I will also mourn the loss of my brother,' he said. 'You want me to beg, Chaim? Here I am, begging. You want my wife to leave me and go to you? She's going right now. You want my business, every penny I own? It's yours. Only give me my son, Chaim. Give me Simon.'

'No,' said Chaim. 'You don't mean it, brother. You mean to fool me. Don't you think I know that as soon as I let go of this boy, the policeman will seize me? They're out of sight but I know they're there. Get up, Bennie. Lead the way. We're going out of the market. Then you will drive me away in your big car.'

He hauled Simon to his feet and Phryne followed a grotesque, horrible procession. Chaim kept his back to the shops and sidled along, using Simon as a shield. Benjamin Abrahams walked ahead, Phryne and Julia behind, and there was still not a thought of what to do in Miss Fisher's mind.

Death under the ground, the Rabbi had said. Beware.

It would be so much easier if it had been her. She would have kicked and fought and could have got away, far enough for a shot to find Chaim's black heart. But Simon was limp prey, going where he was pushed.

They stumbled down the stairs and into the main hall of shops. Phryne heard twittering from the birdshop, and a sleepy voice demanding 'Polly wants…' before it fell silent in its usual indecision. The stench of rotten oranges, Phryne knew, would forever call up this nightmare suspense, the sight of the boy's blood, and the miasma of hatred which surrounded Uncle Chaim like a rank mist.

They had almost reached the door when it crashed open, and Chaim flung himself back against a wall with Simon in front of him.

The knife was against his throat. Julia bit her knuckle to stop a scream. Benjamin Abrahams swore.

'Don't come no closer,' screamed Chaim.

A figure out of a Talmudic story, preternaturally tall, bearded, his gaberdine slick with water so that he looked like he was wrapped in metal, raised one hand and pointed at Chaim.

'Thou shalt do no murder!' he boomed, and the voice echoed in the empty market. Lightning flashed and thunder cracked like artillery behind him, and Chaim slashed wildly with the knife. Simon whispered '*Schma Yisroel.*' Chaim faltered and missed. For a split second he was a little off balance, and Phryne saw her chance. She dived forward and tackled Simon, knocking him down and out of Chaim's grasp.

They rolled across the floor and into a corner. Simon buried his head in Phryne's breast and shuddered and she held him tight, unable to look away from the Prophet Ezekiel in the doorway.

Lightning flashes silvered his hair and made a carved stone of his face. He took another step, and cried again, 'Murderer! There is the mark of Cain upon you!'

Chaim Abrahams screamed and stabbed with the knife, and this time he did not miss.

Phryne saw both figures fall. The Rabbi Elijah collapsed into Yossi's arms, but Chaim Abrahams, who had stabbed himself unerringly through the heart, lay where he fell.

Chapter Sixteen

'I challenge you,' said the young man, 'to tell me the whole of the Torah while standing on one leg.' 'That which is hateful to you, do not do unto your neighbours,' snapped Rabbi Hillell. 'All the rest is commentary. Go and learn!'

—Leo Rosten, *The Joys of Yiddish*

It was a terrible argument.

The Abrahams were forbidden celebration by the requirement to sit *shivah* for seven days to mourn the death of their brother and uncle Chaim. Equally, Chaim had killed himself only after he had tried to kill Simon, and Simon was alive and Chaim was dead. A suicide was denied ordinary burial and mourning; the body was in any case being held by the police for post-mortem and a subsequent inquest. Then again and on the fourth hand, suicides were not condemned as murderers if the balance of their mind was disturbed, and there was no doubt that Chaim's mind had been disturbed, but also there was no doubt that he had murdered poor Shimeon. Confusion was becoming endemic.

Rabbi Elijah was recovering in hospital from his heart attack, and was not available for comment. Phryne finally extracted herself from the argument and went to telephone the gentle and wise Rabbi Cohen, to whom she explained the whole situation in confidence.

'Tell them that the law requires them to mourn a life lost, but it also requires them to rejoice in a life saved,' said the old man's voice, a little shocked and a little amused.

'A party?' suggested Phryne.

'Just a small one,' he agreed.

So it was a small luncheon party. Simon was sitting next to his mother, who would not let him out of her sight. He trusted that this would wear off soon, because Phryne was taking him out to dinner and he had hopes. The only sign of his ordeal was a small cut on his throat which had required only two stitches, some scraped rings around his wrists, and a certain hollowness about the eyes, seen in those who have looked into the face of death and been saved by a miracle. Occasionally he could still feel the cold breath of the blade as it sliced past his face, and the strength of Phryne's body as she bore him across the floor.

He was glad that he had not seen Chaim die. He was still puzzled about Chaim. No one had ever hated Simon before. Uncle Chaim? It seemed impossible.

There were potato pancakes and a tasty boiled fish. There were little pies made of spinach and a multitude of interesting sandwiches. There was also excellent coffee in the big pot and endless supplies of tea.

The students had occupied the sofa and were eating as though they did not expect to see a good meal until next year. Julia Abrahams was passing them more plates, and wondering if there was any real prospect of filling them up.

Mrs. Katz, almost extinguished under her favourite hat, was delighted to be in such respected company. Her husband Max sat next to her. She slapped his wrist and told him, in a loud whisper, not to blow on his tea. Mrs. Grossman, in an equally flowered hat, was enjoying the luxury of eating something which she had not cooked (though she privately considered that her gefillte fish was better). Detective Inspector Robinson, with a commendation from the Chief still echoing pleasantly in his ears, was eating little biscuits and thinking how uncommonly well Miss Fisher looked, considering the immense risk she had taken diving across the floor under a madman's knife. Phryne had put on a violet dress with a black chiffon overlay: the colours of Victorian half-mourning. Jack Robinson wondered if she had done it on purpose and decided that she had. She was a woman who savoured nuances.

'Well,' sighed Benjamin Abrahams, 'it is all over. It is not well over, and I will never forgive myself for not noticing how Chaim felt—for not noticing Chaim at all.'

'To think of Chaim hating us so much for all those years,' sighed Julia. 'I should have seen. But he never touched me, never spoke to me, Bennie, so how could I know?'

'*Ai-ai-ai*,' said Mrs. Katz. 'Such a sad thing.'

'But now it is over,' continued Benjamin Abrahams. 'Chaim *alav ha-sholom* did it all.'

'No,' said Phryne. 'Chaim didn't. Perhaps you weren't there, but I asked him about the other things. I asked him about Mrs. Katz's robbery, the burglary of my house, the man who tried to steal my purse. No, said Chaim, all I had to do was wait until Miss Lee was hanged—the bastard!—and I could buy the book. No, Chaim didn't do those things. And it is not proper to load him with all available sins just because he is dead. But the person who did them is in this room.'

'Who?' demanded Robinson.

'I shall ascertain. Mr. Abrahams, if I may?' He made a gesture for her to continue. She walked to the middle of the room. 'I have three questions.' She held up three fingers. 'One. Mrs. Katz, do you recognize any of the young men who tied you to a chair and robbed your house?'

'I don't like to say,' said Mrs. Katz. Her husband said, 'You tell them, if you know.' Mrs. Katz looked up from under the brim of the black hat and said, 'Maybe he looks a little like one of them. But I really didn't see them to know again. One of them had a scarf over his face.'

'Yossi,' said Phryne, 'you really wanted your formula back, didn't you?'

Yossi hung his head. 'I didn't mean to hurt you,' he muttered to Mrs. Katz. 'I didn't know that he'd left you tied up. When I found out I went back, but Miss Williams was already there.'

'You broke my plate,' said Mrs. Katz sadly. 'And I can't get no other. If you had asked me, I would have told you that I didn't have your paper.'

'What would the rabbi say about this situation?' asked Phryne.

'He would say that Yossi should serve Mrs. Katz in some way, to repair as far as possible the damage he has caused, the fear and the injury,' said David Kaplan.

'Of course, we could just lock him up,' said Robinson.

Phryne asked. 'Hush, Jack, you are a spoil sport! I'll find your major offender for you; can't you let a few little fish through the net? Yossi has a great future as a chemist. He and Mr. Abrahams are going into business and I expect them to be very successful.'

'Well, since there was no official complaint made...' temporized the Detective Inspector, and allowed Phryne to sit him down again. She perched on the arm of the chair.

'I could make you a pair of shoes,' said Yossi suddenly. He knelt down and took up one of Mrs. Katz's feet. 'I'm a good shoemaker. These look tight and they hurt, *nu?*'

'I can't tell you how much,' said Mrs. Katz. 'All day on my feet, cooking, washing. Agony,' she declared. 'And good shoes so expensive.'

'I can make you a pair, you won't know you're wearing shoes,' said Yossi, and grinned. 'Like air on the feet.'

Mrs. Katz clipped him lightly across the ear and said, 'See that they are.'

'Very nice,' approved Phryne. 'Will you make me shoes as well, or wasn't it you who climbed into my room and handled all my underwear?'

'Me,' said Yossi. 'A pair of shoes, you'll want to stand all day to feel how nice they are.'

'Good, and I don't need to clip your ears, either. Do I get a second pair for the attempted theft of my handbag?'

'Not me,' said Yossi.

'Who was your co-offender?' asked Phryne gently.

Yossi's mouth, which had softened into a smile, shut like a trap.

'You won't say, eh?' He shook his head, implacable. Phryne had a certain implacability herself. 'There are other ways of finding out. Second question, and the ladies present should pardon my lack of modesty. Yossi, Kaplans and Cohen. Think about your fellows. Are you sure that they are all circumcised?'

The young men blushed. They avoided each other's eyes. There were some mutterings among the Kaplan brothers and after comparing notes, David Kaplan said, 'We are all five of us circumcised. That's because we're Jews,' he added, with elephantine irony.

'Are you sure?' asked Phryne.

'You had three questions,' commented Benjamin Abrahams. 'What is the third?'

'That I have to ask in private. I am going into the other room, and each of the five should come in one at a time. Make sure that they do not communicate the question to each other when they come out, Jack. Yossi, we start with you,' and she took him out of the drawing room and into the parlour. The door closed with a quiet slap.

After a couple of minutes, a very puzzled Yossi emerged and David Kaplan took his place. He was followed by an equally bewildered Solly, his brother Abe, and Isaac Cohen. He came out after two minutes, and Phryne Fisher had him in a polite armlock.

'You were infiltrated, Yossi,' she told the young man. 'You thought that he was an undercover Zionist, willing to give the money to the cause. But there are undercover men and undercover men, and this one meant you no good. You were intending to kill Yossi after you got the formula, weren't you?' she asked, relinquishing her hold to Jack Robinson, who swung Isaac round to face the company. 'Who are you working for, I wonder? I'd say you were political rather than greedy, so you're more likely to be Russian than American. Going to the lengths of having you circumcised sounds like Russian lunatic thoroughness. That must have stung. You nearly got away with it,' she told him. 'You cleaned your shoes before I could find any of Mrs. Katz's china in your soles. You had a getaway car arranged when you failed to snatch my handbag. I wonder if, when we search you, we'll find your other passport? You can't have come here just because of Yossi. You must have been here all along.'

'Yes, yes,' snarled Isaac Cohen. 'My name is Ivan Vassiliov. Of course I was here. Four years I have been here. I was sent to infiltrate the Jews in Melbourne, the young counterrevolutionaries, the Zionist conspiracy to overthrow the revolution. I learned the language, I learned the customs, I read Torah. I was a very good Jew. When I found out about the compound, I received my instructions. I had orders to kill the inventor when I had his invention. The revolution needs it.'

'You were going to *kill* me?' asked Yossi, bewildered. 'You were going to kill *me*?'

'Of course. With you dead and the formula in my hands, who was to say where it came from?' asked Isaac reasonably. 'I tell you, the New Russia requires it.'

'But, Isaac,' he protested, and Ivan Vassiliov turned in the policeman's grasp and spat in his face.

'Filthy Jew,' he snarled.

'That's quite enough of that,' said Robinson. 'Come along. Immigration'll want you after you get out of jail,' he said to the young man. 'They'll deport you smartish and I hope the Russians have joy of you. Nasty piece of work,' said Robinson, and shoved the struggling ex-Cohen from the room.

Yossi was led away to wash his face. Julia Abrahams said helplessly, 'But he seemed so nice.'

'*Zeeser Gottenyu!*' Mrs. Grossman fanned herself. 'Sweet God, a Russian! In my *house*, yet!'

Mr. Abrahams went to the cupboard, poured busily, and passed around small glasses of strong sherry. Everyone sipped and gradually started to recover from the shock. The voices rose to fever pitch then began to die down.

'That's the last revelation I have for today,' said Phryne. 'Not a nice one but it is the last. Everyone else in this room is definitely who they say they are.'

She looked around. The students were clumped together. The three Kaplans had the advantage of knowing each other from birth. Yossi was well known. Everyone was now known, except this strange woman who had seduced Simon and solved the mysteries.

There was something that everyone was dying to know but no one liked to ask.

Mrs. Katz took another biscuit and nudged her husband, who shrugged. Julia Abrahams looked at her husband, but he was staring into his glass. The students shifted and muttered but did not speak. Then Simon rose from his chair and came to sit next to Phryne.

'I have to know,' he said. His parents looked fondly at him. Simon could be relied on to ask the question on everyone's lips. *Such* a good boy.

'Phryne darling,' said Simon, forgetting that his mother was listening. 'Tell us. Please. We have to know.'

'What?'

Simon took Phryne's hand in both his own. 'How did you know that the spy was Isaac Cohen, I mean, Ivan Vassiliov?'

'A spy can learn a language,' said Phryne. 'A spy can study Torah, be circumcised, and can acquire a protective veneer of shared history or shared study. But one thing cannot be faked. You can authenticate an Englishman by asking him to sing *Humpty Dumpty* or *Old King Cole* or asking him about the *Old Woman Tossed Up in a Blanket*. You can verify a Pole by asking him to say a little prayer, which every Polish child learns at its mother's knee. Orphaned, lost, brought up by wolves, every child born in Poland knows his Our Father.'

'So?' asked Julia Abrahams.

'So I just took them into the next room, and asked them to sing me *Raisins and Almonds*,' said Phryne.

Bibliography

If anyone would like to duplicate my research, here are my sources. I have made one deliberate anachronism: I moved the Society restaurant to Bourke Street four years early.

u/r = unknown reference—I had given the book back before I noted the reference.

Album of Melbourne Views 1925 (author's collection)

Amirah: An Un-Australian Childhood Amirah Inglis Heinemann, Melbourne 1983

The Australian Jewish Herald 20 September 1928

A Book of Household Management Mrs. Beeton Ward Lock, London 1901

The Book of Werewolves Sabine Baring-Gould, Causeway Books, New York 1973

Bridging Two Worlds: The Jews and Italians in Carlton Arnold Zable et al., catalogue, Museum of Victoria undated

The Castle of Otranto H. Walpole, Penguin Classics, London 1989

Celebrate Jewish Festivals Angela Wood, u/r

Dawn of Magic L. Pauwels and J. Bergier, Panther, London 1964

Dictionary of Alchemy M. Haeffner, Aquarian Press, London 1991

Education of Hyman Kaplan L. Rosten, Penguin, New York 1968

Eliphas Levi and the French Occult Revival C. McIntosh, Rider, London 1972

Experimental Magic J. Brennan, Samuel Weiser, New York 1981

Fortune Telling B. Rakoczi, Man Myth and Magic, London 1970

From Moses to Qumran H.H. Rowley, Lutterworth Press, London 1963

The Heir of Udolpho Mrs. Radcliff, Penguin Classics, London 1981

The Holy Bible, King James edition

The Holy Kabbalah A.E. Waite, Oracle, London 1996

Jewels and Ashes Arnold Zable, u/r

The Jewish Problem Louis Golding, Penguin, London 1938

The Jews in Victoria Hilary L. Rubenstein, Allen & Unwin, Sydney 1986

The Joys of Yiddish Leo Rosten, Penguin, New York 1959

Living Traditions I. Becher, Mallard Press, New York 1993

Man, Myth and Magic, an encyclopedia ed. R. Cavendish, Purnell, London 1972

Melbourne Markets 1841–1879 u/r, State Library

Melmoth the Wanderer Sebastian Maturin, Penguin Classics, London 1989

Murder Australian Style Jim Main, Unicorn Books, Melbourne 1980

The Murdered Magicians Peter Partner, Crucible Press, London 1987

The Mystical Quabbalah Dion Fortune, Aquarian Press, London 1987

Natural Rubber and the Synthetics T. Tryon, u/r Bailleu Library, Melbourne University

The New Standard Jewish Encyclopedia ed. I. Wigoder, W.H. Allen, London 1977

Paracelsus: Magic into Science H. Pachter, Collier, New York 1961

The Religions of Man H. Smith, Perennial Library, New York 1958

The Return of Hyman Kaplan L. Rosten, Penguin, New York 1970

Teyve's Daughters Sholom Aleichem, trans. Frances Butwin, Crown, New York 1969

Trial and Error: an autobiography Chaim Weizman, Hamish Hamilton, London 1949

The Torah D. Charing, Mallard, New York 1994

The World's Great Religions Time Life, New York 1986

Maps and journeys—the City of Melbourne, Carlton

film: *Bitter Almonds: The Jews in Melbourne*

Yiddish Words

alav ha-sholom (m) or *aleha ha-sholem* (f): may he/she rest in
  peace
bubelah: baby
dreck: rubbish, dirt
feh!: an exclamation of disgust
gevalt: (equivalent to) enough!
Goldene Medina: the Golden Land, Australia
gonif: a thief
Gottenyu: God or Lord
Kaddish: prayer for the dead
kasha: cooked cereal
kasheh: questions
mazik: a clever little devil
megillah: the whole long tale
meshuggener: an idiot, a fool
meshumed: an apostate
mezuzah: a charm placed on a doorway to sanctify a house
miesse meshina: an ugly fate or death
mitzvah: a blessing, a good deed
mispocheh: family
nu: a multitude of meanings (*sim to eh?* in Greek or *Ar* in
  Australian)
nudzing: nagging

schlemiel: an idiot
schlimazl: an unlucky idiot
shah: silence
Shabbes: the Sabbath
shalom aleichem: Peace be unto you—a greeting
shemozzl: a mixed-up mess
shiksa: a non-Jewish girl
shivah: a period of mourning
Torah: the Book of Laws, the bible
zayde: grandfather

To receive a free catalog of Poisoned Pen Press titles, please contact us in one of the following ways:

Phone: 1-800-421-3976
Facsimile: 1-480-949-1707
Email: info@poisonedpenpress.com
Website: www.poisonedpenpress.com

Poisoned Pen Press
6962 E. First Ave. Ste. 103
Scottsdale, AZ 85251